TESTAM

WORLDS
_A_T WAR

SAMUEL C. KINGSBURY

TESTAMENT

WORLDS AT WAR 1

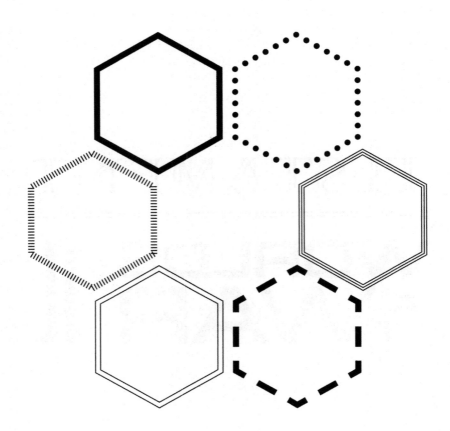

Prologue

These are dark days in the brutalist state of Kappa; the state civil wars, having raged for centuries, had torn the world to shreds; there was not a soul alive who had not felt the effects, the terror and the anguish. The ruling party had brought the people to their knees; comply or die; each and every child is conscripted to the state armies; fight or face the threat of retribution against family and friends. Non-compliance was not an option. The Kappa state armies were fighting on two fronts: to the west they fought a vicious ground campaign against the state of Omega and on the eastern shores they fought the Central state navies.

Over the centuries Kappa has seen brief periods of stability. Normally just long enough to rebuild the necessary infrastructure to begin the next war – there has not been a time over the last thousand years where there were not at least two warring states and often the other states would use that war as an opportunistic time to wage their own fights; everybody fights; everybody is taught to fight and taught to hate. From the age of three you are trained in a field that best serves the state, from your third year in the world to your seventh it is physical, mental and military teachings. By this age all children can strip down and reassemble a machine pistol; are indoctrinated to systematically hate those that are different, and to kill anyone who does not conform to the beliefs of the state. History teachings are added in your eighth year in the world: the children learn of the six states. The central state that once stood as a giant gleaming city that rose to the clouds, the very beating heart of the world that housed the non-conforming, radicalised, inhuman central ruling party and that now there stands in ruins in what once was splendour. The Delta state was the centre of industry; Omega was farming and agriculture; Sigma and Theta were the workers and Kappa state housed and trained the military. No person alive knows the true beginnings of the wars, some states teach it is a religious war, others claim it is being fought for precious minerals and wealth, and Kappa children are taught that they fight to rule the world as they are the superior beings.

From the ninth year onwards you are taught a skill that is needed by the party; for some it is merely more fighting and soldiering; for some it is medicine, others science, chemical warfare and nuclear physics; at age 14 you are assigned a position. Most get posted to one front or the other; more meat for the grinder. The lucky ones are posted to the science core or medical core, and then there are the others; the children either culled or sent to become breeders. At the age of 13 the bottom five percent of every class and the top five percent of the girls are removed from the teachings, the children are told they have been re-assigned but they all know the truth. Those that are physically unfit to perform a duty, that cannot serve the party, are culled and the special girls are sent to the generals and other party hierarchy to be used to breed, create better, more intelligent children to improve the armies of the state in the generations to come.

In the centuries past the armies of Kappa had gained control of both Delta and Theta states, their inhabitants put to work or killed for non-compliance, building the machines of war and necessary infrastructure. The workers had been for centuries building the great shore defence; a 100-foot high and 40-foot thick wall of solid rock and stone with giant defence cannons. The workers were deployed in factories to build tanks, vehicles and munitions. They were often worked or starved to death. Until recent times the people of Omega state had had a treaty with Kappa, to supply food and other essentials for the protection of the Kappa armies. This treaty had been in existence for centuries, but as the Kappa armies grew, the demand on Omega also grew. Until the point that their own people were starving. Omega have been trying to fight back against the might of Kappa, but farmers versus trained soldiers was never a fair fight. The war with Omega is nearly concluded; the Kappa armies have advanced within 20 miles of their capital Khristade, capturing everything and everyone in their path. Soon they will control Omega and all in it.

01

General Hades

Geneal Hades' motorcade was barrelling towards the western front to join with the Kappa forces and lead the final push into Khristade. As the armoured cars passed through an outlying village there was a sudden jolt and a full stop; the lead spotter had noted potential dissidents gathering in the market square. The elite brigade 99 of the Kappa armies, the General's personal protection, disembarked the motorcade en masse, charging fast towards the people shouting for them to line up against the building walls or risk death. A few of the terrified villagers ran but were systematically picked off by the soldiers. Those that weren't killed immediately were dispatched shortly thereafter. A single shot to the head for each, men, women and even a small child. The soldiers showed no compassion or remorse; the remaining villagers, scared for their lives, were lining up as ordered. Once order was established, the General's driver opened the door of the armoured car.

General Hades stepped out; he was a brute of a man, standing almost seven feet tall with shoulders the width of a bull. He wore all black and a half mask that covered grotesque scarring on his face. Hades was the son of a low-ranking Kappa officer, the only survivor of the battle of Castleton, an enemy stronghold during the Theta wars. His father was rewarded for his bravery by being given a single unit of breeding stock, and from that coupling came Hades. An only child who would spend hours during his informative years torturing unfortunate creatures and beating smaller children; a child so horrid he was even shunned in Kappa; his father eventually growing so ashamed, he gave Hades over to medical experimentation. The chemical programme had left him physically scarred, but made him the man he was today, massive in size and shockingly brutal in nature, crazed and violent. Hades had used his newfound strength to ascend the ranks quickly and become general and head of state for all Kappa.

Hades strode quickly across the square to where the soldiers were keeping the villagers. "You will conform to the laws and beliefs of Kappa State," he bellowed. "All men, women and children will be used as workers for the benefit of Kappa State. Those who do not conform will be culled, those who do not comply will die," he sternly added.

There was silence, the villagers too scared to move or make a sound. Brigade 99's commander conferred with the General and with immediate intention ordered the other soldiers to remove the elderly from the group, to take them away. The villagers stirred and cries rang out as the soldiers dragged the chosen villagers away. A child ran from the group and spat on the general's boot.

"Leave them alone," the little boy shouted, undeterred by the menacing form of the general.

Quickly grabbing the child by the hair, the general screamed out: "Who does this belong to?"

A woman ran from the crowd, pleading with the General. "Please sir, please don't harm my boy. He knows no better. Please sir, we will conform."

"Are you willing to sacrifice for the state?" Hades calmly asked, but the woman wasn't sure what to reply.

"Answer me!" the general screamed.

"Yes, sir, yes, sir. Please don't harm him," the woman quickly replied.

"Do you think me some kind of monster? I'm not going to harm the boy," the General said with a wry smile appearing across his face.

He quickly drew his side arm and fired one shot. The bullet struck the boy's mother directly between the eyes, blood and brain matter scattering to the floor as the woman's body dropped in a heap. The boy screamed and wriggled free of the General's grasp, running to his mother's body.

The elderly villagers had been taken to the side of the road, lined up along a ditch with a small number of soldiers in rank directly behind them. There was audible pleading and praying to the gods. A loud call of "FIRE" and with a crisp series of bangs the villagers were dispatched face first into the ditch. The elderly villagers were seen as not useful to the state, they were killed to ensure they didn't use valuable provisions that would be needed by the Kappa armies. There was shock and sadness throughout the remaining villagers, but they knew that any resistance would lead to more deaths and further sorrow. Some of the men were ordered to cover the bodies in the ditch, they reluctantly shovelled dirt onto their mothers and fathers; there would be no proper burials for these villagers. The soldiers were ordered to separate the remaining villagers; men were taken away, shackled and loaded onto trucks. They were likely heading to the munitions factories or the eastern sea defences. Women were gathered together and then sorted, the older less beautiful women and all the children being ordered into the fields to work, with the younger women and girls held in the village's church for the pleasure of the General and his senior staff.

The trucks carrying the village men left. With order gained, and the General pleased by the example set for the villagers, he and his senior staff headed to the church. The doors of the church were flung open, a small group of women huddled together scared by the unknowing of what to expect next. The General strode towards the group, his boots making a thumping sound on the wooden floor as he took each step. Stopping to peruse the women, taking his time to carefully choose the prettiest. He reached in and grabbed a young woman by her flowing golden locks, dragging her from the huddle and away from the other women. Hades pushed the woman through the door of the church's meditation room and slammed the door behind them. Grabbing her by the front of her dress, he swiftly pulled the dress from the terrified woman's body. She screamed and tried to push him away, but the General being a hulking beast of a man was far too strong, and knocking her to the floor he repeated the Kappa state mantra: "Comply or die".

"I would rather die," the woman proudly stated as she got to her feet.

The General didn't utter another word. Pushing the woman to her knees, he pulled a large-bladed knife from his belt and slit her throat from ear to ear. Blood gushed from her wound as she grasped for air. The general wiped his knife blade on the back of the woman's head and watched as the life drained from her body. Thirty-eight dead villagers was the sum total of that afternoon's work. This type of mindless death was all too common in these state wars, and death and destruction followed the General and the Kappa state army like sheep following the herd. The Armies of Kappa were merciless killers who flaunted the power of life and death.

02
The Final Push

The motorcade pulled into the forward operating base of the Kappa armies. The base was located approximately ten kilometres behind the western front, which by now was starting to hit the outlying villages that surrounded Khristade. General Hades stormed into base command, the soldiers quickly jumping to their feet and saluting.

"Update!" Hades ordered.

"Yes, my General," the base commander replied with gusto. "Fourth battalion has successfully taken control of the southern power station with minimal resistance. The eighth Brigade has closed within two miles of the capital's outer western defences, and the 10th and 19th divisions have taken control of the Omega telecommunications centre."

The commander swiftly moved around a large plotting table and began updating the General on the other troop movements. "The 20th tank division has decimated the opposition field troops along the western edge of the city. Rocket battalion one are in position to strike at the capital centre. We are awaiting the withdrawal of brigade four before beginning the first attack."

"Strike now," the General ordered calmly.

"But...." one of the ranking officers began to say.

The general reached out and started to throttle the officer. "But—" the general repeatedly screamed in the officer's face as his hands choked the life out of him. The officer's body dropped limply to the floor as one of the junior officers ran to the communication panel and began to order the rocket strike. "Rocket battalion command; strike; strike!"

"Send brigade three into the city on the eastern edge, deploy the tank battalions into the city streets. I want the city by sunrise," Hades ordered as he left base command.

Towards the eastern edge of Khristade, the eighth battalion had entered the streets of Janstade, one of the outlying towns on the edge of the capital. The 17th brigade was commanded by Captain Marcus. He was a secret foreigner, born to a Kappa breeder's affair with a Delta Doctor. Although indoctrinated with the same education as other Kappa children, his belief was weak. Maybe being of a Delta parent allowed for him to think differently from the others, to have his own thoughts and beliefs. Marcus looked like he belonged; he had finished within the top five percentile of his education class, a tall and lean man with all the common Kappa features. Chiselled looks with dark hair, a very well-spoken gentleman in a brutes' army. A brave and courageous man; through all the Kappa teachings to hate and to kill, he kept his humility, his compassion and his honour. A very calm man on the exterior, but he lived in constant fear of being outed as a non-believing half breed. An intelligent man, but no thinker, he was prone to making rash decisions that would often put himself in harm's way; living each day for that remote chance that Kappa would be beaten, that he could live a normal existence in a quiet world without war and constant fighting. Marcus dreamed of the day he could be himself and not pretend to be a Kappa; not pretend to be a mindless, vile monster. As he led his troops into Janstade, he could not turn aside the thoughts of all the brave Omega farmers his men had killed, the women and children either murdered or maimed. He tried to lead his troops well, tried to avoid unnecessary conflict, but the bloodthirsty killers under his command thrived on it, boasted of head counts and confirmed kills. Were rewarded by his superiors for brutalism.

As Captain Marcus moved his troops through the empty streets of Janstade, there was great hesitation within his every action. Moving troops slowly and deliberately attempting to avoid areas where the local people may have been gathered, or were hiding. His hope was that the people would hide and not resist the flowing surge of Kappa troops pouring into the streets. "Dissidents at ten o'clock" rang out. Gun fire ensued as the Kappa troops opened fire on a group of unarmed locals that were running for cover, to a large, old warehouse-looking building.

"Cease fire, cease fire!" Marcus pleaded with his troops. "Stop firing! They are unarmed civilians."

It was too late: the Kappa soldiers had moved unnervingly towards the crowd, firing at a rapid rate. The locals never stood a chance; the soldiers swarmed the bodies to ensure that all were down for good.

Captain Marcus was anguished inside. He ordered his troops to retake their positions in the group, and to move out of Janstade and towards the eastern city defences. He was relieved when the Kappa soldiers didn't encounter any further local Omegas as they reached the edge of town.

"Set a perimeter and encamp until further notice," Marcus ordered.

The captain was not in this war for the glory, and whereas others may have pressed on and attempted to take the eastern defences, he was not going to without further reinforcements. The captain radioed into battalion command, requesting a further brigade be dispatched to his location, to allow them to breach the defences and push into Khristade. As the soldiers were waiting for reinforcements, one of the junior officers, Lieutenant Titus, approached the captain.

"You must keep your emotions to yourself!" Titus whispered. "To Kappa, no man, woman or child is a civilian. They are all enemies of Kappa and should be treated as such."

The junior officer was speaking out of turn, but Marcus was appreciative of Titus's candour. In the Kappa armies, soldiers were not permitted to engage in friendships or any form of relationship, but Captain Marcus had grown close to Titus. They had bonded over common thoughts and beliefs.

"You must allow the men to be Kappa," Titus pleaded with his captain. "You are lucky the men didn't turn on you back there. It's likely your words will be reported."

Captain Marcus had lived in fear for years and his latest actions only strengthened that fear.

"You need to find an excuse to get away from here," the young lieutenant suggested.

"It will be fine. The men were too busy killing those poor people to notice anything I said," Marcus nervously stated, unsure who he was trying to convince: Titus or himself. "Anyway, I'm not leaving here without you."

If anyone knew of Marcus and Titus's friendship there would be no second chances, no mercy and no trial; just death. They were taking a risk just talking.

"Brigade 99 approaching from the rear, Captain," Marcus heard over the radio.

Panic started to set in. Marcus had called for reinforcements from eighth battalion, but brigade 99 were not part of eighth. They should not be here. "What are they doing here?" Titus asked his captain.

"The General is wanting to claim the glory of this victory, and he has sent the 99th and his son, to lead the charge," Marcus replied. "Make ready and prepare to join with brigade 99."

Titus was now in full panic mode. He worried greatly about the safety of his captain and friend; this summed up the man that Titus was. Unlike other Kappas, he believed in honour and kindness. The young lieutenant was a very handsome looking man, slightly less chiselled than Marcus, but tall and a very well presented individual. Unlike other Kappas, he was furnished with a head of curly blonde hair and lighter features. "They are here for you, someone has reported you."

"It is fine. Just act normal and stick by me," Marcus calmly answered.

Brigade 99 was led by Commander Tiberius, the General's oldest son. His troops tore through the rear line of the eighth and kept going. Not stopping to check in with the duty officer and not reporting to Captain Marcus. Proceeding straight towards the front line and straight towards Omega's defences. Large gun fire started to ring out around the town; it was soon accompanied by small arms fire. All of it directed from the front line of the Omega eastern defences towards brigade 99.

There were loud whistling sounds overhead. Marcus and Titus looked up to see rocket fire directed towards the Omega defences. Huge explosions sounded, one after the other as the barrage of rockets rained down on the large defensive guns protecting the outer limits of Khristade. The rockets and large arms fire did nothing to deter brigade 99, they ploughed forward, ever closer to the walls surrounding Khristade.

"Join at the rear of the brigade and press forward," Marcus ordered.

"For the glory of Kappa" was the only reply.

The mixture of rocket fire, the elite forces of brigade 99 and the sheer mass of the 17th brigade made short work of the Khristade defences. Kappa forces were now entering the city, and soon came further confirmation that other brigades had breached the defences and entered the Omega capital. A voice appeared on the radio – battalion command were sending further instructions to Commander Tiberius. "Brigade 99 commander, return to forward operating base."

"Confirmed," Commander Tiberius replied.

"Enact capture protocol," the crackly voice then stated.

"Confirmed" was again Tiberius's only response.

The majority of the 99th brigade left the front line as quickly as they entered, but left two of their armoured cars trailing. The cars pulled up about 30 metres short of Marcus's position at the rear of the 17th brigade and soldiers disembarked their cars, guns raised and trained on Marcus. "Captain Marcus, Kappa officer 24978. You have been judged as a non-believer, come peacefully and your death will be quick and merciful," Tiberius shouted.

Two gunshots rang out, Commander Tiberius dropped to his knees and then planted face down in the mud as blood began to pool around him. Marcus looked sideways to see Titus holding a still smoking, large calibre gun. He had shot the general's son.

"What have you done?" Marcus cried out in disbelief.

Marcus drew his firearm and repeatedly shot the Kappa soldier driving the closet transport, quickly pulling his body from the door and climbing into the driver's seat. "Titus, hurry," Marcus pleaded.

In those brief few moments of commotion, created by the shooting of Commander Tiberius, Marcus and Titus had secured the transport and were attempting to hastily exit Janstade.

03
Running

The third battalion had broken the Omega defences on the eastern side of Khristade. The sheer volume of the battalion made it impossible for the defences to hold, and the third battalion en masse was now storming the city streets, closely supported by a tank battalion. It was mainly grunts on the streets that day; in the Kappa armies those who do not make command are just grunts, thrown in at the deep end of any fight. Grunts are the first into every battle and their average life expectancy is just 16 years old. Not even seen as worthy enough for names, they were just numbers, but nicknames were common. One Kappa soldier on the streets of Khristade was 76349 or Blank, as a few of the other soldiers referred to him. Due to the sheer numbers within third battalion, it had allowed him to go relatively unnoticed. So much so that Blank had never fired his weapon. Blank was not your average Kappa soldier, shorter than most and a little portly. With light coloured hair and green eyes, he didn't fit, it made him unpopular with the other soldiers, who to a man all looked true Kappa – tall with dark hair and eyes. Blank had not done well in his education, barely surviving the cull; it was touch and go to the final days of selection; he had to best a fellow struggler in a fist fight to earn one of the last remaining places in the graduating class. The young girl whom he beat was taken away and executed along with the other class failures; shot in the back of the head and dumped in a mass grave, like a piece of garbage. Blank had been assigned to the third battalion some ten months previous, had been sent to the front lines a day after his 14th birthday. He was a strange boy, not indoctrinated enough to be vile and monstrous like his peers, but not a good person either. He didn't get on well with anyone and had the foulest mouth in all the Kappa ranks. He didn't believe that killing was the right choice, yet often chastised himself for thinking about choice. He was not fully consumed with hate, like many of his fellow Kappa soldiers, but enough damage had been done to make him confused about right and wrong.

Blank was advancing with the other soldiers into the city of Khristade, with the standing order to terminate any Omega seen on the streets. Loud recorded messages played over the radios. "Stay in your homes and disarm; any Omega citizen caught on the street will be killed. Kneel on the floors of your homes, hands above your heads, and submit to search and seizures."

As the small brigade to which Blank belonged moved towards an open square, a group of Omega residents were seen attempting to flee the city. The brigade began firing; several volleys were fired, killing many of the citizens. Several others stopped and dropped to their knees, hands raised high. It didn't matter: they were shot where they knelt. One of the division commanders grabbed a small child who had been trying to hide under her dead mother. The child looked like an Omega of about 10 years of age, blonde hair and the biggest blue eyes with soft facial features. The poor girl was screaming, howling like a demon. "Blank; come get your first one," his commander ordered.

Blank approached, pointing his gun at the child; his hands were visibly trembling, sweat was pouring from his brow. He knew that if he defied the order that he would join the child in one of the mass graves.

"Not my first, Commander, not a pathetic child. I want it to be a leader, a soldier. Someone worth killing," Blank stated with determination.

"Every enemy of Kappa is worth killing," the commander bellowed. "Even this pathetic child. The Omega turd needs to be put down like the animal it is. Now kill the turd or I will kill you."

With a deep breath Blank raised his gun to the head of the child. Her deep blue tear-filled eyes staring back at him. He felt like he could almost see her soul floating behind her eyes. His finger pressed gently against the trigger, building the nerve to squeeze his finger and end the child's life.

"All commanders, all commanders. Priority order incoming" blared over the radio. "High value target incoming to your area of operation. Kappa officers 24978 & 28113; travelling in an armoured car and approaching your area. Capture only order."

The commander grabbed at his radio, stumbling over his words. "All units return to division; two HVT on approach to our operating area. Kappa traitors have killed Commander Tiberius. Capture only order has been enacted. Take them alive."

In all the ruckus Blank had grabbed the girl away from the commander's grip, and grasping her by the hand had run. He was running as fast as possible away from the rest of his brigade, dragging the child along behind.

"Run faster, you must run faster. Otherwise we will be killed," Blank shouted at the child.

The child was pulling hard at the soldier's hand and shouting at him. "We must go this way, my family were heading towards home and the escape tunnels when you found us. It's this way," the child screamed, dragging Blank back towards the area they had just escaped.

"Back towards the soldiers?" Blank questioned. "No fucking way are we going that way."

"We must," the child moaned. "I have to get home, and we must escape the city."

"Fuck, fuck, fuck!" Blank shouted as the pair stopped in their tracks and turned to head back towards the army. "No fucking way are you going home; show me how to escape this city."

"I must go home first," the child grumbled.

"What the fuck is so important?"

"Family artefacts."

"Pictures and jewels, no way. Show me how to get out this fucking city."

The division commander had moved his troops to form a kill box around the approaching armoured car carrying Captain Marcus and Lieutenant Titus. The car was approaching quickly, and the soldiers were determined to stop the murderous traitors.

"Capture only," the commander reminded his troops. "Our general wants to exact his own form of revenge on the murderous scum traitors."

04
The Beginnings
of a Group

Blank and the child had skirted around the back of the soldiers that were lying in wait for Captain Marcus.

"That poor sod?" Blank exclaimed to the child. "We should warn him or kill him. They will do the most unimaginable things to him when they catch him."

The child ran across in front of the armoured car. Standing tense and closing her eyes in anticipation of being hit by the speeding car. Inside the car Marcus slammed on the brakes, coming to a sudden stop mere inches from the child. Blank ran across to meet the child and the stopped armoured car.

"Don't know what you have done, but those bastards are waiting for you – and if you want to live? Follow the girl!" Blank exclaimed hurriedly.

Marcus and Titus disembarked the car and began running after the girl; she had already set off towards the escape tunnels and a way out of the city.

Gun fire was hitting all around the three Kappa soldiers as they ran after the girl, towards what they were made to understand was an exit route from Khristade. The third brigade were chasing hard behind the soldiers. Firing volley after volley.

"How much further?" Marcus exclaimed.

"Not far. Just a little bit longer," the child replied.

The three Kappa traitors were tiring and the soldiers were closing down on their position. The gun fire getting closer and closer.

"This way!" the girl shouted as she darted off down a little side alley. The captain, lieutenant and Blank followed. They had run into what appeared to be a dead end.

"What the fuck is this?" Blank cried out.

"In here; quickly, before the soldiers see you," the child yelled.

The girl and the three men rushed towards a small hole that had been covered by a grate. The girl first, then Blank and Marcus. Just as Titus was about to climb into the hole, the sound of a loud shot pierced the evening air. Titus went down, hit in the chest. Blood started to soak into Titus's tunic; he was losing blood quickly. Marcus dragged Titus into the hole and closed the grate, bolting it from the inside. He dragged his friend a few yards into the darkness of the sewer-type tunnel, looking like it had not seen a soul in a very long time. "Titus, my friend," Captain Marcus said softly.

"It will be fine, it's not too bad. I'll make it," Titus slowly replied, as blood began filling his mouth as he tried to speak. "You need to keep up with the others; I can catch-up."

"We have time to rest, we can catch them up after you have rested," Marcus replied with a lump forming in his throat.

Marcus was holding Titus closely. He knew his friend would soon pass, and he was not going to leave him in these final moments.

Captain Marcus placed a tender kiss on the head of his dead friend, closed the lieutenant's eyes and wept. He released Titus from his embrace and gently settled him on the ground, stood and quick footed it down the tunnel. He ran into the darkness in the direction that the others had disappeared. When Marcus emerged from the tunnel, night had fallen. He was unsure of his bearings, but noted that Blank and the child were crouched behind a dilapidated wall, and that there were bright flashes and loud bangs in the distance behind him.

"Over here and keep your fucking head down," Blank whispered.

"Where is your friend?" the child asked.

"He didn't make it," the captain said sombrely. "Where are we? And who are you people?" he then snapped.

"We people are Blank and this is..." Blank paused – he didn't know the girl's name.

"Inga," the girl replied. "You are a Kappa officer?"

"I was a Kappa officer. The 99th came for me. My friend; my friend shot Commander Tiberius so I could escape them," Marcus replied, before Blank filled in some of the details.

"Your friend killed Commander Tiberius? There was a capture order for you both and the kid decided to help you."

Inga, Marcus and Blank were about two kilometres outside of Khristade. They had emerged from the escape tunnels in what was once a field of wheat, but now just a bowl of mud and dirt. They were stuck between the third brigade to the north and to the south were the medical and science divisions, along with the base of Kappa operations.

"We can't stay here long, we have no idea if the third or 99th followed us," Marcus proclaimed. "We can't go west as the eighth battalion is to the south-west and third brigade is to the north-west. We need to head east, to the eastern shores and attempt to escape to Sigma. The last I heard there was no war there."

Blank looked quizzically at Marcus and sarcastically replied, "That is over five hundred kilometres across land controlled by a vicious group of killer soldiers, who want to torture you and kill me and the girl. If we make it across the five hundred kilometres, we then have to cross the sea, and then hope Sigma is not at war, and hope that they will welcome us? Sounds like just a great plan."

"Any better ideas, grunt?" Marcus sternly replied.

The two men squared up to each other appearing to be readying for a fight. Inga stepped between them. "Do you really want to fight each other? We have thousands of people trying to kill us, and now you pair want to do the same?"

"Sorry, child," Marcus replied.

Blank shrugged his shoulders and grumbled under his breath. It had been decided that without any better alternatives that the little band of three would head east, attempt to avoid Kappa and anyone else for that matter whom they had to assume would be gunning for them, and escape to the eastern lands.

05
Science officer
416732

Wherever there was a Kappa battalion, a science division and medical division were always in support. They operated out of giant moving convoys; hundreds of trucks fitted with all kinds of equipment. Operating theatres, medical stations and science labs all constantly moving with the army's advances. The science division attached to third battalion had been edging closer to Khristade; as the battalion took to the city streets the science division was approximately five kilometres east of their position. The medical division would tend the wounded officers; any grunt soldiers injured were either left or dispatched without thought. The science division would prepare the rockets and other artillery, maintain equipment and develop new technologies to further Kappa's agenda for world domination. Science officer 416732 Aurora was a low ranking chemical weapons officer; she had finished in the 90th percentile of her education class; not high enough to be automatically taken for breeding; but good enough to not be sent to the front lines. A naturally attractive young woman, but she did her utmost to hide her looks, behind a pair of thick rimmed glasses and ill-fitting uniforms. She was petrified an officer would take notice of her and have her sent to a breeding centre, so masked her looks and quite deliberately maintained a higher than optimal weight. Aurora was another hidden foreigner, born to a Kappa father and Delta mother; she should have been disposed of at birth, but her father was a high ranking commander in the Kappa armies and forged her details; she looked very Kappa and as a child acted very Kappa, so was easy to hide in plain sight. When Aurora hit her teen years, something changed; a realisation that there was more to the world than Kappa edicts and laws. She worked hard at her education and was smart enough to finish in just the right percentile to find a good station in the ranks, where she knew that one day she could try and influence the direction of the wars. She was still young, around 19 years of age, having been sent to the science core at age 14. Working there for five years, she now worked under Captain Quirinus developing what Kappa leaders referenced as project testament. They were tasked with developing a weapon that would only kill the enemies of Kappa, and leave all Kappas, food sources and the ground untouched. Project testament had been in development for many years; the science division had tested many iterations of the weapon on innocent civilians but had never found the exact formula for success. The last tested formula had killed Omegas and Deltas, had not scorched the ground or harmed Kappas, but the weapon referred to as Keystone had bonded with water to create a toxic poison that was deadly to all. Captain Quirinus and Science officer 416732 were now working on formula 11356. A new version of Keystone had been developed and they were hopeful it would prevent the toxicity issues of the previous formula.

Captain Quirinus was readying the formula for the first test. Science officer 416732 was preparing the gas chamber for its next set of victims. "Aurora, can we load the chamber with test subjects please?"

"Yes, my captain," Aurora responded.

Several shackled test subjects were moved through into the chamber, Captain Quirinus loaded a gas canister and pushed an innocuous button on a control panel. The colourless and odourless gas was released into the chamber. The test subjects were unaware of the pain and suffering they would experience momentarily. Nothing was happening; with formula 11355 the subjects were crippled over in excruciating pain, and gasping for air and in just moments – but formula 11356 had no effect.

"Aurora, check the flow of the gas," Quirinus complained.

"Gas flow is fine, 10 bar pressure. All systems check and are showing a green status. It must be the keystone," Aurora replied in a frustrated sounding tone.

"Turn it off and return the test subjects to their accommodations," Quirinus demanded. "And expel the chamber."

"My captain; we should be thorough, test this formula across the board. Those were only Omega subjects."

"Do as you are told, girl, and don't ever question my orders again!" Quirinus screamed back at Aurora.

"Yes, my captain," was her only reply.

Captain Quirinus was checking the data from the earlier test; he was troubled by what had happened, or as it appeared not happened. The change to this keystone was significant – it may have resulted in a less pronounced effect on the test subjects but not to the extent of zero effect. He checked the data and then checked it again. There was a puzzling sequence in the formula. Quirinus moved to a set of medical refrigeration cabinets and grabbed two of the vials being stored. The captain inserted them into a large machine that would compare the vials. He impatiently waited next to the screen for the results. As the results appeared on the screen, Quirinus was taken aback by what has was seeing. "It couldn't be," he said quietly to himself.

"What couldn't it be?" a female voice questioned.

"Aurora, I didn't hear you enter the lab. Take a look at this!"

Aurora made her way over to the screen and stood next to Captain Quirinus.

"Do you see what I am seeing?" the captain questioned.

"Yes, my captain, the sequence is completely wrong."

"But who could have done this? Why would they have done..." The captain stopped mid-sentence; he couldn't talk. His limbs were going numb, he stumbled backwards and fell into a desk before sliding to the floor. It was becoming more difficult for him to breathe. Looking up at Aurora, he was puzzled – why was she was not helping him? As his eyes began to blur he noticed a long syringe in the hand of his female assistant.

"Sorry, Captain, but you didn't offer me any other choice."

Aurora stood for a little while until Quirinus was no longer breathing. She hurried to destroy as much information and as many samples she could. She knew there was not long, so grabbing a bag, she swept all the samples into it and hurriedly set the terminals to self-delete. There would be backups and copies, but it would take time for the Kappa science officers to retrieve them. Aurora had to do all she could to hinder the scientific advances and keep the Kappa science division from creating a workable keystone solution. Taking the bag, she bustled along the outer walkway to an adjoining lab that has the facility to destroy and contain samples. The young woman scanned a security badge and entered the lab, she threw the samples into a furnace and ran round a desk to the control panel. Hurrying to set the furnace controls for a 30 second delay, Aurora calmly left the lab and prepared to jump from the moving vehicle, picked her spot and leapt. Landing with a hard thud, Aurora rolled away from the convoy and down a slight decline, into an area well covered with bracken. Glancing back up to see the furnace exhaust fire.

Alarms began to sound on the trucks; bells rang and lights brightly shone into the night. Soldiers disembarked the trucks and began hunting across the ground. Aurora stayed silently hidden, watching for the lights and moving slowly when able to do so. She was edging further away from the convoy and the soldiers, and when clear of the lights she would rise to her feet and run a few metres before ducking down again. When the moment arrived, the science officer ran as far away as she could, only stopping briefly to remove her Kappa tunic and any items that could identify her as Kappa. It would be light soon and the young women needed to blend in, make it difficult for Kappa patrols to easily identify her; they would know of her betrayal. She needed to quickly find help.

Aurora was tracking along a minor river, staying far enough off the main route to remain unnoticed, but close enough to allow her to gather her bearings. As she made her way through the brush on the riverside, she noticed a small group making their way along the opposite bank. The sight of the three strangers struck Aurora as odd – there were two men and a child. The men were not Omegas, they were wearing some parts of Kappa uniforms, but what were they doing with a child? And why were they away from their units? She continued to track the group for a few miles. It became obvious that they too were avoiding Kappa river patrols, and staying just far enough away from the river and parallel roads to suggest they were hiding just as she was. Approaching a small bridge crossing, Aurora decided that help was what she needed, and three souls hiding from Kappa would seem to be good help. Little did she know that the three strangers were more wanted than her! Officer 416732 reached the bridge and began to cross, hoping deep down that the strangers were as they seemed.

"Hello," she nervously blurted out. "I'm Aurora; I am hoping you might be willing to help me?"

"Stop, come no closer," an important sounding voice proclaimed. "Where is your allegiance?"

"I am a Delta child," Aurora began to say as the three strangers moved into focus; the two men had their sidearms trained on her. "I have escaped a Kappa transport and am looking for help. Please can you help me?"

"I am Marcus, I too am a Delta child, born to Kappa control. What service did you perform?" Marcus asked abruptly.

"Science officer," Aurora replied. "I jumped from the medical and science convoy north-west of here."

Although there was uncertainty from Marcus, he had a voice in his head telling him that Aurora could be trusted, and because of them both being of Delta origins, he should help her.

Aurora was wearing very little, so it was not difficult for Marcus to see she was unarmed and there was no clear sign of any type of communication devices. He agreed that Aurora could travel with them. The now expanded group returned to the undergrowth along the riverbank and continued downstream.

"You would have to be fucking mad to want to travel with us," Blank bluntly stated to the young science officer. "He has a capture order, direct from General Hades, hanging over his head, and I'm a deserter and a traitor who helped an enemy of the state."

"An enemy of the state? You mean the little girl?" Aurora replied with laughter. "And what did he do to get General Hades's attention?"

"He murdered the General's son," Blank nonchalantly stated. "Well, his friend did, I think. Every soldier in the Kappa army is looking for him."

Aurora was a little impressed. Although now knowing she was likely in more danger with the group than without, she enjoyed the thought of Hades being in pain, and felt reassured that she was with the man who had helped inflict that pain.

06
The taking of
Khristade

General Hades was furious, he was raging with anger. His son had been killed and those guilty were free. Having trashed the forward operating base command, killed two subordinate soldiers and ordered the execution of the entire brigade that incompetently allowed his son's killers to escape... General Hades had lost children before. Many had been killed like heroes fighting for Kappa and doing their duty, but for his son to be struck down like an insignificant in the turd-filled streets, and by one of his own no less. It had enraged the general to his limits. Everyone would carry the price of this betrayal, everyone would pay through sufferance. The first on his list was the sniper who had killed Titus. "I wanted him alive," the general screamed at the third division commander. "Who did this; who shot him?"

"It may–" was all the division commander could say before Hades pulled out his side arm and shot him.

"It may, it may," the general screamed into the face of the commander as he lay bleeding to death from his wound. "I don't want may be. I want the man responsible here in front of me before the hour is out."

The general was on full tilt, ordering almost every brigade onto the streets of Khristade. He wanted the capital and would make an example of any man, woman or child that stood in his path.

Khristade had once been a beautiful city, that was left unaffected by the wars over the last thousand years. It stood as a shining beacon of history. Old buildings littered the narrow streets of cobbled walkways, wooden framed houses and shops made the streets look like something out of an old oil painting; but now the city was in ruins, tank battalions were rumbling down the narrow streets. They were approaching the capitol building, the state leaders were gathered inside. If they surrendered, they would likely be executed, but if they fought, many more brave Omegas would be killed. The council leaders wouldn't let that happen, so they raised the white flag above the capitol building and sent an encrypted communication to all their fighters to flee the city and to not engage with the enemy. As their last act, the leaders would try to save as many of their people as possible.

The capitol was surrounded, the white flag was fluttering above the main tower, the Omega leaders were being marched into the street. This is where they would be tried and punished, as enemies to Kappa. There would be no opportunity to plead their cases, they were the enemy and deserved no mercy.

The general had travelled from the forward command base to the capitol; he strode from his car to the first of the Omega leaders. "How do you plead?" he menacingly asked.

Before the man had a chance to reply, Hades screamed, "Guilty. Death by hanging."

A group of Kappa soldiers created a noose from a tow rope and flung it over a light post; the man was dragged to the post and strung up, taking only a few moments of thrashing for the man to perish.

"Who is the leader?" Hades asked, but nobody stepped forward. "Who is the leader? Do not make me repeat myself again."

An elderly women stepped toward the cruel general. "I am the leader; do as you must," she said bravely. "You will not get the satisfaction of us begging or pleading for our lives."

"You will be taken to the roof of your capitol building. Take in the sights of your beloved city burning to the ground. Then you take a walk off the edge, willingly or otherwise. Take her away," the general ordered.

The woman under guard had reached the top of the capitol building. Khristade was ablaze, fires and smoke filled the night's air. The Omega council leader was made to watch as her fellow councillors were tried and executed.

"How do you plead?" General Hades asked the next Omega, but again without giving her the chance to reply. "Guilty," Hades yelled with a sense of joy. "Death by beheading."

A soldier drew a long-bladed knife from his belt and approached the poor women; two soldiers held her down, kneeling face towards the floor. The soldier swung his knife with all his might, and again and again. At the fourth swing the woman's head was removed, and a soldier picked it up like a trophy, lifting it high up to ensure that the council woman atop the capitol building could see the anguished face of the recently decapitated women. One after another were all executed until all that remained of the Omega leaders was the old woman stood on the top of the capitol building.

"You turn my dear," the general bellowed with a smirk.

Without a moment's hesitation the woman cried out "For all Omega" and stepped off the ledge; she plummeted six storeys, no screams or cries. She died on impact with the cobbled stone street below.

"Burn it to the ground," the general ordered as he stepped into his car and was driven away from Khristade.

07
The Remnants

A small brigade of eight Omega soldiers had been fighting their way towards the capitol building when they heard the order to flee. They knew there was almost certain death if they tried to help their state leaders, but it was their duty. Although mere farmers, they had fought bravely; the brigade were the most special of the Omega forces. Led by senior officer Captain Balder, it was his decision to make. He knew his soldiers would lay down their lives, but they had been ordered to escape, to live to fight another day.

"We follow orders; we live to remember their sacrifice," Balder ordered. "We will track along the escape tunnels from the capitol building, pick up anyone who did make it out. Then we get out of this bloody city."

The group moved out on a route designed to cross paths with as many escape points as possible, knowing it would not be easy, that they would almost certainly encounter many enemy forces, but Captain Balder was determined to rescue as many as possible. Balder is the most decorated officer in the history of the Omega defence force. One of only a handful of full-time soldiers that operated within the force, a hero to the people of Omega. He had fought battles for the citizens and kept peace within the state. His fame was mainly due to the battle of Denstade, an encounter with a Kappa army unit that had secretly infiltrated the town. When discovered, the Kappa unit took the townspeople and threatened their very existence. The stories tell that Captain Balder single handedly saved every Omega life within the town, whilst it burned to the ground. Since the Kappa invasion, Balder had fought several skirmishes against the invaders and won each hard-fought victory, a master tactician and fighter; the truest form of Omega hero. Now a man in his forties, bearded with blonde-brown hair and the typical Omega blue eyes. Tall, but not Kappa tall and very fit; all his years within the defence force had left Balder hardened to the world, and portraying a gruff exterior with everyone; everyone bar his wife; the captain would have jumped in front of a speeding truck or dived onto his own sword to protect his beloved Ava. His second was Commander Torsten, a dairy farmer of huge size and strength. There was Sergeant Sten, an arable farmer with the look of a man who had experienced a very hard life. Erik and Hilda were new to the team, teen siblings and the grandchildren of Omega's lead council woman. The final three positions in the group were made up of Ulf, Ivar and Freyja; three farm hands who had been members of the Omega auxiliary military forces.

"Ivar, find high ground," Balder ordered. Ivar was the best deer hunter in Khristade and had developed the skills of a veteran military sniper. Acknowledging the order, he ran off into a building. The others fanned out, moving from one position of cover to the next. Steadily covering ground and moving towards the first escape tunnel. Balder signalled for the team to halt and lower; he had spotted two Kappa soldiers running through the streets and a further brigade in pursuit. His team were all in cover as the two soldiers ran through their sights, Balder ordering the Omega team to not engage the enemy, knowing a whole brigade was in close proximity. The brigade crossed their path, moving too briskly to notice the seven soldiers hiding in cover.

"One Kappa down," Ivar signalled.

"Confirm last," Balder quickly responded.

"One Kappa officer taken down, silent kill."

Balder was irked, he had ordered no engagement, but was not about to argue over open comms. He moved the team out, again moving tactically from cover to cover until they were a block from the first escape tunnel.

"Kappa swarming the tunnel," Ivar reported.

"Move on, go to route two," Balder ordered.

Balder was annoyed that his team sniper had potentially alerted the Kappa troops to the location of the escape route by killing the officer, but what could he do? He wasn't going to engage a whole brigade with a handful of farmers.

The Omega team moved through the streets uninterrupted until they reached escape route two which was positioned only two streets from the capitol building at the centre of Khristade. Ivar reported a large enemy presence surrounding the area adjacent to the escape tunnel entrance.

"Several captives, all deceased," he reported. "Wait one minute. She is on top of the capitol building. Fuck, no!"

"Stay professional and report what you see," Balder commanded over the now silent radio channel.

"Sorry, sir, but it was the council woman."

"Grandma?" Hilda screamed.

"They fucking threw her off the roof." Ivar had witnessed the Omega leader dropping from the roof of the capitol and falling to her certain death.

Hilda was in tears and Erik was consoling his sister.

"I understand it is tough, but we have to stay professional. We are soldiers, loss and death is the only certainty of war," Balder calmly stated, before ordering his sergeant to check the tunnels.

Sten moved to the escape route, lifting the grate that protected the tunnel entrance; he jumped down and was confronted by an elderly man, an unidentifiable man carrying a large book.

"Stop, don't move a muscle, who the fuck are you?" Sten shouted, raising his gun menacingly at the man.

"Well, who the fluff are you?" the man nervously blurted back.

"Sten, Sergeant in the Omega defence force."

He was gesturing with his gun for the man to move forward and into more light, but the man didn't budge. "Fucking move into the light," Sten yelled. "I am required to check you for weapons."

As the man nervously moved forward he stammered over his name. "I'm Frode, historian to the Omega council."

"Then you're very lucky to have found us."

"Well, well yes I suppose I must be."

After the two men had climbed from the tunnel, Frode introduced himself to the team. The task of discovering the truth had become a 30-year obsession for Frode; the Omega leader pushed him to delve deeper to discover the truths of Omega. Frode was an old man now, long scraggy hair pulled tight in a ponytail, and a grey unkept beard. He looked more homeless man than confident courtier to the highest official in the land. A very well educated, well spoken man. A rarity in Omega, he never worked the land or tended fields, Frode had been educated by his father; a councillor and high ranking Omega official. He had grown up in the central office of Omega and had known the leader for his entire life. When she took office, her first act was to create the position of Omega historian and hand Frode the keys to all the libraries of the land, but in those 30 years he had not discovered any real truths; all the documents and books seemed to contradict each other and his frustration was growing; this had led him to bicker and argue with the leader just days before the Kappa invasion. The old man recognised Hilda and Erik from pictures in the offices of their grandmother. He could tell from their sullen looks and the tears in the young girl's eyes that something dreadful must have befallen her; his last words to his friend of 60 plus years were the hateful rantings of a tired old man, who had lost his faith. Frode explained how he had escaped, and about the courage of the council leaders. It was their actions that had allowed others to escape the Kappa soldiers. The team were within feet of the Kappa armies, and they had seven more escape routes to cover, seven more places where they hoped to find other Omegas to lead out of Khristade and to relative safety.

08
The Book

The team were moving as quickly as they could whilst trying to maintain their cover. Passing escapes routes three, four and five without finding any further survivors, they had almost given up hope of finding anyone else. Balder was hurrying his troops as they had been slowed by Frode. Much older than the rest of the team and slowed further by the enormous book he insisted on bringing along.

"You should drop the bloody book," Balder bemoaned.

"I shall not be leaving this behind. If the book stays, I stay," Frode passionately responded.

"You are slowing the team, putting us all at risk."

"I will not be leaving the book," Frode stated emphatically.

As the team approached escape route six, Ivar, who was maintaining overwatch, radioed to Captain Balder, that a large number of troops were moving around the area ahead. It appeared to be a staging post for further battle operations. From the elevated viewpoint it looked to be a whole brigade between the team and the next extraction point.

This encouraged Balder to change his plan. "Divert to tunnel seven. We will have to miss six; we aren't going to fight a whole damn brigade today."

Ivar was asked to guide the team south-east and along the river to escape access seven, which he obligingly began; they turned and shuffled through a very long narrow alley. The passage would lead the Omega team down the river and along the bank to the escape route. As the team reached the end of the alley and turned to make their way down to the river, all hell broke loose.

Overwatch had not spotted a large enemy force on one of the river crossings, but they had spotted the team. Beginning to fire on their position, heavy machine gun fire and other small arms rained down on the team as they scrambled to find cover and return fire.

Balder had grabbed Frode and dragged him into cover. In the scramble the old man dropped his book. In the commotion the old man started to crawl on his belly back towards the book.

"I must get the book," he cried.

"Leave the bloody book and get back in cover, you stupid old sod," Balder shouted

"You don't understand, I must get the book."

Balder grabbed Frode's leg and dragged him back to cover, ordering all team members to fire on the enemy position, as he dived out and grabbed the book. With a swift and precise rolling motion, Balder had grabbed the book and returned to the relative safety of the wall he and Frode were crouching behind.

"Abort mission, abort mission. Use route seven, evacuate to route seven," Balder barked

Escape route seven was only a hundred feet in front of their position, but it felt like a thousand. With the well-oiled precision of a much more seasoned and veteran team, one by one they were able to make it from their position to the entrance of escape route seven and into the tunnels. The team waited at the entrance to provide cover fire for Ivar as he left his elevated position and charged towards the escape route. With all the team and Frode in the tunnel, they quickly made their way out of the city, setting mines and other traps along the way to ensure they were not followed.

The team were into open land around Khristade. The tunnel had led them to the north-east corner of the city's outer limits. Balder and his team were relatively safe for a minute, enough of a moment to plan the next move and for all the team to take a breather. But Balder couldn't plan, he was overcome with frustration towards Frode for putting himself in danger.

"What is it with that bloody book!"

"This bloody book, it is a thousand years old. It tells of a time before war, when the gods ruled the planet in peace and serenity," Frode passionately stated.

"A bloody story book; I risked my neck for a story book," Balder moaned, becoming more irate.

"Not a story! History, our history, the history of Omega, Kappa, Theta, all the worlds. It tells of the great gods ruling over all from their citadel in Central city."

"What a load of bull crap," Sten blurted.

"No, our leader believed in this. She had me spend the last 30 years deciphering and decoding this language, she believed it would give reason to the wars and give answers to how they must end. Bring peace back into the worlds. She believed and you should too. Even in the darkest of days she had faith in our history, and that this literature could lead us to find the answers to cure this world."

"Grandma thought this to be true?" Hilda questioned.

"Yes, your grandmother, the greatest of us all, believed this to be true and believed that it was a vital key in finding the answers to end these wars."

Balder was not a trusting sort; he only believed in the two certainties of death and war. "What would you have us do? Hike across the world to find this citadel?" he sarcastically asked.

"Yes, I believe the book leads us to the citadel, and the citadel leads us to the gods. Who will lead us back into a world of peace and prosperity."

The captain was having none of it. He dismissed the idea out of hand – he was not about to risk his team's life for a story in an old book, that a strange old man had suggested their beloved leader believed in. He needed more than just hearsay and a dusty old book;

he required hard facts. Balder moved the team out, heading towards the outer limits of the city. Where they would find a few remaining buildings suitable to lay-low. He was hoping to find some safety and much needed time to assess their next move. The Omega team were homeless, state-less and lacking in numbers and arms.

09
Spoils of War

K hristade was ablaze; the Kappa soldiers had taken to the streets and set alight every building they could; hundreds of years of untouched history was going up in flames. Commander Crispus was leading fourth brigade through the streets, with flame units torching homes and businesses alike. The commander took great pleasure in the destruction of Omega, and to him there were no rules of engagement, no mercy for any enemy of Kappa, and his troops were allowed all the spoils of war. Crispus was depraved, a bloodthirsty and cruel man, and he encouraged his men to be the same. As the Omegas fled the city, the men of the fourth brigade murdered and abused anyone that crossed their path. As a group was seen fleeing to the north-west, the fourth brigade moved to intercept them. The Omegas were civilians, were mere farmers and shopkeepers, and this group was no different – several small families that had been hiding together in a house. The house was now aflame, and the group were running, unarmed and carrying several small children. They were scared and running for their lives.

The Kappa soldiers of fourth brigade had closed in on the group, having already run down two of the families and murdering the men without conscious thought, capturing the women and children. The other families fought, they fought hard to try and evade capture, but were no match for the soldiers; all were killed or taken prisoner. The ones unlucky enough to avoid immediate death were knelt down in a line with hands bound behind them. There was one certainty about their situation: they would suffer. Commander Crispus approached the civilians. He ordered the families to be grouped together so he could begin dispatching the youngest family members. Murdering the children in front of their families was pure pleasure for Crispus and torment for the Omegas. His sick gratification was easy for all to see.

During Crispus' education he had not been the smartest, not finished near the top of class and should never have made Commander, but his insanity played well with the teachers. If ever given an opportunity to fight, he would savagely attack the other children. On one such occasion in a combat drill he had beaten two of his classmates to death with his bare fists, and during the final war game he had led a squad into a savage battle where he ordered the vicious killing of his opposition group's leader. He only did this to reduce the pool of potential officer candidates. Crispus fought and murdered his way into the position he now found himself and nothing would stop him. The Commander was striding up and down the line of Omegas; his eyes told of his depraved thinking, dreaming up all manner of disgusting brutalities he could order against his prisoners, his face twitching and ticking with anticipation.

A soldier stood next to Crispus dropped to his knees and blood started pouring from a wound in his chest. Then another went down, and another. Gun fire erupted all around the Kappa soldiers; Crispus stood his ground, didn't blink as the bodies continued to fall all around him. He screamed orders at his men, barked expletives as the Kappa bodies were piling up. Captain Balder was shouting orders to his troops as they fired on the enemy; his team had a clear line of sight to the Kappas from their position, hunkered down on the city's edge in one of a few untouched buildings. They had the tactical advantage, high ground and good cover. The captain ordered his sergeant and three other soldiers to attempt a rescue of the Omegas that were being held. "Move swift, remain in cover. We will provide covering fire from this position. Get as many as you can."

The Omega soldiers moved from the building, maintaining cover and moving in a direct path towards the Omega captives. Each Kappa soldier that they encountered was swiftly dealt a deathly blow. Balder was maintaining overwatch and systematically picking off any Kappa in the team's path. Sten and his group had reached the Omegas, they freed some who ran immediately towards the direction Sten had appeared from. Others just knelt, weeping and praying over their dead children and loved ones. Sten grabbed one woman, pulling her along behind as the team made a hasty exit.

"Somebody kill them!" Crispus screamed as he himself picked up a large weapon and started to rain fire on the escaping Omegas. He hit two before Sten could turn and return fire. He hit the Kappa commander in the leg and shoulder, but Crispus didn't flinch. He replied in kind, hitting Sten, then two more shots struck the soldier and he was down, blood pooling around him, coughing and spitting blood as he lay stricken in the dirt.

A shot was heard whistling in the air as it passed the Omegas civilians, the shot hitting Crispus true and centre, this shot finally putting the commander down. The defence force all began firing in the direction of the commander, shot after shot hit his now limp carcass. They were determined to make damn sure he was down for good. Freyja ran to check on Sten, but he was dead. The defence force had saved a few Omegas and killed the butcher Crispus, but at the cost of losing their sergeant, ally and friend.

The team said some very quick words and left their friend's body where it lay, hastily leaving Khristade with the Omega civilians. The team were headed towards an outlying village called Ramstade. It was a large village with plenty of potential hiding spots and had already been raided by the Kappa forces. It would hopefully allow the civilians some protection and the team some much needed time to rest and re-group.

10
This must end

The Omega defence force now numbered seven, they had lost Sten in the last encounter and were still reeling from the loss of their friend. Held up in Ramstade for the last 12 hours, the team had rested and were readying themselves to move.

"This must stop, the killing has to end. What did Grandma sacrifice herself for?" Hilda cried whilst being comforted by her brother.

"There is nothing left! Khristade is a burning husk of the place we all lived in and loved. We have nothing left," Erik stammered tearfully.

"We must fight back," Commander Torsten proclaimed.

"Fight with what? We are only seven " Erik angrily shouted.

Frode was attentively listening to the conversation, wanting to speak and to remind everyone about the book. That the Omega councillors believed in the book. Believed it would lead them to the answers that could save the world and free them all from the killing. Free from the wars and from the destruction that had filled their lives.

Balder was determined to fight on. "We shall re-group, find other survivors and mount an attack on the Kappa base of operations."

"Find who? Find them where?" Erik angrily blurted out.

The conversation quickly descended into an argument. There were many points of view – some of the group wanted to hit back at Kappa, whereas others wanted to hide. Erik thought it best to escape Omega and head to the old Delta state; they could blend in and survive. Freyja was keen to stay in Omega and try to build a resistance.

Frode had heard enough – if everyone else could voice their opinion then he felt it only right to speak up. "We need to head to Central state and find the citadel. That will give us what we need to end the war forever!"

"Mad talk from a stupid old sod," Balder bemoaned. "Belief in stories is the ramblings of people without any real hope."

"Grandma believed in it. Are you calling her mad or a stupid old sod?" Erik questioned whilst aggressively posturing towards Balder.

"What am I to do, boy? Ask you all to risk your lives on what is an impossible journey, just because a crazy old man with a book suggested it? We do not know your grandmother believed in this, we only have his word," Balder replied whilst attempting to de-escalate the situation.

"Haven't heard anything better," Ivar grumbled. "Why not? Have nothing to stay here for."

Further arguments erupted; there was no clear agreement and Balder had had enough.

Balder was walking around the old farmhouse where the team were resting. He was lost in his thoughts and was not as attentive as normal. The lack of concentration had allowed a man to infiltrate the area and to within feet of Balder.

"Sir, please don't be alarmed. My name is Marcus and I mean you no harm and offer no misgivings."

Balder span on the spot and draw his sidearm.

"I am unarmed, sir," Marcus calmly stated whilst holding his hands in the air.

"You are a Kappa officer! Why shouldn't I shoot you where you stand?"

"Sir, I was a Kappa officer, but I am no more, and I truly mean no harm to you or your companions. We tracked you here with the hope of finding help."

"We?" Balder questioned.

Marcus explained that he had travelled with another Kappa soldier, a Kappa science officer and what they believed to be a child of Omega. They were looking for help to escape to the east, where they believed they would be safe.

Balder ordered Marcus's companions out into the open. The first to emerge was the child. Inga introduced herself and told of her escape and the help she had received from Marcus and Blank; she told Balder that the men were good and that the Kappa armies were hunting them. Blank and Aurora also emerged, also pleading with Balder for help.

Balder asked the three Kappas to disarm themselves and move into the farmhouse. Once inside, he relayed the story to his men. They were reticent to accept a tale from the Kappa soldiers, but the child looked Omega and why would she lie? Although a little unnerved, a majority of the Omega defence force agreed the strangers could stay and rest. They could refresh themselves and then be on their way.

"Those Kappas should feel lucky we didn't take um outside and slit their fucking throats," Ivar grumbled as he left the room. "Nasty smell in here, I'm going outside."

Later that evening, Balder and Commander Torsten were discussing options. Balder was very much against the mythical quest that Frode was suggesting, but Torsten thought that if their beloved leader had faith in the story, then perhaps they needed to have faith in her and believe that maybe it was possible to end the wars.

"We should put it to a vote," Torsten suggested.

"This is the Omega defence force, not a democracy," Balder bluntly replied.

"This is not a normal situation; don't we have to give the men choice? We cannot order them to sacrifice anymore."

"They have sacrificed much, but who hasn't?"

Torsten had no answer, as everyone had given everything, but he was adamant that they had to offer them a choice. They would offer two choices: stay and fight, or follow the mad old historian on his quest for all the answers and a potential end to the wars.

The votes were cast as a silent ballot, pieces of paper were handed around to the seven Omega soldiers, who all quickly cast their votes.

"Four votes to three in favour of Frode's plan," Torsten stated.

"Then I guess we have a very long journey ahead of us. We will need provisions and ammunition, and it would be good to find a map. We also must decide what to do with them?" Balder questioned as he pointed towards the Kappa soldiers.

"Excuse me, sir, but what is this plan you are speaking of? Could we not be of some help to you?" Marcus politely asked.

"We are heading east, to Central. That is all you need know."

"That is the direction we had planned to travel, we are good soldiers and we will follow orders. If you could please see yourself to allowing us to join you expedition?"

"You will do as you are told and no weapons," Balder replied in a stern voice, exerting his authority. "We move out at first light. Erik and Hilda, find some provisions. Torsten, you're on ammunition; and someone find me a map or drawings, anything that can help guide us. Freyja, find our newest recruits some clothes – we are not travelling with Kappa soldiers."

The team set about their duties and in a matter of a few hours they would be heading east, through occupied Omega and the enemy state of Kappa. They would have to navigate the eastern shore defence and cross the sea to Sigma and finally Central. They were 12 souls; 12 people that would begin this quest.

11
New friends

The team had left Ramstade two days ago, their progress painfully slow. Balder was beginning to question his decision to allow the old man and the girl to join them on their journey. The 12 deliberately avoided main transit routes and expansive open ground, having stuck to little used paths and tracks to avoid encounters with opposition soldiers or any desperate travellers. No one was an ally, everyone was to be treated as an enemy. The country was filled with desperate folks who could turn on the group, in the hope of some reward or benefit. Captain Marcus had been using the opportunity to engage with the Omega defence force, having struck up brief conversations with all the team members, excluding Balder. He had made it quite clear that he had no inclination to speak with any Kappas. Others within the Omega team had not been as closed off – Freyja and Ulf had both listened to Marcus's story, and the early seeds of acceptance were starting to blossom. Hilda and Erik were less accepting, the raw emotions from their grandmother's death were still fresh. Their faces told a story, anguished looks anytime either Aurora, Blank or Marcus spoke.

Aurora and Blank were keeping to themselves; brief interactions with Inga their only conversation, having given up making nice with the Omegas. Feelings were running high on both sides and the Kappas felt aggrieved at being treated like the enemy. This annoyed them somewhat – they had sacrificed to fight against Kappa; traitors back in their world and traitors in this world too. Marcus was more pragmatic; he was older than Blank or Aurora, and had more life skills. Knowing the importance of friendship and camaraderie, he intended to help the Omegas and attempt to live in a world of peace.

Approaching the next obstacle in their path, as the end of a forest path approached there was nothing in front of them but wide open farmland. Flat and true without a single ditch or hillock. To circumnavigate the mega fields would cost a day or two, so the choice was clear: they must cross. Balder sent Ivar and Ulf to scout for the narrowest section of field.

"I would estimate that we are only a mile or two from the Kappa forward operations; we should be extra vigilant," Marcus whispered to Freyja. "I would think we have travelled no more than four miles per day; so eight total; and the Kappa army's medical and science divisions always lag no more than ten miles behind the main attack force. They will almost certainly be close by. Crossing here is not a sound tactical move."

Freyja nodded in appreciation of the information as she jumped to her feet and took her newfound knowledge to Balder. As soon as the young soldier opened her mouth, the Captain leapt to his feet and stormed towards Marcus.

"Tactically inept, am I?" Balder angrily shouted.

"I am merely trying to assist. The convoys are out there and the sound tactic would be to avoid them," Marcus replied calmly.

"If you want to assist then tell me exactly where they are?"

"The convoys will be no more then two miles off our current location, on a well-used but not main transport route. An ancillary route perhaps. There are no more than three to four miles between each convoy, and they will never cross paths."

"I can use that information."

"You should ask Aurora – she will have more detailed knowledge."

Balder didn't utter another word and certainly not a thank you. He moved over to where Aurora and Blank were sitting, grumbling at them before producing a paper and pencil. Handing the writing implements to Aurora, he demanded that she mark the likely positions of the convoys.

Marcus was pleased he was able to assist; he was constantly looking for ways to gain trust and offer insight that would help the cause. Freyja looked towards Marcus and gave him a little head bob, a silent thank you of sorts.

Ivar and Ulf had returned, Ulf had found a narrow opening about ten minutes south of their current location, with a hedge to cover on one side. The distance across the field was about two thousand metres with more forest on the adjacent side. The diagram that Aurora had scribbled suggested that the nearest convoy was about a mile further south. The enemy would be very close, but it was not an impossible position. The group moved to the location Ulf had scouted, and Balder sent Torsten, Ivar and Erik further south to monitor for convoy movements.

"You three keep watch south, when everyone is clear across the field backtrack to here. We will cover your crossing." Then raising his voice a good few decibels so everyone could hear his instructions: "Everyone stays north side of the hedgerow. Hilda and Freyja take care of Frode, and you, Kappa soldier, the little girl is your responsibility."

Torsten, Ivar and Erik moved to the southerly position as ordered by their captain. When the soldiers were in position Balder sent the first small group across the field. They would cross in small groups to avoid unneeded attention. Frode, with his escorts, crossed the field without alarm. Marcus, Inga and Ulf went next, Marcus carrying the young girl on his back to speed up the crossing. They reached the safety of the far side in a fraction of the time Frode's group took.

Balder and Blank were left, and as they started across the field Balder's radio lit up with chatter.

"Kappa troop movement south, south-east; moving at a rate of knots" blared across the radio.

The message repeated twice before Balder confirmed he had received the message and ordered everyone to stop and cover. The group already across the open space were in forest cover and safe from enemy spotters; Balder and Blank were out in the open and in serious danger of being seen. Thinking quickly, Balder ordered Blank back to their previous position – if they were spotted they had to draw attention away from the rest of the team. Blank and Balder dived into the undergrowth just short of the main forest as gun fire began whistling past them. The captain grabbed at his radio. "Do not return fire, I repeat, do not return fire!"

He made the assumption only himself and Blank had been spotted and returning fire would allow the enemy Kappa soldiers to identify the team's other positions. Balder grabbed Blank by the collar and dragged him up and into the forest. As they ran through the undergrowth, Balder handed Blank a side arm. "Don't have any funny thoughts. Use that on me and my team will skin you before breakfast. Move back into the forest and head north," Balder ordered his Kappa companion. The pair began moving faster and deeper into the cover of the trees, heading directly away from the Kappa position.

A brigade of troops had disembarked the convoy and were in pursuit of Balder and Blank; they ran directly past Torsten, Erik and Ivar without noticing them and charged into the undergrowth. Tracking approximately 250 metres behind Balder and Blank, every 20 paces the troops would halt and fire a volley of shots towards what they assumed was the position of Omega Captain Balder and his companion. The shots ripped through the foliage as the Kappa division advanced through the forest. Balder and Blank were taking refuge in a ditch around 400 metres into the forest, and the Kappa soldiers were approaching fast. Balder signalled to Blank to move right. He would have an alternate line of sight towards the approaching soldiers. It was two against 16 but Balder always fancied his chances in a shootout.

Blank had found a good spot and was preparing himself for the fight. He was a very reluctant soldier and was sweating, hands shaking with nerves as the enemy approached. Balder peeked out of his position just as the first of the Kappa soldiers fell, shortly followed by another; they were falling like silent dominoes. Panic set in to the Kappa troops, this was the moment to attack. Balder lifted his gun and started to fire, and Blank joined him, advancing quickly towards the remaining Kappas, firing at will. The Kappa troops had been caught out by Ivar advancing behind them, it was him that had begun the killing, his silenced rifle doing its deadly work. In a few flashes of rifle muzzle the fight was over. Ivar was sweeping around the Kappa troops, ensuring they were all down for good, he found one that was not quite dead. He pulled out a knife and ended the soldier's existence with no hesitation, a knife inserted upwards from under the soldier's chin.

Balder was pleased with Blank and his Omega troops, a poor example of a Kappa soldier and three farmers had just ended the lives of 16 real Kappa soldiers without breaking a sweat. Balder approached Blank and snatched the sidearm away from him. "Good work, soldier" was all the captain said as he strode past.

Balder thought it best to not immediately re-join the teams; he sent word to Ulf to begin moving out, and that himself and his four remaining companions would re-join them later; the team would press on without their Captain, would move north-east to stay in cover. Balder and the others would track around the long route. Balder wanted to ensure that if other troops followed, his men would lead them on a merry dance away from the main group that had the slow moving Frode and Inga. Both teams were on the move. Balder and his group moved north through the forest and on the other side Marcus, Inga, Frode and the other Omegas headed north-east, hoping to find a safe path to re-join the teams soon.

12

First Impressions

Marcus was walking towards the front of the group, that contained Frode, Inga, Hilda, Freyja and Ulf. He was deep in conversation with Freyja, with whom he had begun to build a workable relationship. Freyja is a worker; brought up as an only child by her father, in a motherless home; her mother having passed on when she was still an infant. Now at the age of 21, and having been taught well by her machinist father, Freyja can fix almost anything. A bright and intelligent tomboy, she works hard and takes great enjoyment from helping others. A very kind hearted young woman, tall and quite plain looking, with the very typical Omega features, long blonde hair and deep blue eyes. Freyja loves her state and was giddy with joy when placed in Captain Balder's unit for her defence force training. She believed it to be the greatest of privileges to be trained and commanded by the greatest of Omega captains. She took to the defence force well, making an excellent impression; so much so that Balder had asked her to join full time on the completion of her training; but before being given the chance to make that choice, the invasion forced everyone into full time combat. She was beginning to accept that Marcus offered good insight, and on the surface appeared not to be a threat to her or the team. If anything, his knowledge of Kappa offered the team a better chance of survival, and if they beat the odds and did reach Kappa territory, his insight would only become more useful. It was more a relationship of convenience, but unlike some of Freyja's Omega team, she did not want to kill him. Marcus and Freyja were discussing why the team were following the ramblings of an old man. Marcus had overheard parts of conversations, giving him enough information to understand that it was something of a religious quest. He was keen to know more, what they thought they might find and why they were willing to risk their lives for such a mission?

"I know that our leader believed in this, that really is all I need to understand," Freyja proclaimed.

"But what in the world do you hope to find?"

"We hope to find the truth, I believe the truth will help us free ourselves from the death and destruction in this world."

Marcus scoffed at the notion that religious truth would somehow set them all free.

"What do you believe to be the truth? What were you taught to believe?" The young woman barked, annoyed with her Kappa companion.

Marcus thought for a moment. He had always held an interest in the world's history, but in Kappa it was barely taught – any historical books and artefacts were destroyed. "What I was taught and what I believe are very different," the ex-Kappa Officer finally replied. "In Kappa we were all taught that Kappa was the ruling race. That we were more powerful than others, and were supposed to rule the world. Our destiny was to lord over all, and that the wars began because others did not accept this, they fought against this."

Marcus continued to describe his early life, that he had to hide his true self, hide that he was of Delta heritage and had to act very Kappa. To become a Captain, Marcus had to be clever, use his above average intelligence to do enough to make a good impression, without performing the incredible acts of violence, brutality and depravity that was the norm within the Kappa ranks. "Those are not my beliefs. I believe all to be equal, and that we were put here for a purpose. My friend Titus once heard from a Delta prisoner that the rulers had created us all, and everyone was created for a purpose."

"Rulers? What are these rulers?" Freyja asked quizzically.

"I would assume they are what you call gods? Delta history portrays them as rulers, but when Delta was taken, all the history was wiped away. Anything that might have described these beings were destroyed. I believe it was Kappa trying to hide the truth; the violence, the killing was all to hide some truth"

"Why would a race of people be so intent on destroying anything that relates to the past? Unless it paints a very unflattering picture of their past?"

Aurora had been listening from a distance and she couldn't help but chip in on the conversation. "It is not just history they wish destroyed, they are trying to destroy everything!"

"What do you mean?" Freyja snapped.

"The Testament project and the Keystone weapon," Aurora responded nonchalantly. "It is what I was working on prior to my abrupt exit. A chemical weapon to end all wars. It will kill everybody but those who are blessed with pure Kappa genetics."

The group stopped in their tracks; they couldn't believe what they were hearing. Anger began to brew. Ulf lunged for Aurora and grabbed her. Holding her by her smock, her face close to his. "You were doing what?" the soldier angrily screamed.

"It doesn't work, it has never worked. I murdered the lead developer and sabotaged the lab before I left. It will have stopped them for a while at least."

Marcus stepped between the two and pushed them apart. "We have all done things, done things to survive. Please calm yourself."

Ulf was a true Omega patriot, he was lead delegate for the farmer workers union, he stood up for his people and fair treatment for all. He had left his wife and six children at home when he joined the defence force and had not heard from his family for some months. He was unaware if they were even still alive and the thought of such mass destruction angered him to the core.

Marcus was attempting to act as peacemaker. Aurora on one side and the other group members stood opposite, looking upon her with anger in their eyes. "I am sure there is more to this, please let her explain," Marcus calmly stated.

Aurora went on to explain that the formula had been in production for as long as anyone could remember, some 20 years or more she believed. The latest formula 11356 had been doctored, changed to have no effect on anyone. Keystone was a crazy pipe dream that was nearly impossible to create, as the complexity of the formula required pure samples of each race of man, which due to inter-race relationships was difficult to find. "Kappa science division were engineering the weapon from old documents of unknown origin. I wasn't important enough to view the pages, but it was the only paper I ever glimpsed that was not destroyed as part of the Kappa purge."

"So it doesn't work?" Freyja asked.

"It has never worked, and I don't believe it will be working anytime soon."

A little more calm was descending on the group, they had started to move again, walking towards their next rest point, but thoughts were running away with Marcus. Trying to piece together all the information and attempting to understand the meaning of all the pieces.

"It is like a box of jigsaw pieces from ten different puzzles that somehow fit together," Marcus commented to Freyja as again they led the team through the forest. "Old fables and a thousand years of muddled teachings do not make a pretty picture."

By the time the team reached the edge of the forest, it had started to rain heavily and was getting dark. Ulf ordered everyone to stop under the cover from the trees. This would be the place to wait for Balder to arrive. It would be a wet, cold and silent night of waiting.

13
Killing fields

Marcus awoke to find that the team was whole again, Balder and the four other team members had re-joined them at some point during the night. He must have been exhausted as he had managed to sleep through the cold and rain and the arrival of the other troops. Marcus was pleased to see that Blank was looking well and that no harm had befallen any of the group. "We will be moving out, following that ditch to the village," Balder ordered.

The team climbed into the ditch and began slowly moving along, as it snaked back and forth across the ground. Ivar and Erik encountered a section that was much shallower than the rest of the ditch, to retain cover the team would have to crawl through this section to ensure they would not be seen. Beginning to leopard crawl across the raised section, Ivar noticed his elbows began to sink into the dirt. It was softer than it should be; like it had been newly deposited in the ditch. A cold feeling came across the soldier as he called back to the rest of the team to not proceed, concerned that the soft ground was a sign of newly laid land mines. Reaching back to his belt and drawing a knife, he jabbed the knife softly into the ground ahead, listening and feeling for that distinct metal on metal clink.

There was no clink, but when Ivar withdrew his knife it had pale red blood on the tip; he plunged the knife and hit something, but it wasn't metal. A different cold numbing feeling rushing across him – this wasn't a newly laid mine field; this was a newly laid tomb. "Captain, we need to find another way, we ain't going this route."

"Mines?" Balder asked.

"No sir, much worse."

Ivar returned to the group. He dragged Balder to one side, not wanting the others to know about the graves. Morale was low enough in the group without this, and it would affect the already tense relationship with the ex-Kappa soldiers. Balder saw it differently: the team could use the anger as impetus towards their end goal. Approaching the team and explaining what Ivar believed he had found, Balder was taking a big risk with the well-being of his team. There was sadness within the group, but everyone agreed that they must offer these poor souls some sort of true burial. Ulf, Torsten and Erik started to dig carefully in the soft dirt that surround the bodies and within a short time the men had cleared the ditch, uncovering the bodies of 20 elderly villagers. Balder tasked Ivar and Erik to overwatch and the remaining team to scout the area and find an appropriate place to bury the villagers.

As Marcus, Blank and Aurora finished burying the final body they were exhausted – digging 20 graves was back breaking work, but they understood why it was them that had to complete this task. Hilda and Freyja had fashioned 20 stone markers to show the resting places of the villagers.

Marcus offered his condolences to Hilda and Freyja as they were laying the final stone. "We are very sorry for the loss of these people."

"Don't you dare! You dishonour these people with your pathetic hollow words," Hilda screamed.

"I meant no disrespect, we are truly sorry for the loss of these people."

"Sorry, you think sorry means anything? Your murderous bastard kin did this, killed these people for nothing other than pleasure. They weren't soldiers, they weren't the enemy. Just tired old folk, who offered no threat."

Marcus was lost for words, truly ashamed of the heinous crimes that Kappa soldiers committed all over the six states and was genuine in his feelings of grief and sorrow, but what words would make Hilda feel better? There were none that would bridge the divide, none that could explain.

The Omegas were angry and Captain Balder decided he would use their anger to make a small dent in the Kappa forces, and exact some revenge for the villagers, help the team move forward. He used the intel provided by Marcus and Aurora to create a plan to attack a small Kappa-controlled outpost not far from the village the team presently occupied. The outpost was once a trading station for the local farmers, where they would purchase seed and tools, but now it was being used as a munitions store. The Kappa army was arrogant and believed that no man would try and attack an outpost, so left them with minimal support. There was no more than a brigade of troops stationed at the munitions store, so it should be easy pickings for the Omegas, and not only would they get some revenge but they could use the munitions to further dent the Kappa armies.

Balder briefed the troops on the plan, silent infiltration and then use the Kappa munitions to destroy the outpost from within. Hilda would stay behind to watch over Frode, Inga and Aurora; Marcus and Blank would join the Omegas in the attack.

14
Attack on
Outpost 85

Balder led the Omega team away from the village, they were armed and prepared for an all-out fight, but if the plan went smoothly not a shot would be fired. They trekked for around four miles to reach the outpost, after setting out just before dark, using the benefits of fading light to move close to the outpost before night fell. Ulf was whispering with Ivar as they travelled, explaining his reservations of the ex-Kappa soldiers and his immense dislike for Aurora. They discussed project testament and the more pressing nature of their quest. Both soldiers occasioned the odd glance back towards Marcus, with looks of anger and disgust.

"It would be a shame if they didn't make it back," Ulf grumbled.

"Sure, no-one would lose sleep over em. I would gladly kill em. The Captain will have me on overwatch, so a stray shot here and there; no one will even know," Ivar replied with a smirk.

"Hey Erik," Ulf called out.

Ulf relayed the plan to Erik, who was very hesitant. It was going to take plenty of persuasion for Erik to agree to be involved. It was Kappa's fault that his grandmother was gone, but Marcus had already proved useful to the mission, and the others had shown they are all against Kappa. Blank had even killed his brother Kappas. Erik distanced himself from the other pair, but agreed to keep his mouth shut; after all, his fellow Omegas were still more important than the Kappas.

The team covered the ground quickly; it was unsurprising considering they had left the old man and the kid back at the village, as it was them that drastically slowed the group. Reaching Outpost 85 the team found cover until the full black of night had set in. Balder gave everyone their final instructions. Ivar and Erik were to be overwatch; Ivar smirked with delight, as his Captain relayed the orders.

"Ulf, you're with Torsten guarding our entry and exit point. Freyja, Marcus and Blank, you're with me. We will find the munitions lockers and give those Kappa troops something of a surprise."

Balder walked along the line of soldiers checking they were ready; approaching where Marcus and Blank were crouched, he muttered further instructions. "Chance to prove yourselves to the men, don't let yourselves down and do something silly, understood?"

The Kappa pair nodded and finished prepping for the attack.

Night had fallen as the team moved towards their objective. Ivar and Erik arced away from the group to find a good perch, from where to watch events from afar. The other men headed down towards the eastern side of the outpost, the walls had been somewhat fortified, but the eastern side had been identified as the weakest point on the perimeter, and that is where the team would infiltrate. Balder led the men down a hill towards their entry point; there was a single search light beaming out into the darkness, but it was easy to evade. Reaching the wall, they started to climb, one at a time quietly up and over. On the other side of the wall was a small grain hut which offered the perfect vantage point.

Balder checked with Ivar and Erik over the radios, which were starting to crackle as the batteries ran flat. Overwatch confirmed they were ready to cover, and Ulf along with Torsten had found defensive positions close to the exit point; they were there to ensure it would be clear when required. Balder sent Marcus, Blank and

Freyja into the outpost as he swept up behind them. It did not take long before the team found the first munitions lockers, staked high with rockets. It would make the perfect target to detonate and it would undoubtably destroy the outpost. Marcus was able to force the locker door and he, with Freyja, entered the locker, setting two rockets to detonate in 20 minutes. Those two rockets would give plenty of bang, enough to set off all the other munitions and give quite the light show.

Marcus and Freyja left the locker and secured the door, before moving to the next. It was filled with heavy arms and ammunition. Forcing the lock and grabbing all that was possible to carry, they secured the door and began their exfiltration, encountering two guards, whom Balder and Freyja put down with swift efficiency; but not before one of the guards had pressed an alarm. Bells rang and lights began to flash.

"All positions open up on the enemy," Balder quickly ordered as the team scrabbled to find some cover. This was just what Ivar had been waiting for; he trained his sights on Kappa troops from his long range position, putting them down like animals. From their positions Balder and Freyja were engaging with the Kappa soldiers. Marcus, now armed with the heavy munitions taken from the locker, had begun firing on the enemy troops; the velocity of the projectiles from his weapon were enormous. The bullets passing straight through solid metal and stone, hitting Kappa troops left and right, the carnage had created a small window of opportunity to exit the outpost. As the team moved towards the exit, Ulf and Torsten were covering them. Ivar used the momentary lull in the enemy's movements to retrain his sights on Marcus. He took a deep breath in and took his shot.

Ulf was on the floor, blood spurting out from a chest wound, as Freyja was frantically trying to apply pressure to stem the flow. The blood wouldn't stop; it was only a matter of moments and Ulf had passed. No last words, no gentle passing, just pain, anguish and lots of blood. Balder dragged Freyja away from Ulf's body, pulled her towards the wall and escaped from the outpost. Other members of Omega team had already climbed up and out. Balder pushed Freyja up the wall and followed swiftly after; they were over the top and out. They all moved quickly away from the outpost and into the cover of the night. The first explosion could be heard, swiftly followed by a second and then a huge series of explosions as each munitions locker went up in flames. As the first boom rang out, the team all dropped to the ground. Balder turned to see the night's sky alight with the glow from the flames spewing upwards from what used to be the outpost, but now nothing more than a fiery mess of rubble.

15
losses

Balder was leading his men back from the now smouldering
mess of an outpost. They had moved quickly to distance
themselves from their target, as those kind of explosions were
bound to bring the unwanted attention of larger Kappa forces. As
the soldiers ran for the cover of a nearby copse, they were energised
by striking at Kappa, but feeling the loss of Ulf and the inevitable
murmurs had begun. Each of the team running through their
thoughts to put together the events that led to the death of their
comrade and friend, but only one man knew the true events that
had transpired. The group stopped in the copse and rested for a
few moments, which gave Balder a chance to begin questioning the
events as they were in his mind. "Ivar, you had the overwatch; what
happened?"

Ivar said nothing and stared at Erik with a look that aggressively
suggested that it would be in Erik's best interest to keep his mouth
shut.

"Well speak up, what did you see? Nothing? You saw nothing?"
Balder angrily asked. He was beginning to lose his temper. He was
normally a very calm man, but he felt every loss and his blood was
starting to boil.

"I was trained on Kappa and saw no movement from their
troops," Erik blurted. "They were stationary, in cover, or dead."

"And you?" Balder added, aggressively pointing towards Ivar.

"Didn't see nothing."

Balder was unconvinced by the answers his men had proffered; if anything the answers had given Balder even more scope for questions. The time did not allow for further interrogation; the team had to move back to the village and regroup with Hilda and the others.

Freyja was running alongside Marcus, mouthing words towards the ex-Kappa captain, but the ability to read lips whilst running, and looking where he was going all at the same time, was not a skill he had picked up.

"I can't understand," Marcus whispered.

"It was meant for you," Freyja replied whilst looking around to ensure no one was listening in.

"You sure?" Marcus asked alarmingly.

"No, it was crazy back there; so I can't be sure. But I'm convinced it was friendly fire and was meant for you. Watch your back."

Marcus nodded in appreciation before he and Freyja continued to run in silence.

Some way behind, Erik and Ivar were also conversing, but the tone was very different to that of their fellow soldiers. "What did you do?" Erik whispered across to Ivar.

"What you suggesting?"

"You shot Ulf, you missed the Kappa and killed Ulf."

"Fuck you, Erik; I don't fucking miss!"

The mood was becoming fiery, but Erik knew what he saw; he knew Ivar had killed Ulf, a married farther of six who had entrusted his life to his friends, trusted his team to stand by him, to cover his back. "I saw you do it, I saw you shoot him. Own up to it or I will for you."

"How the fuck would you know anything about shooting, you jumped up little prick!"

Erik stopped and pushed Ivar, he fell back and rolled over a couple of times. Jumping to his feet, he threw a punch towards

Erik, which landed square on his jaw and knocked the young Omega soldier to the floor. Ivar jumped on Erik and started to throw punch after punch.

"You fucking prick, don't you dare accuse me of killing my friend," Ivar screamed at Erik as he continued to land punch after punch. Balder ran over and grabbed the aggressor, dragging him off the now bloodied Erik, restraining him by locking his arms behind him as the sharp shooter continued to scream at the young soldier. "Your Grandma jumps off a fucking roof and now suddenly you're a big man. Suddenly become an expert soldier, who knows everything about shooting?"

"You killed him, I know you killed him," Erik slurred through his heavily bloodied mouth.

Balder was now aggressively restraining Ivar, pushing his head to the floor and ranting at him. "It was you? You killed him?"

"No, I didn't; he's got it wrong," Ivar screamed.

"He's pretty convinced it was your shot that killed your friend. Killed your own man. Was it?"

"It was by accident, he moved into my sights."

"There were no Kappas anywhere near Ulf, what were you aiming at?"

"There was a Kappa, Kappa scum was dead to rights. He moved into my sights."

Balder knew there was no enemy in Ulf's direct vicinity and knew that Ivar was still not being truthful. He tied Ivar's hands to the front with a lead and ordered the team to move out, they had to keep moving; for all they knew Kappas were tracking them. Torsten dragged Ivar along by his restraints, whilst Captain Balder helped Erik; a very good looking young man, with the typical Omega features, mid length blond hair and the bluest of eyes. A typical teen, very strong willed, but with strangely unnerving dedication to his family, his friends and his state. He had spent his adolescent years protecting his younger sister from the constant demands of life in the public eye, and working for his grandmother, the leader of Omega. A very slender, but muscular young man. He prided himself on his fitness and could be considered quite vain; often distracted by his own reflection. The son of a farmer, but sitting at a desk was more to his liking; his three months' training in the defence force had opened his eyes and taught him much about how to live and how to be a man.

The team was moving slower than before, but still at a good clip and it was not long before the team arrived back at the village. They were broken and dysfunctional and the Omega Captain was conflicted. The presence of the ex-Kappa trio would be of help in the long quest, with their knowledge too valuable to lose, but their presence was pulling his team apart. They had barely made it 20 miles and already lost two of their own, and he now had to now deal with Ivar. Society had fallen, there were no courts of law, there was no Omega defence force leadership to preside over military laws, and there were no prisons. It was Balder's decision alone on how to punish Ivar for his betrayal, for the murder of Ulf. The decision played on Balder all through the night, not sleeping a wink, thinking through his options. By morning his decision was clear: this was not to be a case of an eye for an eye. Balder and the team had seen too much death to further add to the toll. Ivar was to be stripped of his military position and would remain unarmed as the team moved forward on their quest, and he would no longer be allowed a vote on any decisions for the group. The team accepted the Captain's words with reservation, especially Marcus and the other ex-Kappa soldiers. With Ivar still in the team, there would be the same inter-state tensions that had plagued their journey, and the almost certainty of further violence.

16
Turncoats

In Khristade, General Hades met with his senior commanders; it was them that now occupied the city's capitol building. Having taken the building and the seats around the council table, sitting where the Omegas they had beheaded, hung and shot had once sat, the General was rampaging. He had continued to wipe out the remaining members of the Omega hierarchy, but it wasn't enough. Hades was determined to make everyone pay for his loss, whatever it cost; but his commanders were concerned that by killing those who ruled, the Kappas would struggle to control the population and ensure that the farming continued. The Omegas wouldn't be able to provide the food for the Kappa armies. The high commanders of Kappa did not often speak-up against the will of Hades, not often voicing opinions; but in this instance it was important that Hades understood that his fierce temper ran the risk of destroying Omega and rendering the Omega farms impotent to supply the necessary resources to his armies. In the eyes of the commanders, they needed to turn Omegas that held sway with the people, ones that could offer the Kappas control over them.

The commanders had been working to identify the Omegas that could be turned, the members of society most easily persuaded. It was a simple enough equation: lead the people on-behalf of Kappa and have a good life, a well furnished life with wealth; or die in a horrific manner. The High Command believed it would be an easy sell, but till now most of the key Omegas had rebuffed the offers from Kappa and chosen the alternative. There were a handful that did turn – the landowners liked the idea of control, the ideal of wealth and prosperity. For the others, the Kappa commanders had to turn up the heat. They began imprisoning families and friends of the identified citizens, and the construction of gallows had begun in the capital's square. The increased incentive had begun to work – one by one the influential Omegas were falling into line, and with this, true control over the people had begun. The unwilling Omegas that turned were union heads and village leaders. The people sympathised with them – with threats to their families what choice did they have? But the landowners were seen as turncoats, traitors who needed to pay.

A new council head had been swiftly appointed; Sigurd was a big fat man with a bald head and dreadful personal hygiene. He spent his life cheating other farmers, stealing small parcels of land, until he was the single largest land owner in Omega. Even before the Kappa invasion he had treated his workers with disdain, but Omega law had prevented him from his malicious ways, as every man was entitled to a fair wage and a home; this annoyed and angered Sigurd. Now there were no rules, he could treat the people how he saw fit. The new council had been constructed specifically to include seven landowners who volunteered to join the Kappa cause, and five others whose families were imprisoned and forced to follow Kappa edict. Allowing any Kappa orders to be council-passed and enforced on the people.

The Kappa overlords had new rules for the Omega citizens and the council were being asked to pass them. The majority of new regulations were quotas: every man, woman and child was given a quota they had to meet. If they did, they would be given minimal rations that would allow them to barely survive, but if the quota was not met, they would not be fed. The same was true for medical treatment –, hit your quota and be allowed basic medical care, don't hit your target and you would not; and it was the same for heating fuel and for water. The first council meeting was called to order by Sigurd, who read the new laws out loud and asked for an immediate vote. Although each member knew the laws would gain the majority needed to be passed, there was still unrest. One man was especially resistant, and felt the need to speak up for the people. He knew his pleadings would fall on deaf ears and knew he risked the life of his wife and daughter, imprisoned by his Kappa overlords; but he must try to plead for what was right. This man was Stellen, a union leader in the old Omega. For his entire working life he had fought for the fair treatment of his members and worked hard to ensure this. Building a relationship with the previous council, he had become trusted and adored by the men and women of Omega.

Union leader Stellen is a man of the people, a true Omega, who fought for each and every citizen's rights. The big Agri-farmers once threatened the livelihoods of the people; the smaller farms and plantations were being squeezed into reducing prices and quality, but Stellen fought the big farms; fought for fair treatment for every man, woman and child; homes and food for each and every citizen, and jobs with fair wages for all. He had the ear of the people and they entrusted their fortunes to him. Stellen was not a wealthy man, but always looked his best. A tall man, slim in stature, almost frail looking; with a bald head and a thick long grey beard that splits in two, like horns protruding from his chin. Stellen had grown-up with Captain Balder and they fought for the people in their own different ways. One fought with words, whilst the other fought with guns and knives; unrelated brothers of Omega.

"We should at least discuss these laws?" he pleaded.

"Whatever is the point in that?" Sigurd sniggered.

"The point, the point is that there is no quota control in these laws. No age restrictions, and the targets are unfairly proportioned in favour of those with the most land. The small village farmers will not be able to meet these targets and will starve to death, whilst the bigger Agri-farmers will be plentiful. These are not fair rules and we should not be voting them into law. We cannot in all good consciousness accept this."

"Oh, shush yourself, you should save your words for those who might actually care. We will be voting, and these laws will be passed," Sigurd bellowed. "And you should mind your words – the General and his commanders hear everything. Now vote!"

The vote was taken and split seven to five in favour of passing the rules into law. Stellen left the council meeting angered by the sham that is this new council. He was determined to do what it takes, at any cost, to impede the rule of Kappa and prevent them from taking total control of his people.

17
Beginnings of rebellion

Stellen had arranged to meet a small group of like-minded Omegas in a farm a little outside of Khristade. He travelled on foot and kept to the woods and other covered areas to ensure he was not spotted by the endless Kappa patrols. His determination to stop Kappa was clear – they had taken his family, but he was willing to risk them and his own life to stop Kappa and General Hades. When Stellen reached the farm, it stood in total darkness, no lights, no fire and no people. Quickly checking his watch to ensure his timing was correct – but it was the right time and the right place – so where were his fellow Omegas? Bad thoughts began to cloud his mind: had they been stopped on the way to the farm, had one of the patrols picked them up, and what if they talked? What fate would be bestowed on his family? Panic was beginning to set-in when a small light appeared through the darkness – it was Bjorn and he was closely followed by Ava. Friends were starting to arrive and a light feeling of relief started to spread through Stellen, but he could not be sure until all seven of his friends had arrived safely at the farm, and all seven had returned to their homes.

Bjorn was Stellen's deputy in the union, a giant of a man, with a gruff exterior but a heart of gold. Before the invasion he would often be found helping other farmers; he would help them even at a detriment of his own farm. Ava was the wife of Omega defence force Captain Balder; she was a petite lady with long light hair and piercing blue eyes. She had not seen her husband in some weeks and knew her association with him painted a large target on her back, so had been hiding in one of the small outer villages, knowing if discovered that her fate would not be kind.

"It is very good to see you both. Any news on the others?" Stellen asked.

"Svend and Yrsa were questioning whether to come tonight. I do not think they will be here," Bjorn replied.

"And the others?"

"Sorry, Stellen, I haven't heard from them. Communication is most difficult and very dangerous."

Time had passed and no others arrived; as they were about to give up hope three figures appeared from the night's gloom. Bo, his brother Arne and their sister Astrid had arrived. The boys were respected farm labourers that had been part of the defence force, fleeing their posts when the leaders had ordered it, going to ground and hiding out from place to place, until they heard that Stellen was looking for volunteers. Astrid is the most beautiful girl in Omega, slim and immensely attractive; with long flowing blonde locks and the bluest of eyes. She looked and acted like a true, full blooded Omega; she had the kindest of hearts and would help anyone with any task, large or small. She donated her time to teach home care at one of the local education centres and loved every opportunity to guide others and make someone else's day a little bit brighter. Although the kindest of souls, Astrid was no pushover and very strong willed. She liked to get her own way in family squabbles and was not afraid to use her feminine wiles to best her brothers in any argument. There was a queue of eligible men waiting for her to turn 21, so they could offer her marriage, but her brothers stood in the way of any man taking a second look at their baby sister.

"It is so good to see you all; my heart is filled with happiness that you five have braved the night to meet me. Let's go into the barn and discuss what we are to do," Stellen whispered. The group moved into the barn where Stellen informed the others of the new laws that were to be enforced, and what it would mean for the majority of the Omega people. His worry over quotas that the people would be unable to meet, he feared they would be starved or worked to death. He explained that Sigurd was now leading the council, and that six other landowners were there by his side, doing Kappa's bidding for wealth and luxury. Stellen questioned the others, he questioned what response they should make and what they could do for the people of Omega state. He spoke passionately for some minutes until Bjorn interrupted him.

"We must relieve Omega of the burden of its new council. Sigurd and the six others you speak of must pay the ultimate sacrifice for their people?"

Bo and Arne roared with approval, but Stellen was taken by surprise –, murder was the first suggestion from his new forum.

"But what good will that do? You must expect some kind of retaliation? Kappa is not going to sit back and accept the killing of its council," Stellen calmly asked.

"But traitors must be punished," Bo emphatically stated.

Stellen was very uncomfortable with the direction in which his friends were heading. "We have neither the means or the men to become assassins, we need to help the people, steal food and medicine, and hinder Kappa in anyways possible, but we are not killers; we are not Kappas. Why should we bring ourselves down to the depths of our enemy?"

There was a brief pause; nobody spoke for a few moments until Bjorn decided to speak up once more. "We should help the people! We can steal medicine, and we can ensure that our friends and family have food, but how long can we do that for, until one, or many of us are caught and punished? If we are going to die anyway, surely it is better to die in a hail of bullets than be starved to death? Or hanged from their gallows in capital square? Thrown off the roof like our beloved leader?"

Ava had been listening, but decided it was her time to offer an opinion. She was a very proud Omega and was willing to sacrifice for the good of the state, for the people that her husband had always sworn to protect. "Sod that loathsome Sigurd and his cronies. If we are to stoop to the level of Kappa, then I say we should kill Hades?"

There was stunned silence around the barn; nobody quite knew what to say or what to do. They were all shocked that Ava, of all people, had made such a bold statement. As the moments passed the group all began to nod; nod in agreement that killing Sigurd would lead to severe ramifications, but killing Hades might just cause enough disarray in the Kappa ranks to actually make a difference, and in the event of Kappa retaliation it would be worth the sacrifice to see Hades dead.

The forum were all in agreement that if they were to act, then that act should be to assassinate Hades. It would be no easy task, but with astute planning and some willing volunteers it might be possible. There were two large challenges: how to get close enough to Hades? And who would be the assassin? They would surely be signing their own death sentence by volunteering. The group was silent, in deep thought when a little voice suddenly came alive.

"I can do it." It was Astrid – she was willing to be the one, the assassin, and kill the general. "The General takes a new girl to his bed every night. They are always young girls with blonde hair; it should not be difficult to ensure I am chosen to be his next conquest."

"No, I forbid it," Bo screamed.

"Someone has to, rather me than anyone else, and I am prepared to meet our gods."

"No, not you, my sweet little sister. It cannot be, we must find someone else," Bo said through his tears that were now streaming down his face.

"Someone else's sister or daughter? It must be me."

Stellen was hesitant to agree with this plan, but knew it was the only plan that made real sense, and Astrid was perfect for the mission. Stellen moved over to Bo and placed his arm around the young man's shoulders, comforted his friend whilst he wept. Ava had gone to find Arne who had stormed off at the first uttering of his sister's plan. He was not in tears like his brother, but it was apparent to all that sadness had filled his eyes. The plan was agreed: on a night in the near future Astrid would be adorned with a small directional explosive device, that she would take into the bed of General Hades and it would be detonated when appropriate. An explosive was the way to ensure that Hades was killed, and the device would be small enough to be more easily concealed than a knife or gun, and based on stories told of the General neither a knife or gun would kill him anyway. This plan would mean a certain death sentence for Astrid, but she was prepared and willing.

18
Assassination

Astrid was spending her last day in the company of her brothers, after having agreed to kill herself for the cause; the cause of assassinating General Hades. The new Omega Forum led by Stellen had decided that the quicker the plot is enacted, the less likely that Kappa are to get wind of the plan and prevent the attempt on Hades's life. Tonight was to be the night and Astrid wanted her last day to be one of happiness, but the time was approaching and Astrid readied herself. Stellen had arrived at the farm, he had sourced the explosive and smallest detonator. Affixing the device to Astrid's chest, he explained to her how the device worked and that the closer she could get to Hades the more potent the device would be. Astrid wore a flowing dress with a floral pattern and plaited her hair away from her pretty face; she was ready. Stellen would take her from the farm and to Khristade, there he had arranged for a friend to offer her up to the Kappa General. The young girl said her goodbyes to her brothers and the other forum members. It was an hour's walk to Khristade, the entire journey made in total silence, Astrid was staring into space like she had lost herself in her own thoughts.

Once in Khristade, Stellen handed Astrid over to his friend Kirk, who took her to capital square. There had been a hanging earlier that day and the Kappa murderers had left the bodies of the slain to swing in the spring breeze, for all of Omega to see. A family had been the latest victims, a man, a woman and three children were the unlucky ones to be swinging that day. Kirk and Astrid walked towards the rear of the capitol building where there was a loading door guarded by two Kappa soldiers. Kirk explained that he would be willing to give his daughter to the General for some food and water. One soldier took hold of Astrid's arm and pulled her sharply towards him, he groped at her breasts, then spun her round, ensuring she was fit for the General. "How old?"

"Sixteen years," Kirk replied.

"Perfect for the General that is," the guard stated whilst drooling over the girl. "Yeah alright you got a deal."

The soldier went inside the door and returned with a gallon of water, some fruit and rice, shoving it into Kirk's arms. "Now piss off! Come back tomorrow, you can collect whatever's left of her," the soldier sniggered.

One of the soldiers dragged Astrid into the building, up two flights of stairs to a dark room that had been stripped of everything but a mattress on the floor.

The soldier left the room, locking the door. Astrid was getting nervous, starting to doubt she would have the nerve to kill, but it would not be long until she found out. The door unlocked and through came the largest person Astrid had ever seen. General Hades was even bigger than she had imagined; the stories told of him made him sound large, but he was a truly enormous man and towered over the petite girl.

"Lay face down on the bed and lift your dress," the general ordered.

Astrid was unsure what to do – she had to face the general for the explosive to work. She began to panic; she was a schoolteacher, not a trained killer; just a 16-year-old girl. Thoughts and doubts started to flow through her tiny frame, sweat was dripping from her forehead, her only thought was to flee, but how to escape the room? Between her and the door was a seven-foot monster of a man.

"Do as I ask. I will not ask again, whore."

Astrid moved towards the makeshift bed and started to undo her dress.

"No time for that," the General groaned.

He grabbed the back of Astrid's head and pushed her down towards the mattress; he held her face down on the bed as he tore at her underwear. Astrid squirmed, and began to fight, kicking out at the General. Hades loved the fight; seemingly enjoying the struggle, it spurred him on to be more forceful and brutal. Hades pushed harder on the back of Astrid's head, as the young girl struggled to breathe face down in the mattress. All her efforts were not enough, all the struggling didn't prevent Hades taking what he wanted. Astrid stopped kicking, stopped struggling and gave in to Hades.

When the general had finished, he moved away from Astrid and towards the door; the young girl saw this as the perfect opportunity to strike. Quickly raising herself from the bed, she rushed towards Hades, holding the small detonator in her hand. There was no hesitation, her determination to kill this bastard was stronger than ever. Astrid was within two metres of Hades, but needed to be closer. In the brief moment between two metres and one metre, Hades swung around and smacked Astrid across the face with the back of his hand; the force was immense and it sent Astrid flying against the wall. She gathered herself and charged again, but by now the General was prepared. He grabbed her hand with such force it crushed every bone and the detonator with it. Astrid, in searing pain, launched again for another attack – even without the explosive the young girl was determined to harm him. Hades was laughing as the girl launched attack after attack. For a man of his size and strength it was like swatting flies; time after time he punched and slapped the young girl away; the general laughed even louder. Astrid crashed to the floor for the fifth or even maybe sixth time as the door swung open, a wash of black uniforms stormed into the room with guns raised and ready to act.

"Leave her," Hades ordered through his laughter. "I like the fight in this little one. Take her to one of the breeding centres – with that fight and those looks; she can be made use of."

The soldiers dragged Astrid away to an awaiting transport, Hades straightened his uniform, buttoned up his trousers and marched from the room towards the council chambers. In the chambers he screamed orders at one of the soldiers. "Find me Commander Orcus, now!"

Away from the capitol building Stellen and Kirk were lurking in the ruins of the old bakehouse waiting for the explosion to come; they waited and waited but no explosion. They feared the worst for Astrid and knew that Hades must still be alive. They sat fearing for what repercussions may be coming. Stellen knew he must inform the others and prepare for the onslaught of retaliations against the Omega people, leaving Kirk and starting his journey back towards the farm with a sadness in his heart. They not only hadn't killed Hades, but had lost one of their own; the boys would be very angry. Commander Orcus had arrived at the council chambers; he was the second most feared officer in the Kappa armies. Everyone was truly terrified of the man; he led Brigade 66, the Kappa armies' secret police.

19
Hades' secret police

The worst of the worst, only the most truly heinous individuals were recruited to brigade 66; they were tasked with finding non-believers and murdering anyone who was opposed to Kappa. All in black uniforms, black helmets and menacing looking black face masks, they were the best trained and most heavily armed force within the Kappa armies. In the armies of Kappa simply killing and murdering does not make a soldier stand out. It is perfectly normal for a soldier to rack up hundreds of kills across any normal year, so to stand out and be taken by 66, a soldier would have to commit acts so atrocious that no ordinary man could even imagine. The men of 66 would torture and kill, and take pleasure from doing so. The worst of 66 was Orcus, who was known to have killed and tortured more than a thousand of his own people, a thousand Kappa citizens dead by his hand. He rarely lowered himself to killing the people from other states – unless it was a high ranking official or leader, he would not be bothered to murder them. Allowing his brigade those kills. In all the madness of the Kappa armies, Commander Orcus might well have been the maddest of them all, a totally brutal butcher of men. Like all Kappas, Orcus was a tall man, dark hair and features, with a muscular physique, he had what people thought to be superhuman strength, often killing with only his bare hands. Stories tell of him crushing children's skulls, strangling women and beating men to death.

The 66th brigade had a maximum of 20 soldiers: a commander, a lieutenant and 18 other men. There was a selection process where the few hand-picked recruits would battle to the death with the underperforming brigade soldiers, to gain their place and the right to be part of 66. The same process was used for command selection, but not in the previous 10 selection cycles had anybody dared to challenge Orcus. Orcus's men had over time built a network of spies and informants within the Kappa ranks, so that any non-believers could be rooted out. It would only take one loose word for 66 to come knocking at your door, and any person that they took was never to be seen again. Tortured for information and then murdered. In Kappa state they operated out of a building known only as the cemetery; with big furnace chimneys rising high out of the building, it was assumed that once killed all of 66's victims were burnt to ashes.

Now operating in Omega the brigade was building a new network of informants from within the people of Omega. Paying for information to those willing opportunists, or threats of violence and murder to prise the knowledge out of the less convinced civilians. They had already built a strong network within the outlying villages, but within Khristade it was proving a more difficult task. The people were still united and most were unwilling to turn on their own, but it was only time until hunger and desperation drove the people into the waiting arms of Orcus and his men of 66. It was only a matter of time before the Omega people started to turn on each other. Orcus had reached the capitol building and was presented to General Hades.

"There was a pathetic attempt on my life," the general moaned. "The girl has been dealt with, but we cannot let the people think that this is something that will not go unpunished."

"What is your command?" Orcus stated, head bowed; grovelling to Hades. "How would you see them punished?"

"Every third family member will be executed," the general stated whilst handing a list to Orcus. "Take the third oldest member of each of those families, those still living within the city walls; and hang them in the square. I want every person in this wretched place to understand that Kappa now rules, and every indiscretion big or small will be punished."

"Yes, my general."

"And whilst you're on the streets, find me those behind this assassination attempt and bring them to me. I would very much care to hand out their punishment myself."

Orcus nodded and bowed before his General, swivelled and marched from the room. Division 66 would be on the streets of Khristade in a matter of moments, handing out the punishment that the General had ordered.

20
Executions

The men of Division 66 burst through the door of a home belonging to a farming family living on the edge of Khristade. The family complied with orders to kneel with hands aloft. There was a father, a mother, a teenaged daughter and two younger siblings, and in accordance with Hades' orders the secret police took the teen and dragged her from the property, her father trying to prevent this was beaten into submission, the soldiers using rifle butts to beat the man until he stayed down. The teen girl was loaded into the back of a transport whilst a soldier posted a notice on the door of the home. NOTICE: For crimes of association with those who threaten Kappa, summary execution is ordered by his most gracious leader – General Hades.

In the next inhabited home from Hades' list, a mother of five was removed and loaded on the transport. Any thought of fighting was quickly put down by the soldiers of 66. The process continued; at each home the third eldest person was removed and loaded onto the transport. As word spread of the people being taken, some families tried to flee. They were met by the might of the Kappa Brigades patrolling the streets. Other families tried to hide, some of the men even offered themselves to the soldiers, to prevent their loved ones being taken, but the brigade was thorough, only taking the third eldest member of each family and anyone who tried to prevent them carrying out their duties was beaten or worse. The transport was full, it carried 36 souls to be executed in capital square. Children as young as 10 were among the unlucky ones to have been chosen. The truck pulled up alongside the gallows and the Omegas were unloaded. Lined up and ready to be sorted as General Hades marched across the square to a small lectern that was positioned in front of the nooses. Waiting whilst the Omega victims were arranged in roughly age order, oldest to youngest. Divided into groups of six, the first were led up the stairs of the gallows and nooses positioned around their necks.

Hades started to speak through a microphone positioned on the lectern. "Let it be known that I am a fair man. Some of those among your kin are responsible for an attempt on my life. These acts that are to be bestowed upon your families are a simple matter of the law, punishment for acts of cowardliness. Your mothers, daughters, fathers and sons will be hanged till they are dead." He paused for a moment, before continuing. "But I will give you all one final chance of mercy: bring those responsible to this square and I will spare these lives. I will enact our law on those who deserve it most and not your families."

There was a lull. The Omega victims had a brief hope that they would not be punished, but no one spoke, no shining knight came galloping into the square to save their lives.

General Hades nodded to the hangman, who pulled a lever and the first six Omega victims dropped hard. A few moments of writhing before all six bodies hung limply from the gallows' ropes; the bodies were removed and tossed into a pile in the middle of the square, and the next six victims were brought up to the marks where the nooses were tightened. Again, General Hades offered a chance for mercy and again no shining knight appeared. Hades once again signalled to the hangman, and this set of citizens were dropped. These deaths were not as clean – two of the six continued to struggle against the tightening nooses, so a soldier walked alongside each and tugged hard downwards on the victims, instantly snapping their necks. The bodies were cut down and thrown on the pile, and the next six were put in place, ropes tightened around their necks. General Hades offered these six victims the same mercy.

"It was councilman Stellen, he is responsible," a young girl cried out before the hangman could drop her to her death.

"Thank you, child," Hades responded as he leaned over and whispered to Orcus, who was proudly stood next to the General. "And where might Stellen be?"

"I don't know, sir," the girl stated through floods of tears.

"Kappa thanks you for your honesty," Hades stated as he waved to the hangman.

The six victims, including the girl who had offered up Stellen as the guilty party, dropped to their deaths, as Hades turned to Orcus and ordered him to take his troops and find Councilman Stellen. He then ordered the rest of the hangings to proceed as he marched back towards the council building. As Hades entered the building, another set of six Omegas were dropped to their deaths on the gallows, with Hades then ordering one of his commanders to retrieve Stellen's family from their prison cell in the bowels of the capitol building. He wanted to enact some of his own brand of retaliation on the wife and child of Stellen the traitor.

21
Hostage rescue

In conjunction with the plans to assassinate Hades, the forum had discussed attempting to free the families being held in the capitol building. Whilst distracted by the attempt on Hades' life there may be an opportunity to free the hostages. Bo and Arne offered themselves to lead such a rescue attempt, covertly infiltrating the capitol building where they had been often as children; their father was a custodian of the capitol when the brothers were young. They would use Astrid's distraction to enter the building and help the imprisoned families escape. Leave the capital and reach the outer villages where they could all hide. Stellen was immensely grateful to the boys for risking their own necks for the sake of his family, and the other families being held. Bo and Arne travelled to Khristade shortly after Stellen and Astrid, and took an alternative route to the others, and followed a little used path, passing through several outer villages where the bothers could rest and hide if they encountered patrols.

Once they reached Khristade, Bo visited with the families of those people he could trust, rallying support and gathering vital resources that would be needed to rescue the families. Weapons, a few medical supplies and some animal tranquillisers that would be used to incapacitate the Kappa guards. It was essential to enter and leave the capital silently. The plan was essentially a simple one: use Astrid entering the building as a distraction to avoid the guards at the loading door. Use their knowledge of the building's unused passages and corridors to make their way unnoticed to the lower levels, where they would free the families and if the situation called for it, use the animal tranquillisers on any guards that crossed their path. Track back along the same routes with the families, hand them off to their friends, who would whisk them out of the city and disappear.

The brothers were hiding in close proximity of the capitol, watching and waiting for Astrid to arrive. They watched as their sister was groped by the Kappa soldier and dragged into the building. It was at this point they made their move, rushing through the loading door unseen and quickly making their way to a side passage that was unknown to most. The bothers swiftly moved along a series of corridors until they made the stairs, where a single guard maintained watch. Utilising an animal tranquilliser gun, Bo shot the guard with a heavily dosed dart, which would have knocked out a bull. The guard dropped to the floor very quickly and Arne dragged him into the passage and bound his hands, feet and mouth using tape. Bo led as the brothers made their way down the three flights of stairs that led to the building's lower floor and the prison cells. Once on the final flight, it was apparent there were a number of Kappa soldiers guarding the prisoners. Stationed in a staggered pattern, making it impossible for the brothers to tackle them all with a single animal gun. They would have to remove at least two of the guards by force. Arne crept in the shadows within striking distance of the nearest Kappa soldier, whilst Bo lined up the tranquilliser. Bo whistled and fired off three quick shots that hit the three guards furthest from the brothers' position. Simultaneously, as the whistle sounded Arne lunged from the darkness and drove a knife through the spine of the guard closest to him; this left one guard, whom Bo jumped from the stairs, grabbing at the final soldier, they both tumbled to the floor. Struggling and rolling around until Bo gained the upper hand, his knife positioned directly above the Kappa's heart. He used all his weight to force the knife down towards the soldier as the Kappa resisted.

The knife penetrated the soldier's outer armour and then cut through his chest and was driven into his heart; he had a look of shock on his face as he took his final breath, eyes wide open for Bo to see the life drain from them. Bo got to his feet and wiped the blood from his knife. He and Arne then secured the tranquillised soldiers. They opened each of the rooms that were being used as cells and freed the Omega families. The brothers handed out some weapons to a few of the prisoners, and led the families back up the stairs to the passage they had used to infiltrate the capital. Moving the families along the passages and towards their escape, pausing at the end, in sight of the loading dock door. The guards were back in position and needed to be incapacitated to allow the families to pass. Bo started loading the animal gun, but Arne stopped him. He whispered, "He touched our sister, I want his head to no longer be attached to his body."

"Arne, this is not the time," Bo replied sternly.

"If there is ever a time, that time is now."

Before his brother could stop him, Arne moved quickly and drew his knife; he plunged it through the back of the guard's neck. Bo had to react fast, grabbing the first thing at hand, a fire axe, and swung it as hard as he could towards the other soldier, making contact with the side of the soldier's head, the sharp axe slicing straight through the soldier's face and removing part of his head.

Both soldiers were dead, both killed in truly gruesome fashion. Arne was still hacking with his knife at the neck of the Kappa, Bo having to pull his brother from the corpse.

"Enough, Arne, that is enough. Help us hide the bodies," Bo ordered.

Two of the Omega prisoners grabbed some plastic and wrapped the Kappas' bodies; they dragged them into the passage and secured the door.

The brothers and the Omega families hastily left the vicinity of the capitol building, filing off to the other families who were waiting to whisk them away. Bo and Arne took care of Stellen's family – they were to take them to the farm where Stellen, Ava and the others had been hiding. They planned a slow road back to the farm, criss-crossing the country to make it more difficult for them to be followed, but first they needed to escape Khristade. The brothers were accompanied by Stellen's wife Sif and his young child; the four of them made their way through the inner districts of Khristade, creeping from building to building, ruin to ruin. The group had managed to avoid three patrols and were approaching the outer districts. The brothers had planned on using the escape routes but were advised otherwise; stories told of several Omegas being caught using the routes, and the tunnels were now patrolled or boobytrapped, so their route would now run through the outer districts and to what remains of the defence wall. Sif and her child were following closely to Bo, whilst Arne led them all through the narrow streets and passages that made up the outer districts of the city. They ran down street after street, through many burnt out buildings, stopping at the old watering hole, a now closed gentlemen's drinking establishment often frequented by farm labourers. The brothers and their companions rested for a while until night had fallen.

General Hades had just finished executing 36 Omegas, and had learnt it was Stellen who had betrayed him, sent an assassin to kill him. He had ordered a Kappa Commander to fetch Stellen's family from the holding cells on the lower floors of the capitol building. It was only then that Kappa knew of the rescue, knew that the families had been extracted and were no longer imprisoned. When the General heard this news he spun into a rage, immediately ordering all the soldiers on Guard duty to be killed, and ordering the commanders to raise the alarm and increase the city patrols.

As the brothers rested, loud sirens started to ring out around the city; they did not know if Astrid had been successful or whether the alarms were for them, but they knew they had to move; had to get out of Khristade as fast as they could. There were seven more blocks and a ruin of the defence wall to navigate first, and they managed this with relative ease. Arne's route had taken them to a point where no wall remained, not even a ruin. They were out of Khristade and on their way to the farm; Sif and her daughter were beginning to become excited by the thought of seeing Stellen again; seeing daddy. The brothers led Stellen's family across the farms and through the villages; it was dark and not easy to navigate, but easy to see patrols and hide when necessary. It was two hours later that the four reached the farm, where they were greeted by a very emotional, but sullen looking group. Stellen was overjoyed to see his family, but Astrid had failed and Hades was still alive. The brothers questioned what had become of Astrid, but Stellen was unable to tell them. All he knew was that there was no explosion and that Hades was already ordering the executions of Omegas by the truck load, his way to exact his retribution for the attempt on his life.

22
Weary travellers

Balder and his team were crossing Omega state, open fields planted to crops and fenced areas of pasture for grazing animals. The numbers of Kappa patrols were lessening the further from Khristade they travelled, but travelling during the day across open land was still impractical, leaving the team with little option other than travelling only in the dead of night. The team was still suffering, fractured from Ulf's death. The Kappas, Freyja and Inga were walking and resting separately from the rest of the group, keeping away from the other Omegas and only communicating with them when absolutely necessary. Balder would often walk for a whole night without uttering a single word. Ivar's actions had created such a rift between himself and Erik that the captain was being challenged just to keep the team together. They were tired, their emotions on full tilt, with the slightest misplaced word creating further tensions. They had forgotten why they were there, forgotten their purpose, forgotten the mission. When the team rested, it gave Frode the opportunity to study the book – he had begun translating passages of information, and the passages told of Chaos, the god of Kappa, and spoke of his ability to smite his armies, referenced only as Testament. Aurora had spoken of a weapon called Keystone. Frode wanted to inform her of what he had discovered, but with such a divide within the team he was unsure as to how to broach the subject, as when Aurora's work was brought to the team before it had caused great unrest.

The team had spent the day resting in an old ruin of a barn and night was beginning to fall, preparation for the night ahead had begun, packing up their very limited supplies whilst Balder plotted their route. There was a glow beginning to appear from the southwest, which Balder believed to be the town of Helostade, which might offer itself as a good place to scavenge supplies, but would be crawling with Kappa soldiers. Balder mulled over the plan in his head as the sun descended below the horizon. He considered a visit to Helostade, as without supplies the team wouldn't get very much further, so it was a risk worth taking. The team left their position as the sun set; they were walking in their normal groups. Kappas with Freyja and Inga, and Balder leading the other Omegas with Torsten dragging Ivar by his rope shackles. Frode was edging towards the Kappa group as he was desperate to talk with Aurora about the Keystone and Project Testament. Frode had taken a couple of miles to idle up to the Kappa group.

"Hi, it's Aurora?" he stammered.

"'Yes, Frode? What can I help you with?"

"Keystone? There is reference in my book to Testament."

"Testament?" Aurora responded. "What does it say of Testament?"

Frode went on to explain that the book referenced the Kappa god, and that Frode's understanding was he had a weapon, which was called Testament; he used the weapon to wield his godly power over his armies, as a means to control them, to ensure their compliance. The book had also mentioned the need to ensure genetic purity within the world; that for Testament to maintain control, the gods must maintain that purity.

"Testament was created to control Kappas? That doesn't sound right. If Testament was the weapon, then what is Keystone?" the medical officer surmised. "All I know to be true is that Keystone kills people; but I was not privy to the endless genetic testing that was completed on all of our test subjects; I was a mere weapons officer; not a bloody doctor."

This information seemed important, but something didn't add-up. Aurora's head was spinning with this newfound information. It could be the answer to everything, it could be total gibberish, nonsense that the old man had mistakenly translated. It might be the answer to end the wars and the complete destruction of Kappa; it might be a scary bedtime story.

Frode and Aurora talked and talked on the journey to Helostade, but with only clues to a larger puzzle, it left Aurora with many questions; she had left the Kappa science division with never having access to the most detailed and important information. She began to list questions in her head.

What was the original purpose of Testament; is it and Keystone one and the same? Had the Kappas found this Testament?

Were they in possession of the key to their own destruction? Did they even know what it was? And why the endless genetic testing?

These questions and more were tossed back and forth between the science officer and Frode. They now surmised that there must be a device or weapon called Testament, and it was almost certainly used to lord over Kappas, if not all of man. That it would kill or possibly affect any true blood Kappas and possibly every genetically pure person within the world. The genetic testing being undertaken by Kappa and the insistence on testing Keystone on all races or man must have been for a reason, and with the book being a thousand years old, Testament must have been created when the states were all original, before cross breeding and interstate relationships had muddied the genetic waters of the world.

The conversation between Frode and Aurora had now drawn outside interest, Marcus and Freyja had joined the talk and Marcus was keen to share the information with the group. They all had their differences with the Omegas, but this information was another bridge toward their end goal, another piece that somewhat proved their quest was not pure folly. Aurora was less keen to share, they only had four possible pieces of a thousand-piece jumble, and she wanted to protect the information a while longer, at least until Frode had translated more of the passages and the jumble became clearer. They agreed to pause the conversation until after Helostade, needing to focus on getting in and out of the town safely and without raising any alarms. Balder brought the team to a halt in a ruin within striking distance of Helostade; his decision was for only a small group to enter the town and gather the required supplies, and a small family would be the least conspicuous group. Freyja, Inga and Marcus would make the journey into town at first light.

23
Helostade

The day was beginning, the sun had just peaked over the horizon. Marcus was preparing to leave the confines of the ruin in which the team had spent the night. He woke Freyja with a little nudge and went to find Inga. They would soon be heading into the town of Helostade. The Omega team had run very low on supplies, very little food and no medical items; to continue their journey it was imperative for Marcus and Freyja to beg, borrow or steal anything of use. Marcus had spent the night puzzled as to why Balder had chosen him to go. Balder himself was better suited, or possibly Torsten. Maybe Balder knew this was a fool's errand and was hoping he wouldn't make it back – crazy thoughts go through your head when you are tired, hungry and a whole nation is hunting for you, and another whole nation hates the sight of you. The trio set off from their temporary base; it looked to be about a mile or two to the outer limits of the town, so the journey wouldn't take long. Marcus was pleased to be away from the group. He had done everything possible to be of help and to offer useful information about Kappa and their troop movements, but it had not stopped Ivar from trying to kill him. He was pleased to be with Freyja, of all the Omegas she was the one that had been most accommodating and seemed genuinely concerned for his welfare.

"Do either of you know this town well?" Marcus asked as they approached Helostade.

"My auntie lives here, I think, my mummy and me visited a few times," Inga replied.

"Your auntie? Do you remember where she lived? She may very well be of help to us."

"I think I do, yeah, I'm pretty sure I remember."

"Then lead the way, child."

The hope was that the team would appear to be a visiting family, so it was time to start acting as such. Freyja held on to Inga's hand as they approached the town, and Marcus followed closely behind them with a hood pulled up to hide his features. The three allies meandered into the town with Inga leading the way, pulling Freyja along by the hand. They walked across five or six streets unimpeded until they found the town centre, a market square like those in the middle of most Omega towns and villages. It was bustling with people packing various crops into large crates and a set of large scales had been erected where the crates were being weighed by Kappa personnel. Each crate was stamped and a corresponding stamp was punched onto a card and handed to the Omega who had presented the crate for weighing. The people looked weary, and each stamp would lead to a disappointing look on the faces of the Omegas.

"Which way, Inga? We wouldn't want to hang around here for long," Marcus whispered.

"I think it is that way," the little girl guessed.

Inga, Marcus and Freyja skirted around the square and off down a little side street. Inga was becoming more excitable as she dragged Freyja down one street and then the next. "It's there, that's my auntie's house" the little girl screeched with excitement.

She let go of Freyja's hand and ran to the door; she knocked and knocked. The door opened and there stood a lady with the typical Omega features of blonde hair and blue eyes; she was wearing a floral dress and a pinafore.

"Inga, is that you my child?" the lady asked.

"Auntie Ingrid!" Inga screamed with joy.

The lady grabbed Inga and wrapped her up with her arms and gave her the biggest hug; they were overjoyed to see each other. "Inga, are you here with your parents?" Ingrid asked.

The little girl's joy disappeared and sadness leaked into her face, tears began to well in her eyes and one rolled down her face.

"Ma'am, the little girl is here with us," Marcus stated quietly. "Our friends helped your niece escape Khristade when her parents were unfortunately killed. I am dreadfully sorry for your loss."

Ingrid grabbed Inga again and initiated an even bigger hug with the child. "Inga, it is so wonderful to see you safe, but what of your parents' house, their belongings?"

"When I last saw the house, it still stood. I believe it to be safe, Auntie," the little girl replied.

"Thank you for bringing my niece to me," Ingrid said with a peculiar look on her face.

Marcus and Freyja thought nothing of the strange questions. Everyone reacts differently to seeing a loved one who was believed lost.

Inga's auntie invited Marcus and Freyja into her home and went on to explain that she had been left alone; her mother, Inga's grandma, had been culled due to her age, and her husband and been taken away by the Kappa soldiers, leaving her to tend their orchard to meet her quota. Marcus and Freyja then began explaining brief details of their mission, that there were other team members hiding out just past the edge of town; that their aim was to reach Central in a hunt for an end to the wars, answers to all the unknown questions. They went on to explain that the reason for their visit was to gather supplies; they needed food and medicine to continue on their quest. The team still had many hundreds of miles to travel and the further they travelled, the less friendlies they would likely find, so this might be the last good opportunity to gather supplies. Aunt Ingrid offered her house as a base whilst Marcus and Freyja hunted through the town; she would also put them in touch with some of her friends, who may be willing to help.

"The majority of my friends have suffered great loss, every one of them would happily stick it to Kappa in any way they could, but may I advise that we wait till after the weigh-in has finished?" Aunt Ingrid suggested. "The Kappa officials will be gone then; it will be easier to move around, easier for you to find your supplies."

Marcus and Freyja agreed with Ingrid's assessment of the situation. "You are welcome to use the house to rest, I have to tend the orchard, pick the fruit. Inga, would you like to help me?" Ingrid asked.

The little girl nodded and they left the house, Marcus and Freyja found a bedroom and settled down to rest in comfort – after spending the previous nights getting what little sleep they could lying on the floor, this felt like pure luxury.

24
A morning to remember

Marcus and Freyja were resting in the comfort of a bed in the home of Inga's Aunt Ingrid; neither could remember the last time they had been in an actual bed. Both rested for a while without sleeping; they had been talking, and the conversation inevitably had turned to project Testament and what the next move should be. Marcus was adamant that they needed to inform Balder of the knowledge that Frode had discovered, that he and Aurora had begun piecing together. A potential picture was starting to form, certainly enough to tell Balder. Freyja wasn't so sure – the slightest mention of these weapons of mass annihilation had caused great unrest within the team. She believed it best to wait until the picture was more defined, until they actually knew more. What harm would it do to leave it a few more days? Give Frode more time to piece together even more of the puzzle? Although Marcus did not agree, he conceded to his Omega friend; the conversation then turned to a more personal nature – Marcus was interested in what Omega was like. And what Freyja had done before the war spilled into her state.

"What did you do before all of this?" he started.

"A farm hand, moving from farm to farm, helping out where needed. My father was a machinist, and when I was young I would follow him from job to job and pick up what I could."

"No schooling?"

"Not really. In Omega life is your school; there are classes that teach basic reading, writing and math. A little history and some religion, but it's only a few afternoons each week."

"You believe in gods?"

"All Omegas believe in the gods who created us all, who gave us purpose and allowed us to prosper. We are all taught of the six world gods, one for each race of man."

"You pray to these gods, have religious gatherings?"

"Some do, but I believe the gods are long gone. Left us all in this pretty mess."

The conversation continued for some time, Marcus learning about the ways of Omega, learning that most spend a few months training in the defence force, and Freyja went on to explain that she was due to be offered for marriage the day after the invasion, but was called into the defence force and it never took place. She was placed in Balder's unit and it was a true honour; Balder was the highest ranking officer, and one of only a handful of full time soldiers. Marcus was confused by the comments Freyja had made about the marriage customs of Omega.

"Offered for marriage?" he asked.

"Yes, when a young women turns 21 years, her parents offer her for marriage. They will pick the best suitor and arrange the wedding. It is our custom, a tradition."

"Best suitor? What is this?" Marcus scoffed.

"In Omega there are priorities, the most land, the best job, the highest rank in our defence force; things like that."

"Do you not have to like the man to form a good couple?"

"That's not our way; it is not something I would have ever questioned. So, what is it like for you?"

Marcus explained that in Kappa there is no marriage, no couples, not even any friends. If you do well and your rank increases, you are offered the chance to own breeding stock. That the young women are kept in a facility and the high ranking officers would buy, sell and exchange the women and use them to bear their children. Freyja was disgusted by the very thought of this arrangement

"You were a captain; you must've partaken in this?" she said angrily.

"I didn't! I refused the offering when I became a commander, and then again when I was given the captaincy of my brigade. Unlike other Kappas, I believe in love, in friendship, and I tried to be honourable. It is why I am here now. A hunted man!"

Marcus then spoke of his friend Titus, told Freyja that he felt a love for this man. He was his only friend and would have done anything to protect him, like a little brother. He was killed when they were escaping from Khristade, he was killed because of Marcus. Marcus's eyes began to fill with tears as he told Freyja of Titus; she put her arms around Marcus and began to embrace him, looking into each other's eyes. Marcus lifted his hand and softly placed it on Freyja's cheek, gently stroking the side of her face. Freyja leaned in to Marcus and tried to kiss him, but he pulled back, unsure of whether this was right.

"What are you doing?" he questioned sternly.

"I have never felt love, for one moment in this forsaken world I want to feel this. Please can you show me love?"

Marcus was hesitant but had become close with Freyja and didn't want to upset her. He leaned back towards her and they began to kiss. Freyja started unbuttoning Marcus's tunic, in a frantic fashion she was removing all of his clothes. He reciprocated but in a more measured way. Within moments both were naked. With the laws and rules as they were in Kappa and Omega, neither of them had any experience of love making. Plenty of awkward fidgeting, groping and grasping at each other preceded an all too brief few moments of intercourse. Freyja reached out and held Marcus's hand, she squeezed it reassuringly, and in that moment Freyja may not have felt that real feeling of love she craved; but did forget the horrors of the world.

25
Supplies aplenty

Marcus and Freyja were awoken by a door slamming. They jumped from the comforts of the bed and dressed quickly. Ingrid called out, letting Marcus and Freyja know it was only her and Inga returning from the orchard. Freyja was first to join Inga and her aunt.

"Did you get some rest?" Ingrid inquired.

"Yes, thank you. It was so nice to spend a few minutes in a real bed. I actually feel rested for the first time in ages, thank you so much."

"I was able to speak with some friends and they are all willing to give you what they have left from their weekly rations; it is not a lot but hopefully it will help."

"That is so very kind."

"The medical supplies you require are going to be more of a challenge – no one has anything," Ingrid said solemnly.

"You have done more than enough to help," Freyja said kindly.

Marcus joined Freyja and again thanked Ingrid for her help. She had drawn them a map of the homes where families would give to their cause. Marcus thought it best for the young girl to remain with her aunt – the little girl was unsure of whether to stay or go; she wanted to go on the mission, but Marcus took the child to one side.

"Inga, it has been our absolute pleasure to have you along with the team, and been even more delightful to have gotten to known you, but I think your auntie needs you more than the team. She is all alone and has no family but you left; we will miss your help, but your place is here, with your family."

Inga argued for a moment – she was desperate to remain with Marcus – but eventually agreed that her aunt needed her more and agreed to stay. The little girl gave Freyja a hug and saluted Captain Marcus, who promptly stood to attention and saluted back.

Freyja and Marcus left the house and began to follow the map, door by door they collected supplies. Canned fruit and vegetables; preserved meats and water filters that would allow the team to clean any water source they encountered. Home after home gave over more and more supplies, more than the two could possibly carry, but at the next home the family could see their struggles and offered their hand cart. The generosity of the families was unimaginable. The duo were approaching the final house on their map; it was very close to the town square which was still busy with people.

"I thought the weigh-in was due to be finished by now? Something else must be happening," Freyja surmised.

"You go to the final house, I will take a look," Marcus responded.

Freyja took the cart and proceeded to the final home, whilst Marcus took another street that led to the square; it was difficult to see what was happening as the crowds were ten-deep with people. Marcus found some steps that led up the side of a property and took two steps up to get a better vantage. He looked over the crowd to see a group of Kappa soldiers circling an officer; the officer was preparing to read out a message from an official looking document.

"The people of Helostade, I am Captain Felix of the Kappa armies second brigade; you will all listen and take notice of what I am here to say. The Kappa armies are looking for two men and a child, these men are responsible for heinous crimes against Kappa and need to be brought to justice." Captain Felix paused for a moment before continuing to read from the document. "From this moment forth, any person known to have colluded with this enemy shall be executed, any person known to have helped this scum will be executed; these three enemies will be brought before his excellency General Hades for punishment, and any person who assists the armies of Kappa in finding these traitors will be handsomely rewarded. Any and all information that leads to their capture will be rewarded."

The Kappa captain stopped and began nailing the document to a post in the middle of the square. Marcus could now see that his face was plastered across the document, along with the faces of Blank and Inga; he hurried from his vantage point and quickly returned to Freyja.

"We have to go, now," he commanded, grabbing the cart and beginning to hurry down the streets and back towards Ingrid's home. "We must get Inga and leave this town now; the child is in danger!"

"What was in the square to have got you so worried?" Freyja cried.

"My face is being plastered all over town, along with that of the girl's. She and her aunt are in danger; we must hurry."

Marcus and Freyja chased along the streets of Helostade and back to Ingrid's home. Marcus thumped on the door and Ingrid answered.

"I was worried it was the soldiers," Ingrid complained.

"You should be worried! Where is the girl?" Marcus exclaimed.

"She went out to play with some of my neighbours' children. I thought it would be good for her to be a child again for a short while; why?"

"She is in grave danger, we must find her and get out of town immediately."

"She will be out in the fields."

"Which way?"

Ingrid explained where the child would be and Marcus ran off to find her, running as quickly as he could, down each street; right turn, right turn then a left, he kept running till he found the field Inga's aunt expected her to be in. There were children but no Inga. Marcus's thoughts began to betray him again, thoughts of the worst possible outcomes for the poor child. He was a calm man, but he was now in total panic mode; he felt like he was spinning round in circles looking for the child, but then a voice.

"Marcus?" a small voice called out.

Marcus stopped spinning and there before him was Inga – she had been playing in a nearby tree.

"You must come with me now, child, change of plans. We all agreed that it would be best for you to come with us, and not stay here with your aunt. Hope that is alright?"

Marcus picked up the child and put her on his back and moved quickly back into town, to re-group with Freyja and leave Helostade. Marcus was still carrying Inga as he and Freyja left the town; they had a hand cart full of food and other supplies and were hastily making their way back to the team.

The three adventurers arrived back at the ruin just prior to nightfall. Balder was pleased with their efforts as there was now food enough for their journey; but was less pleased at the news of the hunt for three members of his group. He knew the Kappas were wanted, he knew they had kicked the proverbial hornets' nest, and he had wished that his team would be outrunning the news, but that was one wish that was not to come true. He gathered up the team and provided his orders for the night; they would be moving northeast, avoiding the town of Helostade and any further towns that they may encounter. It was now far too much of a risk to approach even Omegas for help. The people were desperate, and they would likely not think twice about giving up two Kappa soldiers for much needed food and comforts, even if it meant giving up the innocent Omega child too. The group moved out from their temporary base, they trudged through the night in the silence that had become custom.

Balder noted that Marcus and Freyja were walking closer than before, he thought that a completed mission, a successful mission together, had made them closer, increased their obvious bond. He led the team across miles that night; they travelled further than on any other day of their journey. Perhaps it was the thought of a good feed in the morning, or maybe it was a good day's rest that energised them. Maybe it was just the increasing lack of Kappa patrols that night; but for all the problems the team had faced, it felt like they were finally making good progress.

26
The last march

O ver the last four nights Balder and his team had made good progress; they had travelled further than expected and were approaching what they believed was the edge of Omega state –, not one of the Omegas had ever travelled this far out before and the land was all unfamiliar. The cobbled together maps they had been utilising had stopped being useful some time ago; they were now in totally unknown territory and Balder was completely reliant on the information he was drawing from the Kappas. Balder was a thoughtful man – to him preparation was everything and the situation ahead could not be planned. He knew Omega well and felt he knew where he should and shouldn't travel, but he had never been this far and no free man or woman in Omega had ever been to Kappa. He began to think that it might be time for a change, and he might not be the best man to lead the troops on this part of the journey. Surely the Kappa captain was best placed to successfully navigate Kappa state, and get his team safely to the eastern shore, but his men would never agree, there would be total mutiny if it was even suggested. Balder could not let the thought lie, he wanted to ensure his team had the best possible chance and in this situation he knew that their best chance was being led by Marcus. It played on his mind all night until the sun began to rise. It was time to encamp for the day and he had spotted a small copse just under the horizon, where the team would rest, only a mile's further walking.

The team reached the copse just as the light of day was beginning to shine bright. They all settled in their normal groups: Marcus,

Freyja and Inga together; Aurora was deep in conversation with Frode – this had become more frequent the last few days since Frode found reference to Testament in his book. Erik, Hilda and Torsten were together, and Balder was with Blank watching over the still shackled Ivar. Balder and Blank had become more friendly since the shoot-out with the Kappas some days previous, Balder now felt able to trust Blank and his very guarded walls had lowered slightly around the Kappa grunt.

Balder approached Marcus and took him to one side. "One soldier to another, can I really trust you, Marcus?"

"Captain, you can trust me with your life and that of any member of this team."

"Really? Any member of this team?" Balder reacted sarcastically.

"Yes, sir, even him. For better or worse I would not purposefully endanger any of your soldiers."

Balder mulled Marcus's bold statement for a moment before addressing his point. "We are moving into unknown territory. No man in the Omega defence force has ever been this close to Kappa. I need you more than ever to ensure we are taking the right path. Are you able to help me do this?"

"I only know what I know, Captain, Kappa moves at such a fast pace and it has been many months since I have been in Kappa. There may be factories where a month ago there was not; there may be base camps and troops where a month ago there was not; there might even be towns where a month ago there would not have been."

"But you know more than I. So as your neck is on the line like all the rest of us, it is only right and proper that you lead the men through Kappa! Big choices and decisions still come to me or a vote, but you should lead the troops, get us to the eastern shore, get us through Kappa and let's try our best to avoid the base camps and towns if at all possible."

"How will you address this with the men?" Marcus asked quizzically.

"There will be a vote for all. Blank, Aurora and I will vote for this, and I am sure you can persuade Freyja?"

"Yes, sir, I think that is possible."

"That would make it four to three; Torsten, Hilda and Erik will never go for it, but are good soldiers and if the vote is in your favour they will comply."

"So that leaves Frode? What will he vote?"

"He will vote for whatever is his best chance to reach Central, and in this case that is you temporarily."

Balder walked off leaving Marcus to explain to Freyja what he wanted. Freyja was very proud to serve under Balder and was reluctant, but as she knew it was what he wanted, agreed to vote with Marcus. Frode was very easily persuaded to vote with Marcus also. As Balder had thought, all he cared about was making it to Central and uncovering the truth.

Balder called the group together and addressed them. "Friends, I want to be honest in my appraisal of the current situation. We are about to cross into Kappa and this is where my knowledge runs out, but we are fortunate to have with us an ex-Kappa captain who knows the terrain well, and knows the people. It is my belief that our best chance to navigate Kappa state and reach the eastern shore is to allow Captain Marcus to temporarily take command of this mission." Balder paused to get a read from the team, but there was nothing but stone cold silence, so he continued. "I will still be in charge! We will still vote where necessary, but Marcus will lead us. He will set our course and you will obey his orders; this is what I want and I would like you all to agree. I understand your hesitation, I understand the hate towards everything Kappa, but Marcus has proven himself to be unlike other Kappas, and I trust him with my life."

There was still total silence from the group, nobody uttering a word. "By a show of hands, all in favour?"

Blank, Aurora, Frode, Freyja and Balder all raised their hands immediately, but Balder was surprised as Torsten also raised his hand, Hilda and Erik too. It was unanimous: Marcus would lead the team across the border and through Kappa state. "What is your first order, sir?" Freyja asked.

"We need to send a scout on ahead, map the terrain and see how close we actually are to the border. We must find the right path to cross. Erik, you and Blank are our new scout team, get your rest and at sunset you pair go find us a safe route across that border."

Erik and Blank agreed without question, they would head out the moment the sun had set.

27
The border

Half the night had passed before Erik and Blank returned from scouting. They had located the border and brought back troubling news. Having scouted approximately 10 miles, they found four watch towers and a solid line of high electrified fence, with spirals of animal wire encasing the top. Each watch tower had 360° views with four heavy arms mounted one to each side and accompanying high powered search lights. There was a heavily fortified gate across a small service road to the south, but the only possible point of egress was one of the towers to the northern end, unlit and appearing to be unmanned it was the only logical choice. Anywhere else along this stretch of border would be impossible to cross without being seen, without having to engage with the Kappa soldiers; and even to cross at the point identified would take precision and a whole bucket full of luck. Marcus believed it best to scout the potential crossing point himself, so he left with Blank and Erik, setting out towards the unmanned tower. As they grew close it became apparent that the tower was not unmanned but under repair, there were a team of slave workers hammering and drilling near the base of the structure and only two soldiers guarding them. The Kappa guards were just ordinary grunts, low ranking nobodies who likely wouldn't even be missed.

Marcus whispered orders to Erik. "Go back and gather the others, bring them along this exact path we have just followed. Bring them to the edge of the lights range, and await my signal."

Erik nodded, quickly and quietly heading back to camp. Marcus began explaining his plan to Blank. "You and me are going to very quietly remove these guards, no noise, we need to hit them simultaneously. No mistakes; understood?"

Blank nodded.

"When the soldiers are down, put on their helmets and act as though you were supposed to be there. How would you like to play soldier again?"

Blank nodded again and the two moved silently towards the soldiers, it took only seconds to disarm and incapacitate the amateur soldiers. Marcus quickly put on the Kappa helmet and picked up a weapon, moving quickly towards the workers, he hushed them like he would a child. Marcus explained to the workers who he was. The workers were Delta, so his own kin; they had been in servitude for some time and were pleased to see the Kappa soldiers get what they were due.

Blank and Marcus were standing over the workers as they waited patiently for the rest of the group to appear on the path. It took about an hour before Blank could see the group hiding down in the long grass at the edge of the searchlights. Marcus had already instructed the workers to make a small hole in the fence which was not electrified due to the repairs. He signalled Blank, who in turn waved the first two team members down from the long grass. Torsten and Ivar moved through the hole and away into the darkness; another two followed and then another two. It was not long before all but Balder and Freyja had crossed over the border. Marcus waved to Blank and the signal was sent, Freyja and Balder making their way down to the fence and through. Marcus then offered the workers the opportunity to follow, but they had family and friends that they could not leave behind. "What will you tell the Kappas about the guards?"

"We will think of something, tell them they ran off or something; it happens all the time. Good luck on your mission, brave Delta."

Marcus thanked the workers and he and Blank made it through the fence and away into the night. The Kappa slaves repaired the hole and returned to the guard station, where they were questioned about the missing guards. The officer of the watch acccepted their story without ramifications. Someone would surely notice the dead soldiers in the days to come but by that time the team would be long gone.

Now in Kappa the Omega team would have to observe more caution than ever; there were not many hours left in the night so the team needed to put as much ground as possible between themselves and the border before day broke. Kappa state was very different to Omega, all the ground devoid of life, endless mud as far as the eye can see with little or no places to hide. The team would need to dig out fox holes to rest and move during the night or day, when energy levels permitted. Marcus's plan was a simple one: move as fast and as far as possible; day or night the team needed to travel. Unlike Omega, there would not be the heavy brigade presence in Kappa itself – their troops were focused in Omega and on the Eastern shore. It would be more support troops and workers guards, who were the lowest of the low, led by old officers who have never been and will never be anybody. As long as the team avoided the major centres and any large scale constructions, they should travel unnoticed.

28
Rebellion strikes

In Khristade the forum had been growing fast, as more of the people were killed by Kappa, the more volunteers were joining. Joining Stellen and the cause. Kappa command was convinced that killing the people would deter rebellion, but if anything it made the Omega people's resolve even stronger. Internally the Kappas were now referring to Stellen's forum as a rebellion; Stellen was now the leader of the Omega rebellion. They had made a semi-permanent base in the old barn, where the group had originally met. There were now 30 individuals living on the farm; Stellen and his family were there; Arne and Bo had become the soldiers of the group and if there was a filthy task to be completed it was the brothers who were leading the way. Bjorn had been joined by his family, his wife and three sons, who were all fighting age and ready to put their lives on the line for the cause. Ava had returned from Khristade – she had gone to the city to gather intel. One piece of information was the Kappa most wanted list, which she presented to the group, reading from first to tenth: "Kappa Officer 24978, a Captain Marcus; 76349, Blank. They are ex-Kappa soldiers who from what I can gather are responsible for killing General Hades' son. Stellen, you are number three, with my husband at number four. This gives me a little joy, as it appears he has been causing Kappa quite the headache. A Kappa Science officer is fifth and a young girl is sixth; she helped the Kappa soldiers escape Hades. Then it is me, Bo, Bjorn and Arne; it's quite the list!"

"It shows we are making our mark," Bo suggested.

"But at what cost, my friends, at what cost?" Bjorn questioned.

The rebellion had certainly made their mark and were causing what disruption to Kappa they could, but the idea to take a shot at assassinating Hades had caused many Omegas to lose their lives, and the more actions the rebellion took, the more Omegas were being slaughtered in the streets. The members of Stellen's forum knew many good Omegas would die anyway, but by pissing Kappa off they had accelerated the timeline of deaths.

The forum had already suffered direct loss – Svend and Yrsa who were no shows at the inception meeting had already succumbed to Kappa brutality. The husband and wife had been found a few days after dead in their bed; gutted like farm animals. They were good folk who did not deserve their end. The rebellion had been secretly moving families away from Khristade; each night Bo and Arne were leading a team into the city and extracting families. Even with all the patrols and Kappa troops on the streets, they had developed a routine that had enabled the extraction of 17 families over the previous nights. The families were spread around outer villages and towns; hiding in plain sight away from the main Kappa forces on the streets of the capital. The following night the team lead by Bo and Arne were heading back into Khristade to attempt extraction of six further families. Maybe the boys got complacent, maybe the patrols changed their routes, but the team never made it back to the farm and the families never made it either; a few days after this attempt word came down from the capitol that a patrol had discovered the brothers and four families, a fire fight ensued and all the Omegas were killed; Bo, Arne and 15 other Omegas all gunned down in the streets.

There were more attempts to disrupt Kappa; destruction of supply compounds, roadblocks and the mining of main routes into the capital were all attempted by the rebellion, but nothing stopped Kappa. For every Kappa soldier that was killed, two Omegas would be strung up in the square, often just the first people that Orcus and his secret police happened upon. For every supply truck or compound destroyed, quotas would be raised; they had now risen to the point that nearly all Omegas were unable to meet the targets, meaning no food or medicine for the citizens. All the members of the forum had lost family or friends; but having begun down this path it was impossible to turn round and head back – they had opened the box of the gods and now it could not be closed, they could not just lie down and give in. They must continue to fight, continue to disrupt Kappa – but there has to be a limit that will eventually be reached.

29
The more we learn

It was the peak of the day. Marcus and the team were resting in crudely covered foxholes that had been dug the night before – after only a couple of days, the energy levels in the team were starting to wane. Travel, dig, rest, travel, dig, rest was the daily routine, and it was becoming something of a chore. So much time was being lost because there was no natural cover, barren mud field after barren mud field was all that Kappa state had to offer. To limit the digging, the team had been split into three smaller groups, Marcus was of course with Freyja and Inga, Blank was given digging duties for Aurora and Frode, who had now become somewhat inseparable, and then the Omegas, Balder, Erik, Hilda, Torsten and Ivar were together. Their holes were all a little spaced out in case of attack, but sound travelled well across the open land. The topics of conversation varied from foxhole to foxhole; Aurora and Frode were deep in conversation about the lab trials Aurora had been a part of, and what keystones had been attempted.

"How many different variations were attempted?" Frode queried.

"Many; I sabotaged variant 11356, so I suppose there were 11,355 previous attempts? But it is not like we were given the full plotted history of the trials."

"How many were you involved with?"

"Around 300, and every time I thought we were close to a breakthrough, I changed something. Only minor variations that wouldn't be spotted. It wasn't like there was time to plan; each variant was tested on five unwilling participants, and on most occasions all five of their lives ended in a very painful fashion, and that's not to mention the hundreds of our own soldiers it would then be tested on."

"Five; why five?"

"One of each race of man. Kappa would launch secret raids to Sigma and Central to abduct people to test on. There was quite the flow of people through the lab."

At this point others in the group began to take note of the conversation, and not in an interested bystander way; it was more like, you were responsible for killing hundreds of people and testing a weapon that could kill us all kind of way.

Erik was the first to speak; he called out from his foxhole. "How many did you kill?"

"It wasn't like I chose to kill those people, I did all I could to prevent it."

"All you could? Sounds like you killed those folk and didn't do a damn thing to stop it."

"You weren't there, you have no idea what lengths I went to; the risks I took to prevent the weapons creation, and if it meant a few people suffered, so that we might all live without the threat of mass extinction; then so be it."

Aurora was fuming; she knew what she had done, she knew that it was her and her alone that had potentially stopped Keystone from being created. "Go fuck yourself, you small minded country hick," she blurted out.

This enraged Erik who jumped up out of his foxhole and charged towards where Aurora was lying low. Everyone leapt from their cover, Balder manhandling Erik to the ground and Marcus grabbing Aurora.

"You stupid uneducated farm prick," Aurora continued; now screaming not much but obscenities at Erik.

"You fucking people don't deserve my help."

"You f-ing people?" Balder angrily questioned. "Don't you dare refer to us as, you f-ing people."

The whole group was now in a full heated argument, so Marcus stepped in to try to calm the situation. "Stop, all of you stop this now; we have all done things, done horrible things we are not proud of."

Ivar then shouted from his bound position in the Omega foxhole. "I'm very proud of all the Kappas I offed," he shouted through his laughter. "Especially the one in Khristade. I can remember seeing him through my scope, and the horrified look on his pretty face when I hit him square in the chest. Fucking strange looking Kappa, with his blonde hair and blue eyes."

No one paid much attention to Ivar except for Marcus. "What did you say?" Marcus angrily questioned.

"Fucking blond haired, blue eyed pretty looking Kappa prick, that I offed in Khristade."

To most this did not mean much, but blond haired and blue eyed Kappas were very rare, rarer than peace itself. There was only one Kappa in Khristade that day that fit that description. "Titus; it was you that killed Titus?"

Marcus drew a knife as he lunged towards Ivar. Torsten blocked Marcus, disarming him and locking him up with arms firmly secured behind his back.

"Let me go; I'm going to cut his blackened heart out. He killed Titus, he killed my only friend."

The whole group were shouting and screaming at each other, and it was hard to tell who was on which side of this argument.

A girl's voice screamed at the very top of her lungs. "Stop! You must all stop this!" It was Inga; the little girl was the only one thinking straight, in floods of tears as her friends were shouting and arguing with each other.

Freyja went to her and wrapped an arm around her, comforting her.

"What are you all doing?" the little girl asked. "There is no enemy here!"

"She is right," Balder stated in a mellow tone. "Everybody needs to calm down."

"But he killed my friend," Marcus cried.

"And you haven't killed our friends or family? You're telling me that in all the years you spent in the Kappa army you haven't killed someone's friend?" Balder proclaimed.

"Yes, you know I have, but I'm not proud of it. I don't take pleasure from it."

Balder turned to Ivar with a look of complete disgust, before turning back to Marcus. "You promised me you would not harm any member of my team, and although I probably agree that he deserves harm for his callous words, you promised me. And as for this other nonsense, we already know she did awful, hateful things, for which there is really no excuses, but Aurora has to live with that. We were not there; we do not know we wouldn't have done the exact same thing, and we now have her on our side, which in my mind gives us at least a fighting chance to ensure that this weapon never sees the light of any day."

The situation had calmed and everyone had returned to their foxholes. Marcus was being comforted by Freyja; he was most upset to have seen his friend's killer face to face, but also upset by his actions, making a point of apologising to Inga for upsetting her. The rest of the foxholes had fallen silent, not a whimper or a sound. Balder contemplated the future of the team, now twice that the team had nearly self-destructed. Like a tinder box ready to blow, the slightest thing could set everything off again, and next time his words may not be enough to calm the situation.

30
Mines

It was night and the team were crossing more dead ground, brown dust upon brown mud. There was a significant light source in the south-east and another directly north. Marcus estimated that north was the city of Dubris and the south was a new construction, possibly a small town or troop base. The team had been wasting great swathes of time having to dig foxholes, and resting all day – travelling in daylight was proving impossible with absolutely no cover. There had to be a better way? An easier way to cross Kappa? Crossing his state led Marcus to think of his childhood, as although Marcus was the result of love between a Kappa breeder and a Delta doctor, Kappa had always been Marcus's home. He had no fond memories of childhood, but could remember his mother, and was remembering some of the stories she told of his father. One particular story that his mother had told, was that his father had been sent away to work the Kappa mines. Marcus was not knowledgeable about the industrial history of Kappa, but if his father went to work the mines, there surely must be tunnels criss-crossing under their feet as they walked across Kappa state. Marcus also recalled that on his monthly visit with his mother, when nearly graduation age, he was told that his father had gone missing. The mines had closed, Kappa had burned through their natural resources and his father had subsequently been sent to the eastern shore, where he fell from atop the wall and into the sea. In Marcus's mind this meant that not only were there a mass of tunnels running under their feet, but a mass of abandoned, empty tunnels beneath their feet.

As the team moved on, Marcus tried to think back to his youth, tried to remember if his mother ever told him exactly where his father had been sent, but he could think of nothing but Dubris. Was that only because they were near Dubris and it was on his mind, or was that actually where the mining hub was located?

"Everyone, stop," Marcus ordered. "We are losing too much time digging holes, and the nights will only get shorter the further we move into the hot season. I have an idea: mining tunnels. I know that all the mines of Kappa eventually joined each other, and I am one hundred percent sure there was a mining hub just inside the eastern shore, but that's where my memory gets a little foggy. I am only fifty-fifty on where the closest hub could be found. Something is telling me there is a hub just on the outskirts of Dubris, that city to the north–" as Marcus pointed to the light in the night's sky.

"We could use the tunnels to travel across the entire country?" Balder questioned.

"That is the theory," Marcus responded.

"But what of the miners?" Erik asked.

"No; they are all long gone, the mines were exhausted when I was a child."

"But we have no idea about the state of those tunnels, and you are not sure there is a hub close to that Kappa city?"

"That is all correct; but I believe it to be worth the risk. The tunnels would have been made strong, they were built by Delta slaves. I'm sure they will still be passable."

"So, the question to the group is this: do we take the risk of moving close to a Kappa city, for a potential way to move easily across the state, have an unimpeded straight shot under the noses of Kappa?"

After a short pause for consideration a vote was held and to a man the decision was to go for the tunnels. Changing direction immediately, the team started heading north towards the city of

Dubris.

The team were nearing Dubris; there was little or no activity outside of the city, and the team were moving fast towards a small rocky outcrop that would offer a relatively safe location to rest, whilst they searched for the mining hub. Marcus and Blank left the group resting to find the mine entrance, and their search did not take long. The mining hub was no more than a mile from the team's location, unguarded but boarded and secured. Marcus instructed Blank to stay at the hub, to start removing the boards from the entrance to the mine, whilst he returned to the group and began preparing them to move to the tunnels. Erik had been patrolling and found a small yard filled with decaying vehicles.

"There might be something useful in one of the trucks – is it worth a look?" the young Omega asked.

"We have about two hours of darkness left; I suppose it can do no harm. The group should move to the tunnels first, only you and me will go to the yard," Marcus ordered.

The main group moved to the tunnels where Blank had created an entrance for them into the mine. Marcus and Erik trekked to the yard and began searching the old trucks.

"Found anything?" Marcus inquired.

"Lots of old crap; wait, I found an old portable Kappa radio. Shit it's still got power."

"Grab it and let's get back to the others; I don't like being out here, I feel we are vulnerable."

Erik and Marcus quick stepped it back to the team and into the mine.

"Everyone should get some quick rest, we move in one hour," Marcus ordered.

Whilst the team was grabbing a quick rest, Erik was playing with the radio; trying to find a channel that worked. He twisted the frequency dial back and forth but was getting nothing but static;

however, undeterred he kept trying and much to his own amazement Erik had found a working channel, it was pure luck as there were only sporadic updates, which sounded like they were from Kappa command. There were only a few intelligible words. "Kappa most wanted number seven captured on outskirts of Khristade." The message repeated a couple of times until a response was made.

"Base command understood."

Erik was intrigued who number seven on Kappa's most wanted list was so continued to listen in. There were large pauses between updates, until the channel suddenly sprung back to life. "Base command confirmed capture of rebellion leader, Ava; Omega defence force captain's wife. Confirm orders."

Erik was shocked; he called to Balder who came quickly to the radio. "Sir, they are claiming they have captured your wife, the rebellion leader?"

"Ava; they have Ava?" Balder questioned.

"That is what they are reporting, sir."

The response was then heard over the radio.

"Base command orders. Bring enemy combatant to capitol building for processing and public execution"

Balder approached Marcus and asked for his leave; he knew he would be letting down his men, and all of Omega, but could not stand by and do nothing knowing his wife was to be killed. For most of the last months Balder had assumed she was already dead; but hearing that on the radio, how could he not try and save her? Marcus understood; he knew of the pain that must be in Balder's heart. He gave his blessing for Balder to leave, but offered the opinion it should be put to a vote, which Balder agreed to, and the vote was taken.

"Men; I must beg of you to take my leave. Ava my love is to be executed and I must do something. I understand that must hurt you all, especially Hilda and Erik. I made you all stand by when the Leader, your grandmother, was murdered, but Ava is my world and whilst I could live in blissful ignorance I could continue, but now knowing of her plight I just cannot stand idle."

The team voted, and all agreed for Balder to be allowed to leave. He was eternally grateful for the love and respect of the team. There was one further decision to make: Ivar asked to be allowed to accompany the Captain in his rescue attempt and Marcus would not allow this decision to go to a vote, instead immediately agreeing to Ivar's request.

Freyja and Erik had been sent from the mine to inspect some of the old trucks in the yard; Freyja was convinced she could patch one up enough to get Balder and Ivar back to Khristade, so picked the best of the bad lot and began working till sunrise. Just managing to turn the truck over as the sun peaked above the buildings in Dubris. Balder and Ivar loaded their gear in the rear of the truck, and after hasty goodbyes they set-off back to Khristade. The journey would be difficult, with a very small chance of success, but Balder and Ivar were determined. The remainder of the team gathered together in the mine, their number now reduced to nine. Marcus was now the leader of the mission to save the world, an ex-Kappa Captain leading a group with the sole aim of defeating his own people, and for the first time since their journey began there was a moment's harmony in the team – even Erik and Hilda seemed to have embraced Marcus's leadership. It was daytime and the team were travelling – not that they knew it, there was nothing but endless darkness in the tunnels of the mine. At least for now the tunnels appeared sound and were navigable with relative ease. The team had four long days' travel ahead, in the dank and dark tunnels running under the barren Kappa soil.

31
Rebellion is only as strong as the weakest link

The rebellion in Khristade was taking a beating, with Bo and Arne gone; killed in the streets, it was left to Bjorn's eldest son Anders to lead the missions. He had only received three months' basic defence force training and was ill equipped to deal with the rigours of leading men – this had led to a sizeable decrease in the number of missions to liberate families from Khristade. This compounded an already problematic situation, as the randomness of the Kappa attacks and executions was making it impossible to pinpoint which families to help and which to not. Many of the forum families had left the farm; deciding they could no longer be part of the rebellion, as for all their efforts the killing didn't stop; for all the families they had saved, many more had been devastated by loss and destroyed by Kappa forces.

Stellen received news from Khristade and was meeting with Bjorn to plan their response. Stellen had learnt that Ava had been captured by Kappa forces on the outskirts of the city, and from what he understood Ava was to be executed but not before Hades' torturers had their turn.

"We must help her," Stellen pleaded.

"We must all get away from here, she will talk and then we are all dead; my wife is here and your wife is here. Our only plan should be to leave this place."

"Ava is strong and I believe in her. It will not be her that dooms us!"

"My family are leaving. I do not share your faith, and forbid you from using my family in any of your cockamamie rescue plans."

"Bjorn; you are giving in to them, choosing to lay down and die."

"I am choosing my family."

"No, you're choosing stupidity."

Stellen stormed off; he was furious with his friend. How could he not want to help Ava, and how could he give up this easily? He was so angry, they had to do all they could to help Ava, so proceeded to go behind Bjorn's back directly to Anders, asking him to put together a mission to rescue Ava. Anders, unlike his father, was happy to try and help, he was willing to still sacrifice if that is what it took. Anders was given only an hour to put together his plan and the required team. There was no limit of volunteers, more than enough young men and women who quickly offered to be part of the mission; Anders selected five Omegas to join him, including his middle brother Lars. The plan would be enacted that night under the cover of darkness, the team would infiltrate the capitol via the same route Bo and Arne used to rescue Stellen's wife and attempt to extract Ava. It was a simple plan, but the risk was great. Time had forced them to make many assumptions, guessing that the guards at the capitol would not have been increased, that the old passages in the capitol building were still useable and that the team would be able to avoid the beefed-up patrols around Khristade.

Bjorn was fuming with rage; he pushed past his sons and into the barn to confront Stellen. "How dare you go behind my back and put my sons at risk for Ava? What gives you the right to arbitrarily make that choice?"

"I didn't make that choice, Anders and Lars are very brave boys and volunteered; they made the choice."

"But you still asked them, you still asked them even though I forbid it."

"What do you want from me? An apology for doing what I believe to be best for Omega? I am choosing my state, my home; this forum needs Ava alive, this state needs Ava alive."

"And I need my family to be safe," Bjorn raged, with tears beginning to well in his eyes.

"None of us are safe, wherever you go, your family will not be safe. You are merely prolonging a miserable existence. If not dead today, they will starve to death tomorrow, unless we continue to fight."

Bjorn was very upset as he turned and left the barn, he grabbed his sons and took them outside. "You are my boys and I love you, and respect your courage, but please think carefully about your choices."

"Father, we love you too; but we have to do this. If we die tonight, be proud of us, understand that our deaths were for a good cause, in the cause of helping others," Anders replied.

"If you die tonight I will never forgive myself, but I am always very proud; I am very proud of all my family. If you must go, then go with my blessing, my boys; and fight to come home to your mother and brother."

The boys left their father, gathered their team and left the farm, having walked from the farm to Khristade on so many occasions, but tonight felt different, there was an air of inevitability, the inevitable outcome of failure, and with failure their deaths. The rescue team had hiked from the farm and to the outer limits of the city; they had a path to follow that would hopefully avoid Kappa patrols; 22 streets to cross, 22 streets of blind corners and dark side alleys to navigate to reach the capitol building. It was on street number 10 that the team found a major problem: a large Kappa patrol; at least a brigade of men, 20-strong, 20 bloodthirsty, highly trained Kappa soldiers versus six undertrained farmers. The brothers and their four Omega companions fought hard and fought well, but that air of inevitability was coming to pass. One Omega down, dead, shot in the head; then another, dead by multiple body shots. A third soon followed as he tried to help one of his fellow rebellion fighters. Anders ordered a retreat, the three remaining team members left the street one by one whilst providing cover for each other, using what little training they had to fight for survival. Anders and his remaining team had managed to put a small amount of distance between themselves and the Kappa forces, they were moving quickly across the streets and were approaching the city edge. They emerged from the final street only to be confronted by another Kappa brigade holding position in the remains of the Khristade defensive wall. Changing track fast, the team moved sideways and back into the city on an alternate street, barging through the door of an abandoned house and taking positions ready for the inevitable Kappa onslaught.

32
Rebellion is dying

A lthough Stellen strongly believed in Ava's ability to withstand the Kappa torture, it proved to be more hope than reality, as Kappa troops, a whole battalion, were pouring into the area surrounding the farm. Soldier after soldier fired volley after volley, literally raining bullets. The rebellion was doing what they could to repel the invaders, having taken defensive positions, everyone, even the children, were armed and directed towards the enemy. They were willing to fight to the very end, to their very last breath, there was no choice now and running was not an option. The Kappas had the rebellion completely surrounded and there was no real hope of winning this battle. In Khristade, Anders and his brother Lars were the final two members of the strike team that were standing. Of the original six they were now all that lived, Tyr had been shot; after making it to the house where the team were barricaded, but thoughts of a brief respite were short-lived. A sniper had picked him off through one of the upstairs windows. Hope of hiding out were now gone, Kappa knew where they were and it would be only moments before they would hit them like a sledge hammer.

Stellen was taking the lead in the defence of the farm; he had organised everyone and passed out all the ammunition they had; they were not well prepared, but at the very least they would take a lot of Kappas down with them. A small group of Kappas approached the near side of the farm, a ringing of gunfire sounded as the Omegas defended themselves. All Kappas were down and with no rebellion losses, a quick win. Another group approached from the rear and in another hail of bullets all the Kappa soldiers were killed, but this raid had caused Omega casualties: two dead, a woman and her child had panicked, tried to move from their position and were hit as they ran.

In Khristade, Anders was saying some last words to his brother. "Thank you, brother, for standing with me; for fighting for Omega and making our family proud."

"We are not dead yet, big brother, I will keep faith until my heart stops beating."

"You are a better man than me, Lars! Love you, little brother."

The talking stopped as the first wave of Kappas tried to barge into the building.

"Short burst; aim high, head shots," Anders ordered.

The brothers withstood the first wave and then a second, but the Kappa soldiers kept charging, troop after troop ran into the barricades seemingly just waiting to be killed. With each soldier the temporary barricades became weaker, and the brothers' ammunition decreased; it would not be long until the Kappas breached the house. Back at the farm the Rebellion had repelled a number of incursions from the Kappa troops, but the cost was high. Eight Omega souls had perished in the skirmishes.

"Bjorn, I am so sorry, my friend, I was wrong, and have doomed us all."

"No, you were right; it is certainly better to die a man than a coward, my old friend."

The fighting continued, wave after wave of Kappas were stopped short of entering the farm. It would not be long before reinforcements arrived, and Kappa were determined to not let the rebellion see another sunrise. With this in mind, Stellen had decided to take the fight to Kappa; he saw the opportunity to perhaps breach enough of a hole in the Kappa lines to let a few of their friends escape.

Whilst they had been at the farm, Bjorn had been making some of his famous home brew; it packed quite the punch and was quite the volatile liquid. In preparation to defend themselves, the rebellion had been making incendiary devices with the liquid brew, and this would seem to be an opportune moment to try them.

"Use them all! Strike at the Kappa line nearest cover, over there in front of the forest. When they go up, ready yourselves to run; I will stay here and do my best to provide cover," Stellen ordered.

"I am staying by your side," Bjorn stated.

Four other men offered to stay and fight with Stellen, with Bjorn's youngest son Arvid given the responsibility for the group who would be attempting escape. Stellen ordered everyone to ready themselves; the bombs were lit. The group tossed the bombs towards the Kappa line as Stellen had instructed, the explosions started, one after another. A wall of fire exploded from the ground and the Kappas who stood their ground were soon alight like torches, the endless anguished screams filled the night air as the Kappa soldiers burned. Arvid had escaped with a number of women and children, making it to the forest and heading away from the farm as fast as possible. It was not long until they reached the far edge of the wooded area where they stopped, as ahead of them were a set of lights moving rapidly towards them – they had escaped one death, but had they run straight into another? Arvid prepared his weapon and stood front and centre, bold and brave, just like his father and brothers.

Anders and Lars were low on ammunition; they had successfully seen off a number of Kappa attempts to breach the house where they were holding position, but they knew it would not be long until their guns were dry, and until Kappa had a free run at them.

Stellen and Bjorn were filled with a brief moment of joyfulness, their friends and family had escaped and maybe they would be able to find safety; then another wave of Kappas were launched towards them. They fought and fought; killing every Kappa to a man, but now only Bjorn and Stellen were left. They made their peace as this truly was to be the end.

33
Return to Khristade

T he cobbled together truck carrying Balder and Ivar had fared well, and by some sort of mechanical miracle it was still running, which was a testament to Freyja's skills. They were faced with the border they had crossed just days previously, but there would be no secret covert crossing this time. Balder was driving and Ivar had mounted his rifle on the top of the cab; he was perched in the back preparing to fire, as Balder jammed his foot as hard as possible on the accelerator pedal, aiming directly for the border barrier, where there were four guards. A rapid pop, pop, pop, pop was all Balder heard as all four guards hit the floor hard, instant death had befallen them. The truck ploughed through the barrier and kept going; the search lights turned on the truck but they were an age too late, as within a few seconds the truck was out of range of the lights and the accompanying guns mounted on the security towers. Balder knew the Kappas would be coming, but there was no time to think; he pushed on, faster and faster, and did not let off the gas until the duo were well clear of the border; and then it was only a moment to take a deep breath before it was full acceleration again. There were lights in the distance; many small lights, like a hundred fireflies. It must be a Kappa convoy. Balder dimmed the truck lights and headed off the road; this would be another real test of the old truck. It was a very uncomfortable ride, but the truck had missed the convoy and was back on track. It would be a miracle if Balder didn't crash or the truck didn't simply fall apart, but there were no thoughts of failure; accelerator pedal was mashed into the floor and whatever will be, will be.

Mile after mile the truck roared on; further and further back into Omega and closer to Khristade. There had been barely a word uttered between the Captain and his soldier companion since they had left the rest of the team, the total sum of their conversation had been a brief check on the status of Ivar and more importantly his rifle. The truck approached a small outpost –, the team had avoided it when they passed by days before, but the road ran straight through what once was a small settlement. Balder could see a number of Kappa soldiers milling around, but what choice did he have? He knew his wife had a limited amount of life left, so on he went. Not lifting his foot, the truck rushed straight on down the road and through the village, Kappas were running and diving for cover as Ivar fired off a few rounds to let them know he was there; the people were moving too randomly to really stand much chance of hitting anything, but Ivar managed to at least wing a few of the Kappas as the truck rushed through and out the other side. Balder estimated they had travelled approximately halfway back home; they had been driving for about 12 hours, and the truck, however good Freyja's fix had held together, needed a rest. The temperature gauges were starting to top out and so the captain pulled off the road and alongside a small stone shack.

"We will take five, give the truck a rest. Get some food into yourself; we are sure to be encountering more Kappas soon and I need you focused and sharp."

Ivar just nodded in agreement, not in the mood to talk. The pair ate and rested; it was mid-afternoon by the time the truck was in a fit state to move again; Balder moved the truck back to the road and then almost immediately mashed the throttle and again set off towards Khristade at death-defying speeds. What appeared to be another convoy was in front of the truck, a string of red lights filled the horizon as they were approaching the convoy fast.

"It must be one of their support convoys; medical and supplies or such like," Ivar shouted down to his captain.

"It could be a mile long, we aren't going through it; so we must go around. You see any turnings?"

"Two hundred metres on your right, but fuck knows where it goes?"

"We will have to take that chance."

Balder took the turn; the road surface was not as even as the road they had left, so Balder had to slow slightly, there was too much risk in damaging the truck, which till now had behaved impeccably, especially when considering it had been left as junk in a field. The road Balder has taken proved to be a lucky decision, as they were able to travel for mile after mile uninterrupted and with no enemy presence.

Night had fallen and the duo were only a matter of a miles from Khristade. It was hard to get a good bearing at night, but Balder knew he was not far from his beloved Ava. As they took a left turn towards a small forest Ivar called down to Balder.

"I see movement leaving that far edge of the trees."

"Kappa?" the captain questioned.

"Not 100 percent, sir, but I don't think so; looks like women and children."

Balder slowed the truck, as Ivar peered down his sights, and as the lights from the truck crept towards the group he called out, "That's Bjorn's boy, the youngest one."

Balder pulled the truck to a stop and called out. "Arvid, is that you, boy?"

Balder stepped down from the truck and into the light; the hush was broken by a sudden gasp, as all the Omega group saw Balder stride forward, the most decorated defence force captain in the history of Omega was there stood before them.

"Captain Balder, it is so very good to see you, but please, sir, you must help my father."

Arvid quickly explained what had transpired, that they had left Stellen and Bjorn defending the farm where the rebellion had been born; Balder ordered everyone into the truck and set out towards his friends' position. Travelling much more deliberately and carefully than before, the truck made its way around the trees and to a safe distance from the farm. They were in range of Ivar's rifle, he could see the enemy through his gun sights and requested permission to fire, which Balder duly granted as he disembarked the truck; he was headed on foot towards the farm.

34
Rising from the ashes

Stellen and Bjorn were down to their final rounds. They knew they could not hold off another attack from the Kappas; they were preparing themselves for the inevitable and saying their last prayers to the gods. Kappas started to fall silently around the perimeter of the farm, one then another dropped to the ground like they had been hit by an invisible bat. Stellen and Bjorn were shocked as the Kappas kept failing, one after another, no sound just immediate death. Stellen noticed a figure approaching from the rear; he lifted his gun ready to fire, as Balder burst through the Kappa line, shooting two soldiers and whacking another with the butt of his gun. Stellen immediately recognised his old friend and lowered his weapon.

"Praise be to the gods," Stellen cried.

Stellen and Bjorn left their cover and joined Balder, quickly retreating back to the truck and embarking.

As the truck rushed towards Khristade, Balder told of the team he had left in Kappa state; he was deliberately a little vague and left out important details, as he did not want to endanger his team with loose talk. All he told of was of the brave Omegas fighting across Kappa to find help for their stricken Omega kin. There was no mention of the losses, no mention of the Kappa soldiers and no details of position or number. Stellen then told of the rebellion and the losses they had faced, that of the brave team who had left the farm that night in an attempt to rescue Ava. Balder took command of the souls onboard the truck, they found a quiet spot and left the wives and children to hide – there was little point in taking them into the lions' den of the capital city.

As the group led by Balder approached the outskirts of Khristade, they could hear gunfire from an adjacent street just inside the now defunct defensive wall. The team disembarked from the truck and legged it to a good position to recce the area; Ivar headed to a high point and took his position as overwatch, as he signalled to the team an approximation of enemy numbers. Bjorn and Arvid skirted around to another street; the Kappas were too busy attacking a house to notice they were being flanked. Balder signalled Ivar to open fire and on his first shot, Balder and Stellen attacked the Kappas from one side whilst Bjorn and his son attacked from the other. The Omegas successfully boxed in the Kappas, they were falling down like pins on a bowling alley, having been taken by such surprise and with such ferocity that the Kappas barely managed a shot in reply before all were dead or dying in the street. Anders and Lars appeared from the house – they had watched on as the Kappa troops were felled; they were mighty pleased to see Balder and their father and brother, but the team wasn't finished yet; there was still the not so insignificant matter of the rescue attempt for Ava. They quickly moved along the streets, being as cautious as possible whilst moving at pace; there was limited resistance, but what they did encounter was dispatched with methodicalness, each Kappa was silently killed and hidden as they approached the capitol building. Balder ordered a full stop a street away from the city square.

"This is as far as we all go, my friends; Bjorn, take your family and get as far away from this place as you can," Balder ordered.

Bjorn did not question the order, did not utter a word, just placed his hand on Balder's arm, then took his sons and left.

Balder then turned to Stellen. "My old friend, this is where you also must leave me, this is my fight not yours."

"This is our fight, Omega's fight, I'm not going anywhere; ten rabid Kappas couldn't drag me away."

Balder smiled and patted his old friend on the back, they readied themselves and checked their weapons. The pair lapped the outside of the square and to the rear of the capitol building, were there were four guards on the loading doors. With a silent signal to his sniper ally, the guards were killed before they were able to raise an alarm. Balder and Stellen entered the building as Bo and his brother had before when rescuing Sif; they made their way along the passages and to the large staircase, executing any Kappa guards that crossed their path, down the stairs and to the basement level. There were no guards and only a single door was closed; that had to be the one where Ava was being held. Balder barged open the door to be confronted by the sight of his wife's limp body drooped over a chair in the middle of the room; it was no wonder that there were no guards. Balder fell to his knees next to his wife's body; he pushed his forehead against hers as tears began to roll down his face, as his eyes welled with pain.

"I am sorry, my friend, but we have to go," Stellen pleaded.

"I can't just leave her here."

"You must, we have to go," Stellen ordered, as he grabbed Balder and dragged him towards the door. The duo exited the cell door and in a split second, Stellen's body dropped to the floor. Balder looked up and all he could see through his tears was a smoking pistol that had fired a shot point blank through Stellen's head, killing him instantly. Balder was forced to his knees; his eyes clearing slightly he could see a tall Kappa officer stood holding the pistol.

"Captain Balder, I presume; my name is Commander Orcus, the general will be so very pleased that you could join us."

Orcus gestured to his troops who lifted Balder to his feet and dragged him along the corridor and up the long staircase. He was dumped in the middle of the council chamber, hands bound; his head held up by his hair as General Hades stormed into the room.

"The great Captain Balder; hero of the people," Hades laughed as he ridiculed Balder.

"Were you aware that your kin pray your name before they swing from my gallows? Their knight in shining armour now on his knees!"

Balder struggled to get to his feet, but was firmly held down by two Kappa grunts. "You killed her; I'm going to rip your heart out," Balder screamed, as he continued to struggle.

Hades was laughing with delight at the sight of the struggling captain. "You let her down! I could see the hope in her eyes to her very last breath; hope that you would come riding to the rescue," Hades said with a smile. "You pathetic creature; look at yourself, you're a miserable failure, you failed her and you've failed your people, and you will tell me everything I want to know."

"I'm not telling you a damn thing," Stellen screamed with determination.

"They all say that, Captain, you are no different to the rest; you will submit to the excruciating pain that I will inflict, just like your pretty little whore did. Now get him out of my sight."

The soldiers dragged Balder from the room and back down to the capitol building basement, they threw him in the room with his wife's body and locked the door. Balder crawled over to the body of his wife and held her; his eyes began to well again as his thoughts turned to happier times with her. It was a long night for Balder as he contemplated doing the right thing and joining his wife with the gods; but he was so enraged that he wanted a chance to right this wrong, he wanted the chance to kill Hades and put an end to all of this suffering. Dark thoughts filled Balder's mind as he spent the night planning ways to kill Hades; the General seemed overly complacent and far too confident, it would only take the slightest opening and Balder would be ready to strike. He prayed to the gods to care for his wife and to offer him just one opportunity to kill the vile and evil General who had robbed him of everything he loved.

35
What we learn only makes us stronger

The Kappa guards opened the cell door; the light was bright and Balder flinched, his eyes closed. Two guards approached Balder and dragged him to the doorway and dropped him at the feet of Commander Orcus. The commander was looking forward to making Balder grovel and beg for mercy, Orcus was outright sadistic and inflicting pain was why he woke up each morning. He ordered Balder to be taken into an adjacent room in the basement of the capitol building; the room was almost empty, just a small metal chair and table stood in the centre of the room under a large round light. Balder was strapped to the chair, hands and feet bound; Orcus ordered everyone to leave the room as he approached the table, placing one solitary item on it, a long, very thin, bladed knife.

"You wouldn't think such a small item could cause so much pain," Orcus stated menacingly before taking the knife and grasping a hold of Balder's right index finger; he drove the thin blade under his finger nail and deep down; the pain was excruciating but Balder laughed through it.

"Early Sunday morning on the farm, taking out the feed," Balder sang over and over.

Orcus repeated the process until all the fingers on Balder's right hand were bloodied and disfigured, but Balder kept on laughing through the pain, kept on singing. Orcus ordered the guards back to the room where they stripped Balder naked and pushed him up against a wall where he was secured to four small rings mounts. One guard took hold of a length of heavy rope with a large knot tidy to one end; with a nod from Orcus the guard began beating Balder, every inch of his body was battered with the rope; lash after lash. The thump as the rope hit Balder was all the Omega Captain could hear, over and over again.

"It's just like being kicked by a horny bull," he repeated over and over, part grimace, part smile etched across his face and a look of evil in his eyes.

The Kappa commander tried everything, inflicting more and more pain on Balder. There were points with the pain overwhelming Balder would fall unconscious, but all Balder stated were farming facts and other nonsense lines of information, and Orcus was becoming more and more infuriated as the Omega captain just laughed in his face, as more and more pain was administered to him. Balder was a very determined man – breaking his body would do nothing, his mind was strong enough to withstand. In a moment of pure frustration, Orcus drew his firearm and pressed the muzzle hard against the captain's temple, Balder rolled his eyes up towards his Kappa torturer, caught eye contact and smiled, silently goading the Commander to pull the trigger. The door of the room dramatically swung open and in strode General Hades; he glided directly over to his commander and smashed him across the face with the back of his hand. "Imbecile" was all the general screamed.

The Commander sulked; not even daring to mutter under his breath as he cowed in the corner. Hades turned to Balder.

"We captured your man, the one with the rifle. It appears he came to rescue his captain; all very touching, very patriotic you might say."

Balder's grimaced smile left his face as Hades continued. "Should we say, he had a terribly weak soul; he told us everything before he left this world screaming like a pathetic Omega child. Your team in

Kappa state using the old mines by means of travel; my traitorous soldiers as your companions; the sabotaging science officer filling your heads with hopes and dreams of destroying me? You really think you can destroy me and my forces?"

Balder broke down, he closed his eyes and prayed for the end; he had now lost his strength to fight, all he wanted was to be dispatched to the gods to see his wife once more. Hades had lost it, ranting and screaming. "The last thing you see in this world will be the annihilation of your precious team; if you think I will end you now, you are very misguided. I am going to tear each of your team apart whilst you watch, and then, and only then will I put you down like the animal you are. Orcus, prepare your team to travel, you are going hunting."

Hades left the room and Orcus followed behind; the Kappa secret police were gearing up to go after Marcus and the rest of the team. There was nothing Balder or anyone else could do; the team were heading for an almighty fight and Balder's only hope was that his team would make it out of Kappa before Orcus and his goons arrived. Balder was placed back into detention and left to his wondering thoughts; hopes and prayers that his team of brave men and women would make it through Kappa and find the answers they needed. General Hades stood on the balcony of the capitol chamber and watched on as black truck after black truck sped from the city square; the Kappa secret police and Commander Orcus were beginning their hunt.

36
Breeders

The team being led by ex-Kappa captain Marcus had been travelling for what they presumed was three days – it was difficult to gauge the time or even which day it was in the blackness of the mine tunnels. Resting comfortably was a new norm, there were no enemies in the tunnels and it allowed the team to relax just a little. Marcus had kept the team on the same path for the entire journey, until reaching a point where there was no straight on; there was a left fork and a right fork, the right was darker than ever with a downward trajectory, but the left offered a tiny glimpse of light. Marcus decided the team would take the left path to take a glimpse of where they were; gather their bearings before heading back down into the tunnels to take the alternative path and continue their journey. Erik, Torsten and Blank were sent down the left tunnel; it was only a matter of a few hundred metres before they found an exit. It was dusk outside and the perfect time to take a look around; the three soldiers broke down the wooden planks nailed over the mine entrance and quietly took a few steps outside. The fresh air hit them all hard, and although dusk, the light was still bright compared to the inside of the mine. Torsten took the lead and sent Erik and Blank off to investigate the area, it was only a short time later the three were back at the mine entrance; re-entering the mine and reporting back to Marcus their discoveries.

"To the south is a small town, looks deserted; maybe an old mining settlement," Torsten reported.

"West is nothing; nothing as far as I could see and to the north is a freakin' castle, a big stone building; perched atop a big rock and a high wall around it."

"A large building with high walls, it will usually be a centre, a breeding centre."

Marcus went on to explain what this was to the rest of the Omegas, who were not aware of the phenomenon. Hilda showed her dislike of the subject by storming off in a huff. The others were disgusted but also intrigued.

"So who uses them?" Erik questioned.

"Any high ranking official in Kappa, most normally commanders and above; that is unless you are being rewarded for a great win or mass killing, then occasionally lower ranking soldiers might be offered the opportunity."

"You were a captain; you must have partaken?"

"I did not, I declined on two occasions."

"So in that building may be the offspring of Hades?" Erik commented.

"In theory, yes." Marcus paused and a concerned look appeared on his face. He had made the assumption that killing the offspring would have been the next suggestion. "We are not about to become baby killers," Marcus stated angrily.

In an attempt to calm Marcus, Freyja held him by the hand. "Is it just Kappa women?" she queried.

"No, if one of the high officials or Hades takes a fancy to someone, they are shipped off to one of the facilities, to be used for fun. Genetic purity is a binding Kappa law, so no children are born or allowed to live."

"Can we help them?"

Marcus mulled over this question for some time before bringing the group to order. "I think we should help them, my mother was in one of these places. I was born in one of these places and it would give me great satisfaction to help."

Marcus continued to explain the facility specifics; that the sites are heavily guarded outside, but there are no guards on the inside, just slaves and the breeding stock. If members of the team could infiltrate the inner facility there would be no resistance, but then getting out would pose a whole different set of problems. As Marcus talked it became clearer and clearer in his mind that there was just no safe way, in and back out of the facility to help those inside. "I don't see a plan, we might be able to get in; but getting out poses another set of unanswerable problems. I am truly sorry but our mission must come first."

The team were not all in agreement, but understood that their mission had to take priority. Marcus allowed each of the team to take five minutes outside before they continued their journey. Erik and Blank were outside when a truck began approaching the facility; they watched as the truck began to weave from side to side, before coming to a quick stop around two hundred metres from the mine entrance. Two Kappa soldiers emerged from the truck, dragging a woman behind them, kicking and screaming as she was dragged along the dusty floor. One soldier picked the women up by her hair, and dropped her on her knees, as the other held his gun to her head. "Behave or I will fucking kill you."

"Then do it, I will be laughing from my grave when Hades guts you like a fucking animal."

The soldier slapped the woman across the face. "You will behave; this facility will not put up with your shit like the last."

The soldiers were preparing to load the woman back into the truck when one caught a glimpse of a figure in the corner of his vision, but as he turned quickly three shots hit him in the body. Marcus, Erik, Torsten and Blank were moving quickly towards the truck, one soldier down and the other followed rapidly after. Blank helped the injured woman to her feet and then moved quickly to take the truck and move it back towards the mine. Erik hid the truck in the mine and the team regathered.

"Astrid?" Hilda asked the rescued woman.

Hilda and Astrid were similar ages and their families were long-standing friends. Astrid was joyous to see a friendly face; but not so that of Marcus, shocked to see Omegas and Kappas together. "What are they doing with you?" Astrid questioned whilst gesturing angrily towards Marcus.

Hilda explained the history of the journey so far, that Marcus was responsible for the death of General Hades's son, that Blank had rescued Inga, and Balder had thought enough of Marcus to leave him in command. Marcus hurried the team back into the mine and on to the other path; trekking further into the mine, into the darkness; their hope was the next time they see light it would be reflecting off the eastern sea.

37
Astrid

The team were in the pitch-black, feeling their way through the mine, but all were at ease, chatting happily; most of the talk was of their new companion Astrid. She was explaining the circumstances that had led her to now be part of the team, how she had tried to assassinate General Hades and after quite the fight was told she was being sent to a breeding facility for the sole use of the General. "The first facility I was taken to was a new building, very white, very clean, sterile looking."

"Doesn't sound like any breeding facility I know of," Marcus commented.

"They ran lots of tests on me, so many blood tests, and also jabs. I realised pretty quick I could do no wrong, caused quite the commotion and they would just put me back in my room. I thought it was because I belonged to Hades but maybe it had something to do with the tests?"

"Can you remember anything you may've heard, any terms or key words?" Aurora asked excitedly.

Astrid remembered hearing the word keystone was mentioned a few times, but she was not at the facility for long; once they had taken a thousand samples she was bundled on to a truck and moved, and that is where the team found her. Aurora started asking questions about Astrid's life and who her family was; she believed that Astrid could be a pure Omega, no pollution of her cells and no interstate breeding in her lineage, and as the keystone required six perfect genetic samples, possibly Kappa took such interest because they believed Astrid was something they hadn't seen. The pure samples were what Kappa believed was the key to finding the correct combination to effectively create Keystone. Kappa science officers had tried thousands of different samples, but none had created the perfect version. Astrid was possibly a different genetic sample; a purer sample that could in theory be a solution to enabling the weapon. It was all guesswork and assumption, but Aurora was fearful that Kappa may be a step closer to enabling a workable version of the weapon.

There were still too many loose ends and unknowns to decipher; what was the key to the weapon? Had the days since Aurora left the science core really been long enough for Kappa to make significant progress, and was their new companion Astrid a missing piece of the puzzle? The decision to use the mines to travel was not helping the cause, as the time spent underground in the dark had hindered Frode's ability to keep translating the book; he passionately believed all the pieces were there and they were slowly pulling them together, but time was against them. They needed to have fitted more pieces before they reached Central, otherwise the mission would all be in vain. The team ploughed on through the tunnels with thoughts constantly ebbing towards the next challenge, the next set of clues, the next unanswered question; but something was different. The floor, it had become crunchier somehow; each step taken, whereas once was silent, there was now a slight crunch to each step. Marcus stopped the team and searched his pockets for a matchbook; he pulled a book from his chest pocket and lit a single match, moving the match carefully towards the floor he noticed white flecks in the ground, sweeping the dirt aside with his hand; it revealed a bone, so he quickly extinguished the match and gathered himself. He ordered everyone to keep moving, sparking up jovial conversation in a vain attempt to cover the noises of bone crunching beneath their feet.

What had happened in these tunnels, and why were there hundreds of bones? These were the questions swirling around Marcus's head as he led the team further and further into the darkest part of the mine. His attention was taken for a moment, there was light ahead; it was faint, but it was definitely light – were the team nearing the end of the tunnel? As Marcus and the team approached the light it became obvious it was not the end, but a large cavernous section of mine with a vertical tunnel spearing upwards from the middle of the ceiling to the world above. Light was directed through the tunnel and illuminated the large open space below. The light was enough to see old mining equipment strewn around the floor and piles of decayed bodies; now nothing more than rags and bones.

"What in the gods' names happened here?" Astrid questioned.

The team began searching through the cavern hoping to find something which might tell them what had happened; Marcus took it upon himself to search through the skeletal remains, whilst the other team members searched through the scattered equipment and other artefacts. Marcus noted the remnants of string or twine and a small metal ring around a toe on one of the bodies; he found another, so called Aurora, who hurried to his position.

"What do you make of this?" Marcus asked the science officer.

"Looks like the remains of a toe tag. We used them on the bodies of test subjects and the bodies that were experimented on."

"These are all experiments; these people were all lab rats?"

"Quite possibly."

"Twenty years ago a closed mine was probably the perfect hiding spot for a mass grave of failed science experiments, but have you ever known anything like this?"

Marcus and Aurora continued to pick through the bodies, hoping to find something more; a clue to what might have befallen these poor souls.

As the team searched through the scattered artefacts they found nothing of note; just old tools and the odd metal lunch pail. In one of the pails was a handwritten noted dated 20 years earlier; the note had decayed like everything else in the cavern and parts were illegible. There was one section that was still intact; reading out loud to the team Freyja did her best to interpret the writing.

"Was told today that this was my last day in the mine, will be moving to eastern shore tomorrow when mine will be sealed; there were no reports of any men feeling unwell but doctors insisted that there was an illness raging through the camp. We are all being treated with daily injections but men are now starting to suffer from fatigue and sickness.

"That's it, I can't read the rest."

No one knew what to make of the letter; without any corroborating information they would never know what had happened there 20 years before –, was it really an illness or Kappa experimentation? Just as the team were about to move out of the cavern and continue on their trek, Blank spotted another light, it was coming from the direction the team had travelled from. It was odd as when they passed through that section there was no light, it was as dark as dark gets. Blank drew Marcus's attention to the light; it was only faint but it was certainly a light, and Marcus hushed the team and listened carefully; he could make out the very faint crunching noises that they had made when walking those tunnels. Someone else was here, and by the amount of crunching quite a few someones were in the tunnels. Marcus quickly gathered up the team and without a moment's hesitation they were running as fast as possible along the route heading away from their unexpected tunnel guests.

38
The Challenge

As the team hurried along the tunnels, the sounds of their unwanted guests were becoming louder; those other inhabitants were getting closer by the moment. The team were moving fast, but it had become obvious it was not fast enough, as the enemy were closing on their position. Minute by minute they gained on them; Marcus ordered the team to start looking for side tunnels or hiding spots. This would have been a challenge in a well-lit city street, but it was almost impossible in the darkness of the tunnels. As the enemy grew closer, voices began to echo; there was not much talking just the odd word barked out. To Marcus the voice was familiar, it was a light bulb moment as he remembered the voice, and it was very bad news for his team. He had to think fast. Haste never normally brings the best ideas, but with few options he had no choice.

"You all keep going, I will catch-up; Torsten, you are in charge," Marcus blurted out.

Before anyone could comment, Marcus had about-faced and started moving back down the tunnels and away from the team. They stood in stunned silence, not knowing whether to keep running or about-turn and follow their leader.

The light was getting brighter; Marcus was closing in on his tunnel guests. He had hoped to make it back to the cavern prior to encountering the enemy. He emerged into the cavern exactly on cue, just as Orcus and brigade 66 entered from the other side, and before anyone had a second to raise a gun or utter a word, Marcus called out. "Kappa Captain 24978, I challenge for the command of brigade 66."

The Kappa troops stopped; they turned to Orcus who had never been challenged before. They stood bewildered, wondering what his response might be. Marcus was no longer a Kappa officer, but had risked that Orcus would not reject his challenge; he would not want to look weak in front of his men. Orcus paused for a moment, thinking hard on the correct course of action, but ultimately he accepted the challenge.

In brigade 66 the rules were simple: a challenge for rank or position will be a hand-to-hand fight to the death, and to challenge for the command would allow Marcus to become the brigade commander and the men would in theory have to accept his orders. Orcus was very tall and an immensely physical specimen, he had a huge amount of strength, whilst Marcus was a slight man; on paper there was only one winner, but Marcus was thinking of the team. Keep the Kappas occupied just long enough to give them the time needed to escape the tunnels and hide. The men of brigade 66 formed a wide circle with Orcus and Marcus to the centre. Orcus removed his shirt to reveal huge bulging muscles and an immense number of dots that resembled small burn marks.

"You see these; one for each life I extinguished, and your life will take pride of place right here," Orcus commented whilst pointing to an unmarked space on his chest. "Been saving this space just for scum like you."

Marcus didn't reply, just stood, stoic in his response. Orcus lunged at Marcus; he slid to the side and avoided the commander. Orcus lunged again, but Marcus danced around, avoiding contact and staying out of reach; he was only thinking of using up as much time as possible. Orcus lunged again and Marcus just stepped out the way in time, causing a great amount of frustration to the Kappa commander.

The sparring continued for some minutes and Orcus was growing more annoyed with Marcus, so with a bark he ordered his troops to move closer, and all stepped forward two paces, reducing the area in which Marcus could move. Now was the time to fight, and as Orcus lunged forward again, Marcus was not in time-wasting mode anymore; he side stepped left and swung a right arm side punch, catching Orcus across the bridge of his nose. A nasty wound opened and blood began to pour down his face; Orcus lunged again, Marcus stepped right avoiding contact, before gauging his thumb into Orcus's left eye, temporarily limiting his sight. Marcus was done waiting for Orcus to attack, he went on the offensive; striding into Orcus, he threw a left kick to the inside of his enemy's right knee, he ducked down and threw a powerful punch to the inside of his left knee. Orcus fell to the floor; disoriented by the blood in his eyes and the powerful shots he had taken to his lower body. Before Orcus had the chance to regain his footing, Marcus rolled around him and took a hold of the commander's head; his arm locked firmly across his throat; his legs wrapped around his body, Marcus leveraged his arm with all his strength. The Kappa commander struggled, but Marcus had his hold locked in; choking the life from the commander, pulling harder and harder; using every last ounce of strength as Orcus flailed around with his arms and legs; then he stopped, a moment's silence. Marcus released his choke hold, wrapped his arms around the commander's head and violently twisted, snapping his neck in one swift motion. Marcus got to his feet and brushed himself down. The Kappa soldiers of brigade 66 were dumbfounded; they weren't sure whether to shoot or salute Captain Marcus, but they chose the latter. Each man stood to attention and saluted their new commanding officer; Marcus threw a tired cursory salute back before approaching the brigade's lieutenant and passing his first command. "You will put to rest all these souls; every man in here deserves more than being dumped in a hole in the ground."

"But, sir, we are hunting Omegas."

"You are doing what your commanding officer orders; and that is to lay these souls to rest," Marcus shouted.

The lieutenant begrudgingly accepted his new orders, before Marcus took his leave and headed back down the tunnel his team had followed; he began jogging as he hurried down the passage, excited to reunite with the team, and worried that the soldiers of brigade 66 would quickly change their mind and pick the not so friendly option and begin their chase again. As he hurried along, his thoughts turned to what might come next; there was a giant wall, miles of sea and two enemy states still between his team and their final goal.

39
Infiltration

Marcus had reconnected with the team. There was surprised delight from all; surprise he had made his way back and delight he had made his way back; there were the inevitable questions.

"Who, what, how?" Freyja asked as she grabbed a hold of Marcus and squeezed him tight.

"It was General Hades' secret police, led by the most notoriously crazy, psychopathic killer, and I simply stopped them" was all Marcus said in a very matter of fact way; he was more concerned that brigade 66 would decide to ignore his commands and follow him. "There is a slight chance they may well still be tracking us. So I think it's best to keep moving," Marcus ordered.

As the team continued to trek through the tunnels, they began to notice a slight incline; the tunnel was starting to head upwards, and shortly thereafter a small dot of light appeared in front of the group. The light grew bigger; the anticipation began to increase as the team approached the end of the tunnel. As before, the entrance was boarded over; but unlike the other entrances, outside the tunnel there were hundreds of people. The mine entrance was only a few feet within the eastern shore defence wall camp and there were workers; hundreds if not thousands of slaves busily going about their work under the watchful gaze of a division of Kappa troops.

Marcus ordered the team to stay away from the mine entrance; they would wait within the mine until they had formulated a plan to infiltrate the workers' camp. Whilst the team waited, Freyja took Marcus to one side. Since his return Inga wouldn't leave him, and Freyja believed Marcus was holding back on the details of his ordeal because he didn't want the child to hear the more than likely gruesome details. "Are you sure you're alright?" Freyja asked.

"My body is a little sore and my mind is a little on edge, but I'm good. Very glad to be back amongst friends."

"Please tell me what happened?"

Marcus was hesitant; he was not proud of killing any man, and where others might have taken great pleasure in ending the life of Orcus, Marcus did not. "Brigade 66 are crazy zealots, they believe in their hierarchy and their commander; they also trust in their challenge system. Orcus was a vile monster, and had never been challenged."

"Was?"

"I challenged him, challenged his command, and as is tradition in that brigade, it was a fight to the death, and I killed him."

"I am truly overjoyed you retuned, but how?"

"You must understand, I have never liked killing. Tried to avoid it whenever possible; but the truth is you don't become a captain in the Kappa armies without being damn good at it! Orcus was very strong, but slow and so overconfident; I ran the percentages and I was no worse than a 50/50 chance."

Freyja moved close to Marcus and pressed her lips to his, giving him a loving gentle kiss. "Glad you made it back," she added.

Erik approached Marcus and Freyja; he had thoughts on ways to penetrate the workers' camp unnoticed. "I have been watching the soldiers; they are on roughly ten-minute rotations and there are quite noticeable gaps; they are small but long enough for a couple of us at a time to move unnoticed into the camp."

"Any ideas on how we would blend in?" Freyja queried.

"There are no chains; no shackles, there appears to be plenty of Omegas; we should fit right in."

"Then we move out in twos when the guards rotate; we stay in those twos and do not deviate. Do not link back up whatever happens, until we find friends who are willing to assist us, or we know our next move," Marcus suggested.

Erik and Freyja agreed. Marcus explained the plan to the others and decided the pairings.

"Inga will come with me; Erik you mind Frode; Freyja, can you team with Aurora? Torsten, if you would take Hilda; which leaves Astrid with Blank. Please all take care of each other; blend in, do the work, and try to make friends."

The plan was understood, and over the next guard rotations Erik and Blank loosened the boards covering the mine entrance, just enough for a person to squeeze through.

"Ten seconds," Marcus quietly ordered, as Blank and Astrid were readying themselves to leave the mine and enter the population of workers. One at a time they shuffled through the opening and away into the camp. Ten minutes later, Freyja and Aurora followed, then Erik and Frode; they all blended in, picking up tools and joining working parties. Torsten and Hilda went next and did the same, joining workers who had finished a shift and were heading towards the mess hut. That just left Marcus and Inga.

"Stay close to me and we will be just fine," Marcus said with a smile.

The pair left the mine, swung the boarding back into place and wandered into a group of workers just starting out for a shift. The team were now in camp, and all without a single raised eyebrow or question being asked. They had immersed themselves into the working parties; some of the group had it easy as they latched on to workers finishing shifts, so were able to get food and rest. Others were not so fortunate and had a long shift in the hot sun to contend with; breaking rock and stone and heaving large sacks of building materials. For Erik, Frode, Blank and Astrid it was a very long, arduous day, but they took solace knowing they were another step closer to their goal. Now, how to get over the wall?

40
The workers

Marcus and Inga had integrated into a working group that comprised mainly young Delta men; they would pass the time telling old stories of Delta, from before the Kappa invasion and before slavery was the only job a young Delta man could expect. In the days before the latest war, Delta was a hub for science, the leaders of industry; the greatest inventions all came from Delta; machinery and vehicles, medical advances and scientific breakthroughs were all born in Delta. Stories were often of their inventors; how they built Delta into the great shining beacon of the world, and the greatest of these inventors was Jargal – he had created the best medical advances, his medicines and treatments had led to a 20-year increase in life expectancy, but the greatest of his accomplishments was that his developments were created for the world. He insisted all his creations were shared throughout the world and for this he was hailed as the most wonderful of men. Delta are good people, which made them easily overthrown; when Kappa invaded, the victory was taken with ease. The invasion completed in just a matter of days, and only another short time until all the men had been shipped to the mines or to work in other Kappa facilities. That was 30 years ago, but to those who lived through it; it was still as fresh as if it were yesterday. There are not many that still survive from that time, but those that do are all located in the hundred-mile stretch of the eastern shore defence wall. Marcus was keen to talk to anyone who lived back then; he believed that they might have lived through the final days of the mines, and be able to answer what had happened to all those souls they had found decaying there.

Marcus had already drummed up support from two Delta workers, Nomin and Duuren; they were well respected in the camp and had a good knowledge of the people, and who might be willing to assist the team over the wall and across the sea. Marcus was guarded with the specifics of the team and the mission; he was wary that spies may have infiltrated the workers, and the longer the mission was kept secret, the better chance they would have of success.

"There are ways over the wall, because there is nowhere to go! Why would you want to go over? You and your friends would stand more chance going inland and finding somewhere to live out your days," Nomin surmised.

"We must go over, and across the sea," Marcus responded.

"The wall won't be difficult; but the wall is there for a reason. The beaches on the other side are killing fields; Central navy monitors all day and all night."

"So we need a boat?"

Laughter broke out between Nomin and Duuren; they knew that even with a boat, unless you were the best of sea captains, your destruction was inevitable.

In another part of the camp Erik and Frode were finishing a long shift; it was their second since entering the camp. "How do these people do this day after day?" Frode moaned.

"They have no choice; it's work or die, it's quite the motivation," Erik flippantly responded.

Erik had been trying to gather support but the workers in his group were reluctant to assist; although they hated the Kappas, many of the workers were comfortable, and had become scared of anything else; they had heard that life outside the camps was worse than the life within. Kappa were rampaging across the world, and thousands of civilians were being worked or starved to death for the betterment of Kappa; life in camp was hard, but the workers were fed and allowed even a few freedoms. Frode had been talking with an older member of the work crew; the man was a loner and not well amalgamated in his team; this man didn't seem to belong.

"Been here long?" Frode asked the man.

"Not long, maybe six month or so," the man replied. "It's difficult to tell, days just drift into each other."

"Please excuse my ignorance and my rude statement; but you look different to everyone else."

"I'm from Sigma, a sailor, my ship was wrecked just off the shore."

The men continued to talk as the evening passed, Frode learnt of the sailor's life in Sigma and that over the last few years they had been developing boats to rival those of Central, causing tension between the states. In an effort to quell the hostilities, Sigma had pledged three ships to the Central fleet in attacks on Kappa; the sailor's ship was one of these three. In one offensive the ship had been struck by the Kappa defensive guns and sunk just off the coast; none but the sailor survived.

"Do you have a name?" Frode asked.

"Amir," the sailor replied.

In worker crew eight, Freyja and Aurora had been given mess duty, and Freyja had taken the opportunity to talk with lots of the workers as they passed through for meals; she was persistent in her efforts to find allies, people willing to help in their bid to escape to Sigma. One such man was Gan; a young man who had been born in the workers' camp, his father was a Theta worker and his mother a delta doctor who had been running the medical centre within the camp. Freyja hoped that Gan could remember when the mines were closed, but he was too young and his parents had passed away some years before.

"You need to talk with old man Altan," Gan suggested. "He has been here forever, I'm sure he would have been in the mines before here. He is certainly old enough."

"Where might I find this Altan?" Freyja questioned.

"He is on the suicide crew; the ones who spend the nights working atop the wall. His shift will be starting soon."

"How do I get on that crew?"

"You have to be mad to go on that crew, highest death rate of anyone in camp. Sure, they would accept anyone crazy enough to volunteer."

Freyja dropped the serving spoon she was holding and ran to one of the guards. "I want to volunteer for the night crew," she blurted.

The guard looked at her quizzically, shrugged his shoulders and nodded. He took Freyja away, leaving Aurora by herself in the mess hut. Freyja was taken to the Kappa soldier responsible for the night crew; he laughed out loud when told that she had volunteered; either way he took her and placed her with the rest of the crew. Once in place Freyja began to ask around for Altan. The workers were hesitant to talk to Freyja, but with some pointing and gesturing Freyja found him; getting his last few moments of rest before the shift started. "Are you Altan?" Freyja asked.

"Who's asking?" the man replied.

"My name is Freyja. I was talking to a young man who suggested you were the man to talk to, who would know about the mines?"

"Maybe" was all the man replied.

"I came through the mines a few days back and saw all the death."

"You were in the mines? Why were you in there?"

Freyja explained that she was with a small unit of wanted men, that were passing through on their way to Sigma, where they believed they could find safety. They had passed through the mine and into the camp; they were working on a way to escape the camp and travel to Sigma, but they wanted to understand what had happened in the mines; all that death, they had to know why.

The man began to be a little less guarded. "I was there the day they closed the mines," he started to explain. "I was once a Delta doctor, worked in one of those Kappa breeding centres, until I was caught with one of the Kappa breeders and was sent to the mines. Worked there for maybe three years before we were told of a sickness, but there was no sickness. People changed, they changed after the treatments were administered."

"Changed?" Freyja asked.

"The people started to change, the Omegas started to become stronger somehow. The Thetas, they started to develop some sort of skin problems, sensitivity to even the tiniest amounts of light; and the Kappas changed, they became even angrier, more violent."

"Were you not affected?"

"All the Deltas seemed to be unaffected. It became chaos in there. Then on that fateful day we Deltas were all taken out of the mines and a Kappa cleaning crew sent in. The mines were sealed and we were brought here."

"What did they do to all those people?"

"It was injections of something, told us it was a cure for the sickness; the medicine was labelled T-991."

Freyja was shocked that an experiment had caused all those deaths, but was this Testament? Had Kappa been working on it all this time? Freyja thought Testament to be a weapon, but what Altan was describing wasn't a weapon, but some form of chemical or medical treatment that changed its victims.

41
Family

Freyja continued questioning Altan – much of what he had told her was shocking, but there were eerily familiar parts to the tale. Where had she heard this story before? Who was Altan and why had he not befallen the same fate as the other minors? "What happened after the mine closed?"

"All the Deltas were sent here, but most didn't last long; an accident here, and one there took care of most my kin. Others were just outright murdered."

"Why not you?" Freyja asked.

"I killed myself first," Altan commented with a wry smile. "Had my own accident; fell from atop the wall into the sea. I disappeared myself, never to be found."

Freyja now was sure she had heard this story before, but let Altan continue to tell his tale. "Hid out for a few weeks, lived off the sea. Then when the opportunity arose, I snuck back into camp and became Altan."

"Who are you really?" Freyja quickly asked.

"That doesn't matter, I am only Altan now."

Freyja was now throwing out more questions; trying to piece together her thoughts. "Do you have a family? A son perhaps? A Kappa officer for a son?"

Altan was taken aback: this girl knew his secret.

Guards entered the hut and ordered the workers to begin their shift; everyone got to their feet and proceeded towards the door.

"Stay close to me, and no more questions," Altan told Freyja sternly.

The crew moved out and started climbing long ladders, Freyja followed closely to Altan until they made the top. "Keep your head down and follow me," Altan barked.

The wall was shaking as the Central fleet fired upon the eastern shore; Altan took Freyja to the thickness section of the wall, where the Kappa defence cannons were mounted.

"We should be safe here," Altan commented. "No one will be able to hear us over the noise and the Central guns don't reach this section. What do you know of my son?"

"He is here, in the camp," Freyja commented. "He is leading the team I am with."

"But he's in the Kappa armies?"

"He was a Captain." Freyja continued to tell the tale of their quest; how the information Altan supplied would help the team scientist and historian piece together more of the puzzle.

Marcus was in camp and under the illusion his father was missing, presumably dead, but here he was, living an alternative life to avoid death and keep the secrets of the mine and the vast Kappa experimentation.

"He will be so pleased you are alive," Freyja stated.

"No one can know he is my son, if anyone discovers my son was a Kappa Captain, life here will be very short, for him and for me," Altan stressed. "You all must leave this place."

"That is the idea," Freyja responded. "We need to get over this wall and across the sea; can you help?"

"I will do what I can, but for now we must work."

Altan and Freyja set about their work; all night they toiled until the sun began to rise. The sound of a large horn signified the end of shift, and all the workers began making their way down the wall and to the mess hut for feeding. In the hut Freyja found Aurora and instructed her to find Marcus and tell him they needed to meet quickly. Aurora asked questions, but Freyja deliberately kept the responses vague; she was not prepared to divulge Altan's identity or the new information about what had happened in the mines.

Marcus's work crew were finishing a shift; he and Inga were heading to the mess hut when Aurora intercepted them; pulling him to one side she explained that Freyja had met a contact who needed to speak with him, and that it might be time for the team to gather. There were endless options for leaving the camp and escaping the wall, but Marcus was no closer to finding a solution for the voyage over the sea, which made him reticent to bring the team together yet.

"We should ensure we are ready to leave before meeting," Marcus explained. "Have you word from anyone else?"

"No; but Freyja stressed the importance," Aurora responded.

"What did she tell you?"

"Not much, she was being very secretive, but I could tell it was important. She insisted that you, me, her and Frode should meet. That is all I know."

"I trust her opinion; we should all gather in the mine. Let us feed, then you grab Freyja and I will find Frode."

Several hours later Marcus was in the mine with Inga and Frode. Frode was telling Marcus he had met a sailor from Sigma; that he survived a shipwreck just off the coast.

"He may be a good ally, he is Sigma so may be a good companion if we ever do make it there."

"Do you think he would join us?" Marcus questioned.

"Anything to get out of here. I am confident he will travel with us, at least as far as his homeland."

Freyja and Aurora appeared, and they were accompanied by Altan.

"Who's with you?" Marcus queried. "I thought it would just be the five of us."

"Marcus, he is why I wanted to meet," Freyja responded. "He was here when the mine closed. I think it may have been experimentation with Testament?"

Altan walked forward and into the little light shining through from the small gaps between the boards covering the entrance. "Marcus, my boy," Altan said. "Is it really you?"

"How do you know my name? Who are you?" Marcus responded.

He had heard stories from his mother but never met his father, he had not even seen a picture. The fond memories Marcus had were from his mother's kind words.

"My son," Altan responded.

"Father? But how? He went missing 20 years ago."

Altan went on to tell his tale, the same as he had told Freyja the previous night. Freyja explained what she had learnt about the mines and the experiments with what she believed to be Testament.

"That doesn't make sense," Frode complained. "Testament is a weapon, the book tells of it being used to lord over the people, control the people."

"I don't mean to undermine your skills in translation, but are you sure?" Freyja questioned.

"Well, I cannot be 100% sure, but it is the only thing that makes any sense."

"It is a thousand years old, does it have to make sense to us?" Marcus asked.

"I have not read the book in days. We were in the dark, and then in the camp, I need more time."

"The pieces are here, and I believe you will figure it out," Marcus said reassuringly.

The group had discussed much but there was still the biggest challenge to overcome, how to cross the sea? The team had been in camp for two days and were no closer to being able to cross that hurdle.

Back in camp Torsten had been talking with a group of Omegas. They were talking of the rumours around camp that Kappa were building a fleet of ships. The talk was that Kappa had captured a Sigma crew from a ship wrecked just offshore and they were being forced to build the ships. Kappa had salvaged the wreck and were using it as the base for their designs. The Omegas also told of men going missing. Men with metalworking experience had been taken from the camp and none had returned; one Omega man told of his son disappearing one night – his son was a machinist and welder.

"Where do you think this shipyard would be?" Torsten asked the Omega men.

"Oh, I really don't know; but it would have to be somewhere behind the wall," one man suggested.

"I used to work the night shift, from the top you can see for miles, there was an inlet just a few miles south. I would guess if anywhere, it would be there," another Omega man proposed.

Torsten had to check if the rumours were true, he had to check for himself if the shipyard exists, and if it does, whether the ships were even ready to sail. One of the Omega men told Torsten how to escape the wall and reach the beach, so Torsten decided, he and Hilda would do just that and escape the wall, checking for the potential shipyard.

42
The Shipyard

It was a misty night and Torsten had decided that tonight he and Hilda would search for the potential shipyard. The beach was a treacherous place, but Torsten hoped the mist would provide a little cover. Hilda wasn't keen to leave camp but accepted that they had to check the possibility – if they could find a ship they would be able to continue their journey and that is what her grandma, the deceased Omega leader, would have wanted. The duo escaped the camp with ease, they made their way through an un-repaired crack in the wall and on to the beach. The sight out to sea was a spectacle, almost beautiful – as the Central cannons showered the wall, the night sky appeared alight with fire. The shells rained down on the wall but barely made a mark; the explosions seemed so small in comparison with the gigantic wall. Hilda and Torsten carefully made their way along the rocky beach, their movement slowed by the huge boulders and old sections of fallen wall that were strewn across parts of their path. The path looked slightly clearer closer to the water, so the duo moved down the beach to the water's edge; as they moved along, the water began lapping over their feet. Hilda screamed as the skeletal remains of a long dead sailor washed up onto the shore and then watched as the tide ripped the body back out to sea. A light began shining on the beach from way out at sea; surely no one heard Hilda's scream above the pounding of the cannons and the shells exploding against the wall, but Torsten and Hilda took cover until the light passed, deciding it was nothing more than a regular sweep by the Central navy. They continued along the beach, keeping close to the water's edge until their route was blocked – a huge section of what used to be defence wall was in their path; it stood 20 feet tall and ran the length of the beach from wall to sea.

"We will have to swim around it," Torsten suggested.

"I don't think so, I don't swim well," Hilda replied with a shaky voice.

"You'll be fine, just hold on to me."

The pair entered the water, Torsten went first and Hilda closely behind, grabbing at Torsten's belt. They had to swim approximately 20 metres out to sea to make their way around the massive rock. The sea was ice cold and Hilda was struggling against the waves beating the shoreline; Torsten was swimming for both, but once around the top of the rock it became much easier as the waves began pushing them in towards the shore.

Torsten helped Hilda out of the water and back onto the beach. They continued to progress towards the inlet where they had hoped to find a shipyard. As they steadily made their way along the shoreline the mist began to clear.

"We should head back in towards the wall; someone will spot us this far down the beach," Torsten suggested.

Moving back up the beach and to the wall, they travelled a few hundred metres until there was no more beach; the wall was at the very edge of the sea.

"This must be it!" Torsten stated almost excitedly.

"How do we get in?" Hilda questioned.

"Swim under the wall, I guess?"

"It's 40 metres thick," Hilda complained. "There is no way I could hold my breath that long, or even swim that far."

Torsten offered to go it alone – he was a strong swimmer and believed the tidal current would assist him getting in, and under the wall. He took a deep breath and dived into the icy water; he swam down a few metres before he could see a way under the enormous wall. He quickly returned to the surface to take a breath and then he went under again. Swimming hard he made it down to the opening and along the underside of the wall; he was trying to count as he went, so he could guide the others if they had to make this same journey. He reached a count of 35 before the colour of the water above him lightened, and he began swimming up. He bobbed his head out of the water for a quick gasp of air and a very quick look. There it was: seven ships in various near-complete states of their builds. Torsten saw sparks flying as workers welded and machined the craft, he now knew the stories were true, but were any of the boats seaworthy and what were the number of Kappa guarding them? Torsten swam quietly over towards one of the ships; it was the only one currently not being worked on. Torsten took a good hard look and to his joy it looked finished, but there was no guarantee. Whilst studying the boat Torsten looked across and saw a group of Kappa officers converging on a raised gangway between two of the craft. Torsten dived under the water and swam across to beneath the gangway; he lifted his head enough to hear the chatter from the officers.

"Are we on schedule to bring down the wall?" one of the officers asked.

"Yes, sir, we are on schedule for day after tomorrow as planned."

To Torsten this seemed like good news – if they were preparing to bring down the wall, the ships would have to be ready to launch; all the work being completed must be only cosmetic.

Torsten dipped back under the water and swam towards the wall; he popped up for one quick gulp of air and then down into the water and under. As the Omega rose out of the water on the other side, Hilda gasped with relief as she saw her friend re-emerge from his spying mission. Torsten conformed the best news to Hilda: there were ships that were ready to launch and in two days they would be destroying the wall, allowing the craft to leave the inlet and move out to sea. The pair took their news and hurriedly began their journey back to the camp. They made their way past all the obstacles, back around the enormous rock that blocked their path and back up the beach. Re-entering the camp, Torsten and Hilda were happy in the knowledge they had gained; they needed to tell Marcus and plan their escape for the night after tomorrow. Torsten used Aurora to pass the new information to Marcus; it was easy to use the science officer's job in the mess hut to pass information between the team members. Marcus was pleased to hear the news and began piecing together the plan. The team would all gather the following night; they would meet in the mine and move out together from there; their numbers would be swelled to 11 with the addition of the Sigma sailor. Marcus's father had declined the invite to join his son and team on their quest; he believed his age would only slow the team and his usefulness was limited. He had made friends in camp and felt the workers needed him more than the team did. Altan was sure that when his son finished his mission there would be a day that the workers of the camp would need his leadership, his experience to guide them in the new world.

The team had gathered in the mine and there was growing excitement for the next stage of their journey; the biggest of the challenges they faced was now a possibility, but there were hurdles to jump first.

"Getting out of camp is straightforward," Torsten explained. "But the beach is treacherous and it is blocked about 200 metres from the shipyard. The only way round is to swim and the current is strong."

"We will need to buddy up; those confident swimmers need to ensure they take care of the less confident," Marcus ordered.

"There are seven ships, all identical, all will be manned and there is a 40-metre-thick wall that will stop us leaving the inlet," Torsten continued. "We have to wait for them to blow the wall before we make a move."

"Any ideas on the enemy numbers on each craft?"

"No idea," Torsten replied whilst shaking his head.

Marcus then began to run through his thoughts, explain the challenges in real life scenarios. "We leave in our swimming pairs," Marcus started. "We make our way down the beach and around the first major obstacle, as described by Torsten. We infiltrate the shipyard in the same pairs; stay together and move at your own pace. We will gather again inside the yard. We board a ship and hide onboard. We wait for the wall to come down and the ships to move out towards the sea; we do not want to get caught in the inlet, having to force our way past six hostile ships."

There was a lot of nodding and agreeable shrugs from the group.

"Torsten, Erik, Blank and Freyja; you'll join me in decommissioning the crew onboard the ship, everyone else stays hidden till we have taken control. We shut in and lockdown as many crew in non-essential areas as possible, and if for any reason we fail to take the ship, Hilda, please try and get the others to safety."

The team moved out of the mine in their pairs, like they had the first day they reached camp. The pairs went from the mine and headed directly for the wall crack that was being used to escape the camp. Each pair made their way down the beach and round the minor obstacles, just as Torsten and Hilda had done two nights before. The pairs made it to the large rock blocking the beach, and each pair in tandem entered the water and swam around. Erik struggled with Frode and his book; helping Frode who was a very poor swimmer was quite the challenge. It left the pair lagging some way behind the others. By the time they reached the inlet all but Marcus and Inga had begun their swim under the sea defence wall.

Marcus carried Inga into the water and after both took a large deep breath disappeared under the sea; Erik and Frode followed moments later, with the book tightly wrapped in waterproof material and clasped under one arm and a hold of Frode's collar in the other hand, Erik dived under the water and began his swim under the wall.

All the teams had made the shipyard. Marcus took a good look around and decided that ship number seven was the best target, although it would likely be last to leave the yard and have to pass the other ships out at sea, it would potentially have the weakest crew and the other six ships would likely be engaged with Central the moment the wall came down.

The team moved quietly to the dock for ship number seven. Marcus went first; he climbed up the side of the ship and onto a very quiet deck, then covered the others as they climbed. All 11 team members were now on the ship. There were two small covered lifeboats on the sides; these appeared to be a good place to hide and wait for the moment to take the ship. The team clambered into the boats and pulled over the covers; there was nothing to do now but wait. The team were taking the moment to rest, all but Frode, who was using this time to read the book for the first time in days; he was keen to review the section that he believed had called Testament a weapon. The information learnt from Altan put his beliefs and translation in some doubt, so he needed to understand the true meaning of Testament, the true purpose and why Kappa had been experimenting for the last 20 plus years.

43
The horrors of home

Bjorn and his family were hiding out in a small farmstead north of Khristade; since they left Stellen and Balder, the family had been in a basement of a farmhouse owned by Bjorn's brother-in-law. They left Khristade and moved as far away as quickly as possible; the whole family had travelled there – Bjorn, his wife and three sons. They had not left the basement in days. There had been news from Khristade, the sickening story that Stellen and Ava's bodies had been hanging in the square for a number of days; Hades had put them on display to show the rebellion was dead. Civilians had been trying to leave Khristade in their droves, but only a few managed to find freedom; Kappa troops had blocked as many as possible from leaving through threats and acts of violence. There had been stories of families being treated like animals, herded and chased through the streets, scared for their lives; some had been chased by packs of dogs and if caught the Kappa troops allowed the dogs to rip and maul the unfortunate souls to death. Others had been made to fight, the troops would pit one family against another; fathers, mothers and even the children being forced to fight to the death or be murdered by the Kappa soldiers.

The stories from Khristade tore at Bjorn – his people were being slaughtered for fun, and as the rebellion was dead there was no need for the people to be treated so, it was Kappa just having their fun, acting like the vile creatures that they are. Many Omegas who were lucky enough to flee the city had been making their way out of Omega, into the hills of Delta, living from the wild, but surviving. Some had travelled north like Bjorn and joined relatives or friends at small farms or workers' camps, offering to work for food and minimal shelter. The streets of Khristade were now literally red with blood and death; Kappa had total control, fear within the outer villages and farms was at the point where families would rather starve themselves than not meet quotas. The true horrors of what has happened in Khristade will never be known; those tortured and murdered will never tell their stories; the young women that have gone missing or been taken will never return to tell their tales. Within Bjorn's family, his sons Anders and Lars were particularly keen to return to the fight, but two boys against an army of men was suicide; their deaths would be pointless.

Although the rebellion was dead, Bjorn maintained a good network of friends and confidants in and around Khristade; he would often hear news and information through this network. The latest information came from a farm in the north-east of Omega near the Delta border; a slave in Delta had escaped and was being hidden at the farm; the story was he had valuable information about the true origins of the wars. Bjorn was intrigued by this news and in wanting to do something other than hide in a basement, he had decided to trek to the farm and retrieve the Delta escapee. Anders offered to travel with his father and Bjorn was happy for the company and help on the journey. Bjorn and Anders left the basement and began the roughly 30-mile journey to the farm hiding the escaped Delta slave. A year earlier, the journey would have been a gentle hike across fields and forest, but in today's Omega a 30-mile journey was like playing chicken with a combine harvester. It was going to be a difficult journey, but Bjorn and his son were experienced outdoorsmen and would be able to travel cross-country and avoid roads and paths. They travelled all night and for parts of the following day; using the forest for cover they were able to make good progress. The journey started to feel almost normal – before the fighting Bjorn and his sons would often go hiking for days; they all loved the outdoors and this little piece of Omega especially. What made it feel even more normal was this area was still relatively untouched – the black fist of Kappa had not smacked and punched the landscape as it had done elsewhere; the water still ran clear, the grass still green and the trees still standing; the father and son enjoyed their walk and took lasting memories of the world the way it was.

Anders and his father reached the farm within two days; they were greeted by friendly Omega faces and were welcomed. The Delta man was hiding in an old cellar and had been well cared for since his arrival, but was very keen to speak with Bjorn. They met in the cellar and the man introduced himself as Batu.

"I was told you had important news?" Bjorn asked.

"History; I have important history," Batu responded whilst tapping himself on the side of the head. "I was a scientist and 20-odd years ago when Delta was invaded, I was forced to work in the Kappa labs, forced to work on project Testament!"

"I have never heard of this, why should I be interested?"

"Do you like stories?" Batu asked with a mildly crazy look in his eyes. "I have a story you might like."

"This man is crazy," Bjorn bemoaned.

"We have come all this way, Father, we might as well listen to his story," Anders suggested.

"Go on then; tell us your story."

"It all began when Kappa invaded Delta. The Kappa science officers found something buried under our temple, I do not know what this was, but it changed the course of our history. Do you believe that Kappa are just merciless killing machines who just want to rule? You couldn't be farther from the truth. You think Kappa are nonbelievers? Again, falsehoods."

Bjorn was beginning to lose patience with Batu. "Get to the point, old man, I've come a long way for this!" Bjorn shouted.

"For 20 years Kappa have been trying to devise a weapon; the keystone if you wish to name it – it will return us to the past; reset the world. Kappa and especially General Hades are true believers; they revere their god and believe they were deserted by the gods because of our hedonistic ways. They believe that in the eyes of the gods all races of man should be pure, Kappa only lays with Kappa, Delta only with Delta. Their weapon will purify the world, any genetic anomaly will be wiped from it, leaving only six pure races of men." Batu took a sip of water and a deep breath before continuing.

"General Hades does not lead Kappa; he follows the orders of his priests, and they will do anything to win favour with the gods, and believe that returning the world to how it was will please them. The things Kappa do are never random; if there is an execution, it will not be pure bloods. Well, unless they have hurt Hades in some personal way. They think the gods will return and reward them with Testament."

"Hades, priests, weapons of mass destruction and whatever this testament is; this is all a little bit much to believe?" Bjorn questioned.

"Believe what you will," Batu responded.

Bjorn got up and left the cellar; he walked outside and started wandering round the farm, gathering his thoughts.

Inside the cellar Anders was frustrated with the old man; he had more questions that needed answers.

"What does this all mean?" Anders asked. "You tell us these random pieces of information without giving us any sort of context. How does it help us stop Kappa? How can we use it against them? That is what my father needs to know."

"You must understand, boy, I only have pieces, I was never privy to all the information; but what I do know I am sharing with you now. The priests believe this nonsense, they believe they are to be saved from this world if they put everything right."

"But Kappa children are taught they are superior and that they fight to rule; you're telling me that's bullshit?"

"Have you been listening at all? This didn't start yesterday; that is what the children of Kappa have been taught for centuries; the new thinking, the priests, the believing again started with whatever they found that day in Delta. The experiments started shortly after and now the weapon."

"They are determined to kill anybody who is not from a pure lineage?"

"That is what the priests believe is the only way to appease the gods."

"And what about everyone who passes the lineage test?"

"They live to be ruled by the returning gods, with Hades and his priests sat at their side."

Anders was sat shaking his head; he knew not what to say or do. Bad enough that General Hades was a crazy vile monster; but a crazy vile religious zealot monster who would not spare a soul to cleanse the world of those he sees as inferior people, who upset the gods? The general wants his reward, he wants to be sat to the right hand of his god and rule over everything and everyone. Bjorn returned to the cellar; he had composed his thoughts and had one final question for Batu.

"How do we stop them?"

44
Home truths

General Hades's motorcade was travelling away from Khristade; he was heading towards the Delta, Kappa border and the temple of Galil; the temple was the first thing to be taken during the invasion nearly 30 years earlier. The temple was a place where the highly religious Deltas used to travel to each year, a yearly pilgrimage to pray for guidance; but since the invasion the temple was now home to General Hades' higher command; the priests of Chaos. The people of Kappa are non-believers, but Hades had found faith when he discovered the priests. After invading Delta and seizing the temple, Hades had used it to hide the priests. They guided Hades' movements to appease their god; he was now merely their puppet, everything he did was for their cause. The temple was heavily guarded on the outside, but no one but Hades was allowed within the inner rooms. The inside of the temple was regal and opulent, lined with elegant depictions made from gold, statues of Galil, looking down from atop the great tower that once stood in Central, and in the middle of the main hall stood a giant crystal representation of the great central city.

Four robed figures appeared in the central chamber of the temple; their hooded robes were old and torn around the edges, tattered and not in-keeping with the palatial surroundings of the Delta temple; the hoods entirely blocking views of their faces. They appeared as faceless monsters, that were willing to kill and destroy all they needed to please their god and bring him back to the world.

"Chaos has abandoned me again," Hades complained. "I have done all that he asks and still I do not reign. All I do is suffer; suffer for his cause and have now had to give my eldest, my favourite son to his bidding."

"We all sacrifice in his name," one of the robed priests responded in a crackly, elderly voice.

"What do you sacrifice?" Hades screamed.

"Do not speak in this tone to your god. We have given 30 years to his cause, 30 years locked inside of this place so that we may learn his will."

Hades knelt with his head down and submitted to the will of the priests. One of the hooded figures stepped towards Hades and placed a hand on his shoulder; his hand was old and wrinkled, all vein and bone.

"The world must be cleansed, only then will our god return and reign, and once again the great state of Kappa will sit to his right hand. What do you say of progress with the weapon?"

"We are no closer today than we were 20 years past. I have failed him and his anger took my son away."

"How have you not found the key?" a priest asked. "What must we do?"

"My lead science officer believes the world is too polluted, that it is too late and the world cannot be saved."

"Heresey!" a priest yelled.

"I will have him killed for his words, my lords," Hades quickly responded.

The priest moved away from Hades, who rose to his feet and moved towards a stone altar near the far end of the central chamber; he put both hands on the table and bowed his head; he muttered a prayer under his breath and backed away. He moved to another chamber and the priests followed. Within this chamber was a glass box and inside the box were the remains of a being. The being was very tall and large in scale. "When you doubt your faith in our god, gaze upon the remains of Galil, that our god Chaos struck down, reaffirm that your faith is true and that he will return to us."

"My faith is true," Hades responded.

Discovering the remains of Galil 30 years earlier, buried under the great Delta temple had been the trigger for Hades to turn to faith; it had caused a change in the direction of Kappa and created the beast that Hades had become. Once he submitted to the will of the priests, his heart became darker, and he was more determined to bring his god Chaos back to the world and reign alongside of him. Everything that has happened after the discovery can be directly attributed to that day. The priests took Hades to the inner most room of the temple. It housed all the relics and artefacts that Hades had taken over the years, those that were believed to have been destroyed were lying in a room, within a temple on the edge of what once was Delta. The priests used the artefacts and the writings within to guide Hades; it was the writings that told of the great reward that was Testament, the writings told of the gods' anger at the state of the world, it was an artefact that depicted Chaos slaying Galil a thousand years before. Under the rule of the gods, each race of man had a place, a purpose. When the gods abandoned the world those men wanted more, the farmers wanted more land, the scientists wanted to create bigger and better things which required more natural resource. All the teachings of the states were in some little way true. People got greedy and that led to a thousand years of war; all of this was written or depicted in the documents and artefacts stored in this room.

Hades was angry; he wanted to know what he was to do. "Priests, tell me how to solve the weapon? How do I cleanse the world without fire and destruction?"

"The text tells us the pure will survive and the disgusting half breeds will perish, and the keystone is six pure samples, one for each race of men. You know this already."

"That is all you have told me for 20 years; you must have found something new to guide me in my mission," Hades pleaded.

"Three men, three women form the keystone and will lead you to the answers you seek."

Hades was obviously frustrated; he turned and stormed out of the room and down the long corridor that joined all the rooms within the temple. He barged out of the front door and slammed it behind him.

"Lock it up," Hades ordered. "Bring my motorcade. I will be heading to Kappa city for the evening."

The motorcade pulled up, Hades stepped into the car and the motorcade pulled away from the temple and headed towards Kappa city, the capital of Kappa state and the home of Hades.

45

The Taking of Kappa Ship Seven

Marcus and Freyja were quietly talking as they hid in the lifeboat on the deck of Kappa ship number seven. "It would be good when all this is over if you and me could find a nice quiet spot somewhere and raise the child. She needs a good home," Marcus suggested.

"I would love that, she's a sweet kid," Freyja responded with a cheeky smile.

In the recent days Erik had become Marcus's confidant – after a difficult start Erik had taken to Marcus and his leadership.

"Why are you doing this?" Erik asked Marcus.

"Doing what?" Marcus replied, thinking Erik was asking about his intentions towards Freyja and the child.

"Leading this team? Leading a bunch of strangers on what could well be a foolish mistake?"

Marcus stopped to think before replying. "It cannot be a foolish mistake as long as it gives people hope, and I still have hope. The mission could be a mistake, but it was this or a hole in the ground," Marcus said with a smile. "Who would have thought, A Kappa, A Delta, an Omega and a Sigma were working together for the betterment of all people. That is why I lead this team; because as long as I do, it gives me hope for the future of the world."

Erik shrugged, he knew the ex-Kappa captain was right; they had travelled a long way, from hate to friendship; from loathing to respect and from certain death to the slim possibility of a war-less life.

The team had been waiting for some time and it seemed like a good opportunity to run through the plan to take the boat.

"Freyja, Erik and Torsten will take the engine room. Blank, Amir and I will take the bridge. When passing any doors that don't restrict our access to the bridge, engine room or weapons centre, you must secure the doors and mark with an 'X'. Once we have the engine room and bridge secured, Erik, Blank and I will take the weapons centre. Blank will be on weapons with Erik; Amir, you are good to drive this boat?"

"If it was designed from the Sigma ships, then we should be just fine. It has the appearance of my old Sigma vessel, so I would think it was a pretty safe bet that I can sail her."

Marcus was content that everyone knew the plan and their jobs, so everyone returned to resting and whispering conversations.

A short while later there was a sudden sideways shunt of the boat. The ship's engines sprung into life and it started to move; that was followed by a huge explosion, so Erik took a quick look, and watched on as the wall began to fall into the sea; huge chunks of rock and cement crashed into the water, creating a huge wave that knocked the fleet off track for a moment. The first of the boats quickly passed through the gap and was out to sea; it began opening fire on the nearest Central ship – ship number one had begun the engagement with the Central navy. That ship was soon joined by craft two, three and four. This was the time for the team to strike. Marcus left their hiding spot first; Erik and Blank followed and Torsten after that. Freyja was last to leave the lifeboat. The team split into their preassigned groups: Torsten leading the team down the stairs towards the engine room and Marcus leading the others towards the Bridge. Each and every door they passed was locked and secured firmly, an 'X' marked on them. Door by door each of the teams moved towards their targets. Marcus's team was the first to reach theirs; entering the Bridge they encountered a total of six sailors; three resisted and were quickly dispatched by gunfire, the others surrendered without fuss – they were Sigma sailors and were not the enemy.

In the engine room it was a similar story, a few Kappa soldiers who were quickly ended; the other engineers and sailors were either Delta or Sigma and did not want to fight; they quickly surrendered and were taken to a room and secured with the others from the bridge. The main areas of the ship were now under the control of Marcus and his team. They followed the course as was already set and prepared to tangle with the central navy. Marcus took Blank and Erik to the weapons centre; there were no surrenders here, all were Kappa soldiers. Blank entered the room and took down the first soldier, Marcus and Erik followed. Erik fired a shot point blank and killed the ranking officer, his blood spraying the weapons consoles with a dark red mist. The Kappa soldiers tried to cover but the Omega team were too quick. Marcus had flanked the soldiers and with a quick burst of machine gun fire had killed the remaining soldiers where they hid. Marcus hurriedly returned to the bridge; the ship was the last to pass through what was the defence wall. The ship quickly picked up speed as it hit the open sea. As the newest Kappa ship captain, Amir wanted to put distance between themselves and the Kappa fleet quickly. He changed heading and pushed the boat hard towards the furthest edge of the central fleet. They took a few minor hits from flack and small arms but passed though mostly unscathed. Kappa ship number seven was now past the Kappa and Central navies and out in open water.

46
Naval Warfare

Marcus and his team were sailing towards the Sigma shore; they had not encountered any other ships since they broke past the Central fleet a day ago. Life onboard was difficult – the team had locked enemy soldiers in the non-essential areas on the ship and two of those non-essential areas were the galley and the bunks. The team were hungry and tired, but spirits were high.

Frode had used the last 24 hours to study the book and check his previous translations; he had concluded that Testament was a weapon, but after talking with Altan it was clear this assumption was wrong and Testament wasn't the weapon being described in the book.

"That makes more sense," Frode called out. "It is a weapon; sort of; it is described as a reward for the true believers, and the wrath of the gods for those who don't."

"So it would reward some of the population and punish others?" Aurora asked, "How would that even be possible?"

Aurora had worked in the Kappa science core for some years and she knew the technology didn't exist to build such a device. She walked away shaking her head, and headed to the bridge where Marcus was on watch. "This nonsense book is leading us down the wrong path," she complained.

"What's that?" Marcus asked.

"Science is the true state, it proves everything. The science just doesn't exist to create what that stupid book describes. If we take our lead from that text, it will be the end of us."

"As long as the book guides us to where we need to go. That is all we need it to be right about. What's that?"

Marcus was distracted by a small dot that had appeared on the horizon. The small dot was getting bigger fast, it was a Central vessel steaming hard towards Kappa ship number seven. He quickly sounded the ship alarm and Amir ran onto the bridge from the deck where he was resting. Amir grasped the wheel and turned the boat a hard right and pushed the speed to full, now heading away from the oncoming vessel.

"Better to run than fight," the Sigma sailor stated nervously.

Marcus was still watching the vessel. "They're not closing; but have changed course to follow."

The onboard radios sprang to life; it was the ship's engine room. "Temp gauges starting to run very high. I don't think the engines can take this punishment," Torsten cried out.

Amir reduced the speed hoping to reduce the strain on the engines, hoping the enemy vessel would have to do the same. He was hopeful of maintaining the distance over the Central ship.

Kappa ship number seven was performing better since Amir had reduced the speed, but it allowed the enemy Central ship to close slightly. It appeared as though they also were unable to keep sailing at the highest speed. Amir was doing his best to maintain the largest possible advantage; he wanted a distance of at least two thousand metres to stay out of range of the enemy guns. Marcus was maintaining watch on the enemy; he could see men scurrying on the deck of the enemy boat. Marcus was no sailor; this was his first experience on the sea, but he could tell that the enemy were preparing some tubes on the left hand side of the ship. The Central vessel took a hard right, exposing their left flank to Marcus and Kappa ship seven.

"There is something in the water," Marcus yelled.

Sailor Amir turned the Kappa ship to face towards what he assumed to be an enemy torpedo, making the profile of his ship as small as possible. "Count down the distance," Amir shouted.

"Three hundred metres," Marcus replied. "Two fifty, two hundred, one fifty, one hundred, now only fifty."

Amir wrench the wheel right, the ship lurched badly. He pushed the engine control lever full forward and the craft reacted immediately roaring fast away from the oncoming torpedo. Amir spun the wheel back around and faced Kappa ship seven directly towards the enemy vessel. He hit the radio button and barked orders to the weapons centre. "Prepare to fire main guns. Straight ahead sixteen hundred metres and reducing fast."

The Central ship began to open fire on the team. Amir manoeuvred from side to side, avoiding major hits, as he ploughed on towards the enemy. "Guns one through four, fire, fire," he screamed into the radio.

The guns on the Kappa vessel each fired, the noise shook the air as each gun boomed into life. Marcus watched as each shot arced in the sky and as they spiralled down towards the enemy. Three of the shells crashed into the vessel with the most incredible force. Each shot pounded the ship, folding it almost in half as it quickly sunk. Fuel began to catch fire on the surface of the sea, instantly burning any sailors who had survived the hits; the screams and anguished cries could be heard from the bridge of Kappa ship seven.

Amir returned the ship to the original heading and fell down in the bridge command chair; relief filled his face as he closed his eyes and sighed. Marcus walked over and patted the Sigma sailor on his back, he left the bridge and went to check on Inga, Freyja and the others. The Omega team were back on course, tomorrow they would reach the shores of Sigma and whatever they might face there.

47

If You Want A Job Done Right

General Hades was in his personal apartment within Kappa central command. Central command is the home and war office for all high ranking Kappa officers. The apartment was not what many would have expected, sparsely furnished with little other than an armchair and side table in the main living space. There was a bedroom that had a large mattress on the floor and a closet that contained only uniforms and dress boots. Where the kitchen should have stood, there was a space filled only with an enormous set of exercise weights. The windows, of which there were many, were undressed: plain glass with no curtains or blinds. Hades lived a very scant existence, he was rarely seen at central command and on the occasion he would visit the apartment was often just used for female conquests. Since he had argued with his priests he had been contemplating his next steps; at first the only thoughts were of fire and brimstone – his anger was getting the better of him. Burn the world if that is what it took to cleanse it from the half-bred filth; but Hades had now calmed a little and his focus had moved back to Keystone and what his scientists could do to move forward. Hades was more determined than ever to please Chaos and bring him back to a better, purer world.

There was a knock at his door.

"Enter," Hades yelled as a Kappa officer strode into Hades' apartment.

"Sir, there has been no contact with Brigade 66 for some time. When they last reported it was from the old mines. They were entering from the entrance near Breeder station ten and had reported they were close on the trail of Omega Captain Balder's team."

"Nothing since? No sightings? Nobody has seen them at all?" Hades screamed.

"No sir, no updates."

Hades had started to pace, with his obvious frustration beginning to boil to the surface. "Can no one be trusted with even simple tasks?"

Hades grabbed his jacket and face mask, he dressed before stomping out of his apartment and towards the elevator. The soldier ran after him.

"Should I prepare your motorcade for a trip, sir?"

Hades gave the soldier a look like: don't ask stupid questions! They entered the elevator and the soldier selected the garage level.

Hades' motorcade was rolling towards Breeder station ten and the mine entrance where the General believed Orcus and his troops were last seen. Hades could still not remove the idea from his mind that perhaps fire was the answer to the problem after all, that Chaos would be happy if the world was anew, if that requires death and destruction then so be it. The motorcade arrived at the mine entrance near breeder station ten, and Hades disembarked the car with a brigade of troops in tow. The boarding over the mine entrance was already broken down and there was a transport hidden in the opening. Soldiers searched the transport truck and found the dead bodies of two Kappa soldiers.

"Who are these men?" Hades demanded.

"Just checking their IDs, sir," a soldier responded. "Looks like they were on breeder transport duty, from Station zero, here to Station 10."

"Who were they transporting?"

"An Omega, sir. Astrid."

The General looked up, closed his eyes and clenched his fist; he took a breath and a moment to calm himself. "What happened to her?"

"She never made it to the station, sir."

"And this was not reported to me? My property goes missing and nobody thinks to inform me?"

"Sorry, sir. Her disappearance was not reported to Kappa command."

As the General moved his troops into the mine, he was showing obvious signs of losing his temper. His soldiers moved along the path and advanced as far as the junction. Without hesitation Hades gestured for the troops to take the left path, which they followed until they found the missing brigade 66 soldiers; they were still in the throes of burying bodies as ordered by Captain Marcus. "What are you doing?" Hades yelled as he entered the large central chamber of the mine.

"Burying these bodies as ordered, sir," responded the lieutenant that had been left running 66 since Marcus killed their commander.

"Ordered by whom? Where is Orcus?"

"Captain Marcus ordered us, after he won the command of the brigade by defeating Commander Orcus."

"Orcus is dead?" asked Hades. "Why would you take orders from a man that is wanted throughout Kappa for killing my son?"

"It is our way, sir. He defeated Orcus, and he became our new commander."

"Foolish idiots." Hades paused for a moment, then he turned to his division commander. "Take them outside and kill them all."

Hades's brigade moved swiftly, and without fuss took each of the soldiers of 66, they moved them back down the tunnels and into the light of day. The brigade 66 soldiers were ordered to start digging a large hole that would serve as their grave. The men were handed shovels and they began digging, but these were the men of 66 and were not going down without a fight. The division sergeant whistled two short blasts and as he did, each soldier turned their shovels to makeshift weapons. A mass brawl breaking out, the 66 soldiers fought well. They killed over half of Hades' troops before the last man was put down. Hades missed the commotion – he had taken a small number of soldiers and continued through the mine and towards the workers' camp and the eastern shore.

As Hades arrived at the end of the mine tunnel, he burst through the boards and into the workers' camp; it was a good minute or two before any of the guards reacted to an armed team storming the camp. Hades held his head in his hands, there was stunned disbelief at the incompetence of the camp guards.

"Who is in charge here?" Hades screamed.

An older soldier walked down from the camp office. "I am, sir."

"Where are these men?" Hades asked, as one of his soldiers held up pictures of Marcus and Blank.

"They are not in this camp, sir. I would know if they had been here."

Hades was furious, what could be seen of his face was reddening and his fists were clenching by his sides. A soldier approached Hades and whispered to him. "Sir, we have received a short wave burst from Kappa fleet command. It's very important, sir."

"Just tell me," Hades yelled.

"Kappa ship number seven has gone missing, believed to have been taken, sir."

That was the final straw; Hades exploded in a rage, immediately pulling his sidearm and shooting the camp commander. Shot after shot, even after the commander was well dead, Hades fired and fired at the stricken body. Hades continued to pull the trigger until after the gun was emptied. He then turned his attention to the poor soldier who had delivered the message regarding ship number seven. He wrapped his giant hand around the neck of the soldier and squashed his throat like it was putty. The body of the unfortunate soldier dropped to the floor. General Hades was still raging. "If you want a job done right!" he yelled. "Get me a ship; I will hunt them down myself."

A soldier ran to the camp office and radioed for a ship to return to the shipyard; also calling for the motorcade to join them in the workers' camp. Hades was pacing up and down, still furious; no one dared speak to him or utter a word.

After a short wait the motorcade arrived and took Hades to the shipyard. Once there, Hades' impatience grew as he waited for a ship that would take him after the Omega team and ship number seven. Ships three and six pulled into the shipyard and up to the gangway. Hades stomped onboard ship three, and immediately took command and the captain's chair on the bridge. "How many soldiers does each ship carry?" Hades barked at the captain.

"Each has two full battalions onboard, sir," the boat's captain responded.

"Head for the Sigma shore and prepare all ships for invasion."

Ships three and six moved off from their moorings and headed back out to sea. The captain radioed the other ships of the fleet, informing them that ship three was now in the lead, and that all vessels should make best speed for the Sigma shore and prepare all troops for the invasion of Sigma state.

48
Sigma

Marcus's team were approaching the Sigma shore and were on edge; they had no knowledge of Sigma, no information on the Sigma capabilities, zero understanding of the topography and no details of the arms that could be borne against them.

Amir was thinking of going home; he had not been in Sigma state for some months. His knowledge of Sigma would be handy to the team, but Marcus was not prepared to keep the man, knowing he just wanted to return home.

"Just point us in the right direction and I would be eternally grateful," Marcus stated with a smile.

"I can help you as far as the capital," Amir responded. "I'm heading there to try and find my family."

"Family?" Inga asked.

"Yes, my dear, a wife, a son and two daughters. I was conscripted to the navy some two years ago, so I haven't seen them in quite some time. I'm just hopeful they are still in the capital."

The little girl was intrigued; she missed her parents and talking about family made her feel a little better. "What are they like?"

"My family? Well, my wife is a teacher, a historian who teaches in the city school. I have known her since I was your age. We've been married 30 years and she is my everything."

"She sounds lovely," Inga responded.

"Leave Amir alone, Inga," Marcus chirped.

"That's alright; it's nice to talk about them, it helps me remember them," Amir said solemnly. "My son is 18; no, he must now be nineteen. He joined the Sigma armed force at the age of 15; I'm very proud of his dedication. The girls are much younger and were still at home with their mother. They are very sweet girls just like their mum."

Inga skipped away and down the deck of the boat. "Cute kid," Amir quipped.

Land had become visible in the distance; it would not be long until the team were again on dry land. Marcus had a frown across his head and a pained expression on his face. "I wish we knew more of your homeland," he said.

"What would you like to know?" Amir questioned.

"Everything. I hate feeling unprepared, and in this moment, I feel totally unprepared. Like I'm walking into the complete unknown, lacking direction. In fact, I don't even know which direction to walk!"

"That is an easy one; keep heading east. You should skirt Akbar City and if you keep going you will find Central and from there you can't miss Central City. You can see the city from anywhere in Central state. It might now be a ruin of what it was, but the city is enormous."

"Thanks. Makes me feel a little better."

"The armed force is mainly young men, they will be just as wary of you, as you of them. They won't fire unless you provoke them. They may try and stop you – strangers are very rare."

Marcus was forcing this information into his brain; concentrating on each of Amir's words like it was a matter of life or death. He needed to know more. "How about transportation? Roads, paths, ground cover? Armed force station positions? Towns, villages? I need to know everything."

"Well, there's very little transportation, over 80 percent of the population live in Akbar. There is a motor rail that joins several smaller towns with the capital. It runs from Cyrus to Daria with the capital in the middle. No roads, but there are hiking routes or paths, the ground is wild scrub and brush. No trees or forests to speak of."

"I am so grateful for your candour. Telling a stranger this information about your people. It is a rare quality you have, trust."

"Just do me one favour. Find your answers and use them to stop Kappa, put an end to these wars that tear us all from our homes."

Marcus was feeling a little more prepared, his frown not completely gone but significantly reduced. He was plotting the best path and considering options for moving through Sigma.

"You will need to change your clothes," Amir suggested. "You will stand out, be easily noticed."

Marcus called for Torsten and Erik; he ordered them to take the clothes from the Sigma sailors that were onboard. The team would do their utmost to disguise themselves as Sigma, help them move through the state without issue. The ship was now mere metres from the shore. Amir brought the ship to a full stop one hundred metres away from a yellow sand beach and dropped the anchor. Marcus ordered the team to dress in the Sigma clothes Torsten and Erik had recovered; then prepare the lifeboats to take them to shore; they would take both the boats and turn the ship over to the Sigma sailors onboard. As the team dressed in the Sigma clothes, nothing quite fitted right – it was especially difficult for the women, having to dress in men's clothes. The team embarked the lifeboats, Marcus commanded one and Erik the other. The boats were lowered into the water and they made for shore. A short ride took them close, before the boats were driven up and onto the beach, the soft sand grabbing hold of the craft and holding them neatly whilst the team hopped out and on to land.

Marcus and Erik took their teams up the beach and inland a little, where they all regrouped. Captain Marcus shared the stories from Amir; he wanted the team to use the information to develop stories that they could use if ever captured.

"Where are you from?" Marcus asked, pointing at Aurora.

"Sigma," she replied.

"Where in Sigma?" Marcus curtly responded.

"Daria?"

"You must sound convincing. How about you?" Marcus said, this time pointing at Torsten.

"I'm from Daria, conscripted to navy about two years past."

"Better," Marcus stated. "You must all be that confident."

Marcus was generally happy the team were at least paying attention. He asked Amir to take the lead as they moved away from the beach and into the relative unknown.

"Take us to your Capital," Marcus asked the sailor.

Amir nodded and started walking due east. It would take a couple of days of fair paced walking to reach Akbar, but the team were eager and happy to be walking again after their adventure on the sea.

49
Enemy territory

Marcus's team had not walked far before they encountered a small force of Sigma soldiers. The team were hiding in an area of brush and the soldiers seemed unaware of the team's presence. The Sigma force was quite large, maybe 30 men and they were heading towards a small banked area to the north-west of their position. The Omega team stayed hidden as the Sigma men moved past them; they were heavily armed and their guns raised. Marcus was worried that the soldiers were sent for them, but they passed without incident and continued towards the bank. The first of the soldiers reached the bank and stopped, led down and crawled up to the top. Once there he peered over and positioned his gun facing out, back towards the sea. All the other soldiers followed suit and within a few moments were lined up along the top of the bank with their weapons trained.

"What is going on?" Marcus whispered from the team's position in the brush.

"No idea, it is strange for the armed force to be this far out from a town or our capital," Amir responded.

The Sigma team suddenly opened fire, rounds and rounds fired upon something that was hidden to the team.

"Everyone, keep their heads down; Amir, come with me," Marcus ordered.

Marcus and Amir snuck around the edge of the bank whilst still maintaining cover in the brush; Marcus was trying to get a look at what was being fired upon. As he rounded the edge of the bank, he could see another force of men defending their position; several were dead already, but some survived and had hidden behind nature features, humps and bumps in the ground.

Marcus questioned Amir: "Who are they?"

"I think they may be Central forces, but I cannot be sure."

"Central, why would they be firing on Central? I thought you were allies?"

"Two years is a long time in this world. They must be at war over something?"

Marcus decided he had seen enough and signalled to Amir to move back to the team's position. They both moved quietly and stuck to the brush cover, re-joining the team. Marcus signalled for the team to move away from the bank, to stay down and move quickly. The team did as ordered, heading as fast as they could away from the warring soldiers.

Marcus informed the team of what he saw, and what he and Amir had assumed. Sigma appeared to be at war with Central, and this would make it more difficult to move freely across Sigma state. A new plan was required, and Marcus wanted to be bold – it would be too slow for the team to be moving only through the brush on their bellies.

"Where is that motor rail you spoke of?" Marcus inquired to Amir.

"Cyrus is probably about four or five miles in that direction," Amir replied whilst pointing south-east.

"Think we will blend in? Enough to board the motor rail?"

"It's possible; if you don't do anything stupid, we might be alright."

Marcus had already decided, regardless of Amir's answer, the team were heading for the town of Cyrus and the motor rail. Marcus again asked Amir to lead the way, and they set off towards the town. The Omega team walked for about two hours before the town appeared into view; they had avoided any more of the Sigma defence force and were about to test their thrown-together disguises. Marcus stopped the team a few hundred metres outside the outskirts of Cyrus.

"Tried and tested technique, everyone, we go into town in small groups; pairs would be best. Straight to the motor rail and board. We go all the way to Akbar and do not regroup until then. Everyone alright with that?"

Everyone nodded and two by two the team entered the town and made their way to the motor rail. Marcus and Inga were the last pair, and as they strolled into town they encountered several Sigma civilians; not one lifted their head or took a second look at the pair.

Marcus and the little girl continued unimpeded through the town and towards the motor rail. The town was small, only ten or so streets, set out in a sort of grid. The motor rail was towards the far side of town, so Marcus and Inga would have to walk across eight or nine streets to reach the transport. As they made their way through the streets, they kept an eye out for both soldiers, and the other members of the team, but they saw neither. As the pair approached the motor rail, they noticed all the other team members already waiting at the side of the track. It was a very simple set-up, a wooden stage next to widely spaced metal tracks with a large building positioned at the far end of the rails. All the team were waiting patiently trying not to draw any attention, making conversation with each other about the weather and other inane things. A loud roaring noise emanated from the large building and an enormous engine started to appear; the engine was pulling many wooden sided carriages, some with seats and some completely empty other than boxes and sacks. The carriages pulled up to the wooden platform and people started to board the seated carriages; the team followed suit, copying the local people exactly. As Marcus was about to board, he heard a woman's scream; he turned and saw Aurora was being dragged away from the rail by two large, formally dressed gentlemen. He watched as Torsten was also dragged away; he had to act. He took Inga by the hand and walked down the wooden stage towards Aurora and Torsten. He noticed a pensive looking Freyja on a carriage and handed Inga off to her.

"Look after her," he said with a smile, as Freyja reached out a hand to stop him.

Marcus proceeded to follow his soldiers away from the motor rail and towards the town centre. As he walked after them he saw the motor rail start moving down the track and away from the town. Aurora and Torsten were taken into an old regal looking building with large wooden doors to the front and bars across each window. He stopped and took a seat on a nearby bench; his mind was only thinking about his next move, how to rescue his men.

"Need some help?" a voice asked.

Marcus looked up and Amir was stood there. "I told Freyja where to go once they reach Akbar, thought they would be fine, whereas you – I thought you were bound to get into trouble and could use my help."

"What about your family?"

"It's been two years, what's an extra day or two?"

50
Captured

Aurora and Torsten were being held in the justice building
in the centre of Cyrus, a small Sigma town at the end of the
motor rail line. They were in separate cells on the main floor of the
building. The cells were concrete rooms with bars on the windows,
a single bench along the back wall and a solid wooden door.

"Why are we being held?" Torsten shouted from his cell, but
nobody was responding.

A large, well-dressed man approached Torsten's cell. "Keep it
down," he grumbled. "You will be put before the justice in just a
short while. He will inform you of the charges."

"I didn't do anything," Torsten complained.

"You will be in front of the justice shortly. Keep the damn noise
down."

Torsten was annoyed and frustrated; he and Aurora were just
a step away from the motor rail and had been grabbed for nothing.
To be so close to the target and be foiled at the last moment was
agonising. Torsten knew he didn't belong in Sigma, but was just
passing through. He had no bad intentions towards them. Two men
approached Torsten's cell; one unlocked the door and told Torsten
to stand. The men proceeded to shackle Torsten's hands and drag
him from the cell and along a corridor, through a set of doors, where
a robed man was sat in a chair raised off the ground with a table to
his front.

"I am Justice Azad. Under Sigma law you have been charged
with being unable to prove your identity. You are believed to be

foreign to Sigma and are not welcome here."

"I am a Sigma sailor who has been held in Kappa captivity for the last six months. I escaped with the woman, the one I was with at the motor rail." He was making it up as he went along, but hoped it was convincing.

"A sailor?" the justice asked.

"Yes, sir," Torsten responded. "I have been away for some time and was heading back to Akbar to find my family."

"And the woman? There are no women in the Sigma navy."

"She was a prisoner like me. She helped me escape and I owe her my life."

The justice seemed receptive to the story Torsten was telling. "You and your saviour, you will be held here until you can be processed for genetic testing. If you are Sigma, the charges will be dropped; and if not, you will be expelled from our land. Take him back to the cells."

Outside the justice building Marcus and Amir were preparing to make a move. Amir had returned from the justice building, where he had discovered what Aurora and Torsten had been charged with.

"They are charged with being foreigners," Amir confirmed.

"What is going to happen to them?"

Amir explained that they would be expelled from Sigma once it has been proven they are outsiders. They would likely have to submit to genetic testing; unless they admit they are not from Sigma.

"If we go in and forcibly remove them there is a chance that people will get hurt, and we aren't here to hurt your people," Marcus commented. "But what choice do we have? I'm not leaving them here."

"You'd be better to wait until they are being moved. Cyrus doesn't have a lab and they will be moved for testing."

"How will they be moved?" Marcus asked.

"There is only way to move anything in Sigma; they will use the motor rail. There will be another departure later today."

"Where is the lab?"

"I believe there is a small lab in Mina, which is around halfway from here to Akbar."

Marcus confirmed his thoughts; they would rescue their team on the journey to Mina. Remove the guards from the motor rail and continue on to Akbar, where they would find the other team members.

Aurora and Torsten where being readied to move. Hands and feet shackled and each guarded by two large men. They were walked across town from the justice building and to the motor rail. Marcus and Amir were watching from a far enough distance to not be noticed. Aurora and Torsten, with their guards, boarded the motor rail in the carriage closest to the motor. Amir and Marcus boarded in the very last carriage – they would bide their time before attempting to rescue their friends.

The motor rail was pushing along at good speed, and Amir estimated it would be 30 minutes until they would reach Mina, so it was time to attempt the rescue. Marcus and Amir started moving along the carriages; the motor rail was relatively sparse of passengers, which was good for the team. They would like to avoid unneeded attention when they threw four large men from the transport. Amir entered the carriage first and was greeted by one of the guards.

"This carriage is taken," the guard said menacingly.

"Sorry, sir," Amir responded. He turned and faced the carriage doorway as Marcus burst through the door, raised pistol in hand.

"I will be asking you to please back away from your prisoners," Marcus asked politely.

Amir moved to release the team, he took a set of keys from one of the guards and unlocked all the shackles. Marcus moved to guide the guards around the carriage and towards the side door.

"I am going to have to ask you four to leave the carriage please," Marcus asked very politely. "We would rather not hurt you, but you do have to leave the motor rail."

Three of the guards seemed happy to accept their fate, but the fourth was not leaving the train without a fight. "I'm not leaving this carriage," the guard stated forcefully.

"Leave or I will be forced to shoot you," Marcus ordered.

The guard made a move and gave Marcus no option. He fired one shot into the leg of the guard, who fell to the floor, grabbing his wound and grimacing in pain. The other guards reacted to the shot, and a fight broke out. Torsten swung the carriage door open as Marcus forced two guards through the opening. They hit the ground and rolled along the brush to the side of the rail and could be seen getting to their feet. Amir was fighting the other guard, punches flying back and forth. The shot guard grabbed Amir by the leg and rolled towards the door; Torsten reached out and clasped Amir's hand as the guard fell from the motor rail. The guard held Amir, who in turn was being held by Torsten. Amir struggled, kicking out at the guard who lost his grip and crashed into the ground. Torsten pulled Amir back into the carriage, where Marcus was making light work of the final guard. A right jab to the face and kick to the midriff, the guard stumbled back toward the open door; he reached out in panic and grabbed Torsten's arm as he fell and both went tumbling out the door. Marcus and Amir desperately reached out for Torsten, but it was in vain, they were too late and Torsten was gone. Marcus looked back from the carriage to check for movement, but neither the guard nor Torsten rose up from where they fell.

"No!" Marcus screamed in despair as the motor rail continued to rocket along the track.

Whilst Marcus and Aurora consoled each other, Amir sat in the corner of the carriage daydreaming about the family he would hopefully see again soon. The team had lost another man; Torsten was a good man, a good soldier and would be missed by the team. The losses made Marcus ever more determined to finish this mission and complete the quest for the truth. They would soon be through Mina and well on their way to Akbar, to meet up with the rest of the team and push on towards Central.

51
Man down

Marcus, Aurora and Amir had arrived at Akbar; the motor rail had just completed its journey from Mina. Marcus had spent the journey consoling Aurora, who had become upset at the loss of Torsten; she had spent enough time with the man to have forged a strong friendship. Torsten was a nice man, he didn't say much, was always offering to help with any task and would have been first into any fight if possible – him being gone would have a severe impact on the team. Amir stepped from the motor rail and took a deep breath of Sigma city air; he coughed a little – he'd forgotten how thick and smoggy city air was. Everything in Sigma was run by fuel-powered engines and it created quite the acrid smell and massive plumes of grey-black smoke that filled the sky. Marcus thanked Amir for his help in guiding the team this far. Amir had saved them all with his naval manoeuvring and was well respected by all the team, but it was time for him to find his family. Amir explained that before he had left the group to help Marcus in Cyrus, he had instructed the team to gather at a local drinking spot. It was a rough and ready joint, but they would not be bothered there. He gave Marcus directions to the spot and said his goodbyes, Marcus shock Amir by the hand and left with Aurora. Marcus was feeling a tinge of disappointment that Amir was leaving, but he understood his need to find his family.

Aurora and Marcus walked through the streets of Akbar without incident; just like in Cyrus no one even so much as looked at them funnily. The pair found the establishment that Amir had described;

it was called the City Baths, a strange name for a watering hole. Marcus and Aurora entered the building and were greeted by a huge room packed with people, sailors, workers and every other type of person crammed wall to wall, climbing over each other to get drinks from the small bar located against the back wall. There were several small scuffles around the room, but nothing too serious and certainly nothing to worry Marcus. Aurora was searching the room with her eyes, trying to spot the team, but there were literally people everywhere. It was then that a hand reached out and gently touched her shoulder; she turned and was face to face with Blank. She reached out and wrapped her arms around the startled ex-Kappa grunt.

"It's good to see you, grunt," she said as a tear began rolling down her face.

Marcus put his hand on Blank's shoulder and smiled. "Where is everyone?" he asked.

"We have a room upstairs, everyone is safe. Where's Torsten?" Blank asked, looking around trying to spot the Omega soldier.

Aurora's head dipped and Marcus shock his head.

"Didn't make it," Marcus said sadly.

Blank led Marcus and Aurora to the room where the others were waiting. There were lots of happy looks in the room. Marcus gave Freyja a massive hug and Inga a little ruffle on the head; she grabbed Marcus's leg and held it tight. Before anyone asked, Marcus told their story, he explained what had happened, and that Torsten unfortunately would not be joining them for the rest of the quest. Marcus made a point of going to each member of the team and thanking them for their efforts so far. He never had a chance to say the same to Torsten before he was lost and didn't want the others to not hear his words, and his thanks. Each person Marcus spent time with was grateful for his words, he expressed what the team meant to him and how he would not want to be in the company of anyone else. The last person Marcus spoke with was Freyja. Marcus took her to one side; he wanted to tell her more than just thanks. Marcus took Freyja outside, they found a quiet spot behind the watering hole. Marcus held Freyja and passionately kissed her, as she pulled down his trousers and wriggled out of her own. Marcus lifted her up and they consummated their love.

"I never want to be without you," the Captain stammered as the pair continued to make love.

"I want to be yours," Freyja moaned.

The pair had learnt from their previous awkward encounter and this moment was not uncomfortable at all. When the lovers had finished, they dressed and kissed. Freyja was giddy with her love. Marcus was more controlled but couldn't hide his happiness when back amongst the others. The Omega team rested through that night, some slept, some talked. Freyja and Marcus slept cradling each other with Inga sleeping to their side. Aurora and Frode caught up on all things Testament-related. In the morning they would be moving out, leaving Akbar and heading to Central.

52
Roads less travelled

The team were preparing to leave Akbar, they had all rested well overnight and were ready to continue their quest, but alarm bells were ringing all around the city. Marcus sent Erik and Hilda to gather intel, to gather information about the alarms and why they were sounding. Erik and his sister went to the bar area of the watering hole which was now all but deserted. They couldn't just ask as about the alarms as it would be a signal that they were not from Sigma.

"What you doing here?" A voice shouted from the back of the room. "You need to get to your stations, go there now!"

Erik and Hilda didn't know what the man was talking about.

"Stations? We are new to the city, just arrived from Cyrus," Hilda grumbled.

"We are under attack, go back to your rooms and take cover, go now."

Erik and his sister hurriedly returned to the others.

"We aren't going anywhere," Erik stated. "The city is under attack."

The team knew nothing of who was attacking – it was surely Central, but what if Hades had been mad enough to follow them and had invaded Sigma? All the team could do was wait and hope.

Outside the city, Central tank battalions were heading directly for the northern side of Akbar; they had broken through the outer defence and were bearing down on the city. Their numbers were great and Sigma had no tanks to defend with, they were dependent on brave young men destroying the tanks with small explosive devices; they would need to manually plant the bombs on the tanks. A number of men from the Sigma armed force were hiding in holes waiting for the approaching tanks – when the tanks were close the soldiers would leave these holes and attach bombs to the tanks. This was a dangerous game, but Sigma had no heavy artillery and this was the only option. Several tanks had been destroyed but Sigma had lost many young soldiers. The tanks were still bearing down on the city. It would not be long and Central forces would be on the streets of Akbar.

Back in the room at the City Baths the team were debating their next move –should they wait out the worst of the attack and then make their move, but if Central take the city it may be more difficult to escape, and if it was Kappa they had to put miles between them and Hades. They felt too close to their target to be stopped now. It was decided that it was now time to make their move, but as they were leaving the watering hole shells began to rain down on the eastern side of the city. It would appear that the east was the city's industrial area and whoever was attacking wanted to cripple Sigma with a decisive strike. The team were again in their room and replanning once more.

To the north the tanks were within metres of the city when they all stopped and began to reverse course. They were within striking distance of their goal and just stopped. The tanks turned and began leaving the area at a great speed; the battalion were heading towards the coast, to the eastern shore. As the shelling stopped, the alarms were silenced; this was the opportunity the team had been looking for. They gathered their supplies and left the City Baths, they hurried down a few streets heading east. Erik was leading the team as they approached the edge of the city centre. Erik signalled for the team to stop – their path blocked by a fire emanating from several buildings that had been shelled in the attack. The team would have to find a way around. Erik led them south away from the fires; they tried every side street heading east but all were blocked or un-passable due to fallen buildings or further fires. They pressed on south and eventually found a passable side street. The further the team moved away from the city centre, the less well organised the streets became; it was like a rabbit warren of streets. The team were hoping to find their way out of the city and back on course to find Central.

53
Invasion

On Kappa ship number three, Hades was discussing options with his highest commanders, who had joined him on the new fleet flagship of the Kappa navy. Hades' fleet were hunting for Kappa ship seven, which Hades believed had the Omega team and the traitorous Kappa soldiers who had killed his son onboard. The Kappa fleet had made short work of the Central navy on the eastern shore and were sailing at top speed towards the Sigma coast and ship number seven. Hades was preparing all possible contingencies: find the ship with the treacherous dogs still onboard and destroy it on sight; sink them into the cold sea water and watch on as they all drowned; and if the team had made land, Hades had 600 heavily armed men ready to invade Sigma and find the scum that form Team Balder. As the boats ploughed through the sea, Hades was discussing invasion options with his commanders.

"Storm the beaches with a full force. Our intelligence tells us there is little in the way of large artillery or defensive capabilities," one of Hades' commanders commented.

"And Central?" another commander asked.

"Our spies tell us they are at war and currently engaged with Sigma to the north and east of their capital. They have two sizeable tank battalions to contend with."

"How do we contend with them, with only ground troops?"

"We will draw them to us. Use the main ship cannons to provide destructive fire."

"Draw them to us?"

"If we send 600 troops on to the beaches, they will come to us. Sigma will wait, they will come for an invading force."

Hades seemed content with the invasion ideas. Hades would sacrifice every one of the 600 men and women in his strike force to get his hands on Marcus and the remaining Omega defence force.

As the ship continued towards the Sigma shore, Hades was distracted; his mind was still stuck on the argument with his priests and what he must do to bring purity back to the world, which would allow Chaos to return and take his rightful place as ruler of the world. Hades' mind was formulating how to wipe the world clean. His preference would be to create the perfect keystone and peacefully annihilate any who do not have single state linage, even if that was millions. If the perfect weapon was not possible, then Hades was willing to compromise, willing to use his vast army to be his spear, to seek out and murder all those that he himself believes to be unfit for the new world.

"Kappa vessel number seven in view, sir," A voice bellowed from the front of the ship.

"Change course to intercept," the ship's commander ordered.

"Sir, the ship appears to be stationary, anchored 150 metres from shore."

"Slow your speed, helmsman. Order all ships to guard the shore at safe distance. We will proceed to intercept ship seven."

The ships in the fleet all slowed and spread themselves across a line a few hundred metres from shore, whilst Kappa ship three with Hades and his commanders onboard headed slowly towards the anchored boat.

"No life craft onboard, sir, and no obvious movement," the spotter called out.

"Helmsman, complete stop. Prepare the boarding team and lower the boats."

The boarding team ran to the deck and boarded one of the lifeboats. The craft was lowered to the sea and it sped off towards ship number seven. The boat settled against the side of the larger vessel and the team climbed the side and onto the deck. They found the majority of the doors locked as they swept the deck.

As the Kappa team broke towards the bridge, there was zero resistance and not a soul to be seen. The team stormed the bridge, where five Sigma sailors were found. They took the men, quickly checking them against pictures of Marcus and Blank.

"You know these men?" the Kappa team leader shouted.

"They were on board, but went ashore some hours ago," a scared Sigma sailor stuttered.

The Kappa team commander reported the findings to the bridge of ship three and waited for a response. "Kappa team leader reports that the targets are no longer onboard, sir," Kappa ship three bridge commander reported to Hades.

"Execute all onboard. Leave no man alive," Hades ordered.

The orders were relayed to the Kappa team who quickly and without remorse murdered the bridge crew of ship seven. They continued to sweep the vessel, one by one opening the locked doors and executing all those onboard, Sigma, Central and Kappa, all shot and killed. After the sweep was completed, a Kappa clean-up crew was sent onboard to remove the bodies. All the dead crew were summarily thrown over the side of the ship, the water turning red around the hull, as the bodies sank to the ocean floor.

On the bridge of Kappa ship three, Hades was making the final arrangements for invasion.

"Prepare all troops to land on the beach. Full arms and supplies for the invasion of Sigma," Hades ordered. "You commanders will lead the invasion on the ground, so make ready to go ashore. You will earn your commissions today, soldiers."

Hades then ordered for the ship to join the line of Kappa vessels. "We will start the bombardment shortly. Ready the guns."

With the ships ready to fire and 600 troops loaded in the landing boats, the invasion of Sigma was imminent.

54
The End is Nigh

The invasion of Sigma had begun, 600 heavily armed Kappa troops had landed on the beach and the cannons of the Kappa navy had begun bombarding the area adjacent to the beach; any Sigma troops guarding against a beach landing would be obliterated. Hades' highest commanders had landed with the troops, whether Hades saw it as punishment for the many mistakes made during the invasion of Omega or he just wanted to make them earn their way in the Kappa forces; the six highest ranking captains who advised Hades were on the beaches, armed and at the forefront of the Kappa forces. The first smatterings of resistance were beginning, Sigma armed forces moved to engage the Kappa troops and prevent them leaving the beaches. The guns onboard the Kappa fleet were firing volley after volley towards the edges of the beach; the Sigma troops were being killed in their masses, explosion after explosion hit their positions, destroying all that stood against Kappa.

Onboard ship, Hades ordered the guns to cease. He wanted to ensure they were ready if the Central tank battalions engaged his troops; this is what his commanders had predicted, so Hades wanted to ensure they were ready and able. On the beach the easing of the cannon fire had allowed what was left of the Sigma forces to regroup and attack the Kappas on the beach. It was a blood bath, true ground war, like meat through the proverbial grinder. Soldiers being torn apart by heavy machine gunfire. The Sigmas took a few Kappas with them, but it was a significant loss. Kappa was gaining a foot hold on Sigma soil.

Towards the town of Mina, Central tank battalions were rolling through the countryside. They had been tasked with reaching the Sigma shore to push back the invading force. The battalion was light of resources, they had heavily shelled Akbar and several of the group had been destroyed by Sigma soldiers at the battle north of the capital, but the tanks roared on towards the shore regardless. Past Mina and on towards Cyrus the tanks moved, three of their number were ordered to peel off and defend the motor rail in the town; if the invading forces took the motor rail it would allow quick access to Mina and beyond to Akbar.

On the beach the Kappas were making small advances but taking losses as they moved. The remaining Sigma forces had retreated to the edge of the sand and continued to try and prevent the Kappas moving forward. Reserve Sigma troops had arrived; they took up positions to cover their fellow Sigmas and provided quite the pushback against the Kappa force. A division of the Kappa troops tried to flank the Sigma reserves, but were pushed back by the sheer numbers that Sigma had sent into the fight. Kappa had suffered losses but still had the larger numbers and better arms. Hades watched on from the bridge of Kappa ship number three. He took pleasure in the very sight of bloodshed, and was enjoying the battle for the beach, especially as his force had the upper hand despite some losses. Losses were nothing to Hades, the soldiers on the beach were lower than insignificant. Kappa ship seven had now been re-crewed and moved away from the shore, Hades had ordered the ship along with ship six to sail back across the sea to Kappa, fill up with troops and arms and return to Sigma. Hades ordered that every inch of each ship be loaded with troops – he wanted more troops, needed more troops to ensure success in Sigma. Ships seven and six would be ferrying back and forth all day and night; within a few hours there would be hundreds more Kappa soldiers on the beaches of Sigma.

The Sigma forces on the beach were sustaining heavy losses but were holding the line; Kappa had advanced up the beach but were being held there; however, if significantly more troops were to land, the Sigma armed force would be overwhelmed. The recent war with Central had reduced the Sigma force and affected supply lines to the troops stationed along the shore. It was beginning to have an effect on the Sigma force's ability to hold their position, ammunition was running low, and so another significant surge from Kappa would break the line and allow the Kappa armies into Sigma.

Seventeen Central tanks were approaching the shore, loaded and ready to fire.

"Battalion command, battalion command. Approaching target orders please?" the tank commander communicated over his short-wave radio.

"Support Sigma shore defence, kill Kappa, kill Kappa!" was returned over the radio.

The tanks were readying to comply with their orders when the sky turned dark. Shell after shell filled the sky, the vast number almost blocked the sun. The shells began to hit hard, pounding the ground around the tanks, filling the air with dirt and shrapnel.

"Abort, abort!" the tank commander screeched over the radio. The tanks started to reverse course, but several were caught by the shells. Tank 11 was hit directly and quite literally turned inside out by the force of the explosion, several others were disabled by shrapnel and one toppled into a bomb creator. Only six tanks managed to pull back, and out of range of the massive Kappa ship cannons.

Onboard his flagship, General Hades was looking very smug; the Central tank battalions were all but destroyed and he could see ships six and seven returning from Kappa; the decks were teeming with soldiers readying themselves to land in Sigma. Hades ordered all of his fleet to send their landing craft to the troop ships; he wanted every soldier on the beach supporting the invasion. As the crafts sailed inward towards the beaches, the Sigma soldiers knew that in moments the Kappa force would be doubled in size and it was inevitable they would be defeated; but they still held firm. The soldiers fought and fought until their very last round was fired.

55
Red Sand

T he brutality of war was plain to see on the beaches of Sigma, the sand was red with the blood of Sigma and Kappa, men and women alike. Sigma's force had been completely decimated; not a single soldier was left alive. The Kappa army had lost many of their force, but reinforcements were arriving regularly from across the sea. Hades had taken a craft onto the beach to proudly stand and soak in his victory; 400 of his men were dead but for Hades that was merely a feature of war, the victory was everything. With the reinforcements arriving, the next step to the invasion would be to take the town of Cyrus and set-up a base from which to push troops further into Sigma. Hades had been informed by his spy network that ex-Kappa captain Marcus and his team were in the capital Akbar and he was determined to get there quickly and finally put an end to the traitor who was responsible for his son's death.

Outside of Cyrus the remaining Central tanks had gathered to protect the motor rail which would allow Kappa access to significant areas of Sigma, including the capital city. The nine remaining tanks were beat-up and battered but serviceable and ready to fight.

"Tank commander, come back, over" a voice read over the short-wave.

"Tank commander responding, over."

"With all haste pull back to border, repeat; with all haste return to Central border, over."

"Understood, pulling back to Central border. Will await further on return, over."

The tanks pulled away from Cyrus leaving it unprotected from the Kappa force being reinforced on the beach. As the tanks roared away, the people of Cyrus were scared – they had heard stories of the sheer size of the Kappa armies and were all desperate to leave. All the citizens began gathering at the motor rail; the people desperate to escape the oncoming invading force. Fighting had broken out at the platform for the motor rail, the men and women of Cyrus were scrambling over each other for the last few spaces on the transport leaving for Akbar. This would be the last transport leaving the town before the Kappa armies arrived.

The people unable to find a space on the motor rail were beginning to walk away from town, carrying limited personal possessions they were abandoning their homes to avoid the Kappa forces. The justice in Cyrus had gathered his guards and instructed them to destroy the remaining motor rail before leaving town. The justice then took his space on the motor rail as it left. Unbeknown to the justice, the guards were unhappy being left behind in the town, so they abandoned their duties and forced their way on the final motor rail carriage, violently removing a family and taking their space. The final motor rail was left untouched and sat waiting for Kappa to utilise. With the Kappa armies now reinforced, a vast group, numbering three battalions, were moving towards Cyrus. The commanders were expecting a fight, but as the troops arrived on the edge of the town there was no fight; the area had become a ghost town. The battalions were able to move through the town unimpeded, through to the motor rail without an issue. The Kappa machinists immediately began working on the motor, and with a little tinkering the motor sprang to life. The soldiers were busily preparing the carriages to transport 900 troops; mounting metal plates on the sides of each carriage for a little protection, and cutting holes for gun placements. By the time the motor rail pulled out of Cyrus, it was prepared for an almighty fight.

The transport had travelled as far as Mina. As the motor rail pulled into the platform, a smattering of Sigma soldiers had taken defensive placements. The firefight began and ended in only a few minutes, the heavy armaments of the Kappa forces were too much – with ten times the troops, the Sigmas wouldn't have stood a chance. With Cyrus and Mina now behind them it was a straight shot to the Sigma capital. Kappa commanders were meeting to decide upon their tactics, but Hades wasn't interested; he wanted all his troops on the streets of the capital hunting for Marcus and his team.

"Every troop will be deployed in the city. The first priority is to find the traitors, kill as many Sigmas as you must, but find the scum," Hades roared at his commanders.

Sigma citizens were streaming from the towns along the motor rail track; as news spread of the Kappa advance the people were panicked into fleeing en masse. In Akbar the battle with Central had left the people trapped – most of the routes out of the capital were blocked and the excess volume of people left the open routes jammed and un-passable. People were crammed in the streets with only a modicum of justice guards attempting to organise and control the population as they fled; this was an impossible task. The streets were like a smorgasbord waiting for Kappa to feast. Crowds were pushing and shoving as they were funnelled into smaller and smaller streets on the outer edges of Akbar. Children were being separated from families; others trampled as the herd desperately tried to escape. Screams and cries filled the air as the merciless reputation of Kappa was driving the Sigma society to act like animals. Order had now crumbled, but a small Sigma force guarded the motor rail platform awaiting the inevitable; soldiers were deserting, leaving only the bravest few to fight. Towards the east of the city, Marcus and his team persevered in trying to escape the narrow complex of streets, the cries of the people filled the air; they now knew Kappa were coming.

56
There is fighting in the Capital

In Akbar the motor rail was arriving, heavy armaments were firing at will. Thousands and thousands of rounds tearing up the city, the people and all that stood in the way. As the transport came to a complete stop, 900 Kappa troops disembarked the carriages and immediately spread out. They had one mission priority: to find Marcus and the Omega team. Whatever the cost and consequences, Hades wanted Marcus, he wanted to rip him limb from limb, punish him for his treachery and the death of his son. The Kappa troops had peeled off into smaller brigades to begin their search. From the information provided by Hades' spies, the vast majority of Kappa troops began the search towards the eastern parts of the city. The remaining soldiers pushed outwards in all directions, forcing the Sigma citizens to flee.

In the west of Akbar fighting had broken out; Kappa soldiers had fired upon a retreating group of the Sigma armed force. The native team had held their ground well and were fighting bravely. With all the troops in the east searching for Marcus's team, no Kappa reinforcements were joining the brigade, which allowed the Sigmas to gain the upper hand. The armed force was dug in well and had the better cover as the fight waged on. In the north the Kappa troops were approaching the local people trying to flee; there were no armed force among them, but the Kappas fired regardless. Sigmas were falling like the leaves in autumn, people were trying to hide and find cover; there were too many people and not enough spaces to disappear into. Kappa were staying true to their reputation and mercilessly killing the ordinary folk of Sigma.

Battling in the east, the Sigma force had driven the Kappas back and into an open courtyard where they were being easily picked off. This was the first win for Sigma in a truly one-sided war but was little consolation for the people of Sigma and their decimated armed force. In the east of the city, twenty-plus brigades were scouring the streets for Marcus and the team. Marcus and his team had been stuck in the cramped narrow maze of streets and unable to leave the city. The team had hunkered down in an old shop; they had been walking the streets, trying to escape the city for hours. The team would cross three streets and find an un-passable route, be turned around and trek four streets back to find another path, and then repeat. Marcus and the Omegas were tired and frustrated.

"We know Kappa are out there, we need to get the fuck out of here," Blank stated.

"I think we are all aware of that, Blank," Erik gruffly responded. "If you aren't helping, shut the fuck up."

Things were getting tense and Marcus stepped in to calm things. "Alright, enough," Marcus stated authoritatively. "We have got this far by being a team, and we will continue to fight on as a team; stop the damn complaining. The first thought in your head should be team, understood?"

The room nodded in acceptance and to a man got to their feet, ready to move out again and start the search for a route out of the city and towards Central.

Marcus was leading his team down yet another street and it was looking good – the street had begun to widen and there was no obvious smoke or fire to the front. Marcus pushed his team on, the street was clearing and excitement was rising for a moment.

"Kappas, Kappas behind us," Erik shouted from the rear of the group.

"Push on, Freyja, take the team forward. Erik, Blank with me," Marcus ordered.

Marcus, Erik and Blank took defensive positions as Freyja led the others forward and out of the city. She was able to lead them clear of the city and into cover provided by an old derelict stone building. Back in the narrow streets the fighting had begun, Kappa were pressing on Marcus's position but Marcus was taking advantage of his Kappa knowledge. He guessed that Hades would be desperate to take him and the team alive, to personally dole out punishment. This allowed Marcus to stay a step ahead of the Kappa troops — knowing you're unlikely to be killed in a battle changes the rules of war. The team were holding their own, fighting back every Kappa advance and killing many men in the process, but brigade after brigade kept pushing forward in an attempt to take Marcus and his men alive. It was decision time as the enemy would not stop until Marcus had been captured.

"You have to get out of here," Marcus ordered.

"No way, boss" was Erik's response as he shot another Kappa approaching his position.

"Follow the damn orders, go now!" Marcus sternly shouted as he stood and left his cover. Blank grabbed Erik by the arm and dragged him away and out of the city. The Kappa troops advanced as Marcus held his hands high and surrendered. A few Kappas landed cheap shots on Marcus as they took him into custody, laughing as they spoke aloud about what Hades would do to Marcus when he got hold of him.

57

Face to face
with the devil

Marcus was being led through the streets of Sigma, his hands were shackled and he was being guarded by a whole brigade of troops, ensuring he would meet the General for face to face punishment.

"You know he would kill you without a second thought," Marcus thought out-loud. "He would kill you all to win a war, or to get whatever it is he wants."

"Keep quiet," a guard responded sternly.

"What would happen to you if I escaped? Hades would slaughter you all without even thinking."

"I said keep quiet," the guard repeated.

"Do you not think your men would want to know how insignificant their lives are? How the slightest mistake will lead to their death, and not a glorious death in battle; but a pathetic death at the hands of a psychopath."

"If you don't shut up…" the guard started.

"You'll do what? Kill me?" Marcus knew that was never going to happen.

Murmuring had begun in the brigade; the men were getting anxious, so Marcus continued to twist the psychological knife. "You there," Marcus said pointing at one of the grunts. "Do you know who I am? Or why Hades invaded a country to find me? Or you, do you know?" Marcus continued pointing to another Kappa soldier.

"You killed the General's son," a grunt replied.

Marcus smirked; he was almost laughing. "Is that what you all think? My team are trying to stop Hades from killing every man, woman and child on this world. That is why he is trying to stop me, that is why he sent hundreds of your fellow troops to their deaths to enable this invasion."

"Bullshit, you're a fucking traitorous liar," the lead guard responded angrily.

"You sure? Willing to bet your life on it?"

The murmurs had now grown to outright open discussion in the ranks.

"Are we sure he is lying?" a grunt asked.

"Of course he is lying, General Hades does everything for the betterment of Kappa; we are Kappa," the brigade sergeant replied.

"You think he cares about any of us?" another grunt asked. "We are just hammers that are sent to hit things."

There was now outright dissent within the brigade. "Have you radioed it in yet? Does Command know we have him?" yet another Kappa soldier cried out.

"We are not letting him go, and the next man who opens their trap will feel the blade of my knife," the sergeant shouted.

The discussion ceased but the murmuring continued. Marcus still saw an out, he had not seen or heard the brigade sergeant radio in his capture – if he was sure about handing him over to Hades he would have radioed it in by now.

"Sergeant, Hades will kill you. You are now living the last few minutes of your miserable life. Do you think it stops with me? He will punish you for allowing my team to escape." Marcus was now in full flow. "You all think this is simply about one damn Kappa captain? However crazy you are, you don't invade a country for one man. How many of your fellow Kappas have been killed this far? Two hundred? Three hundred? More? All that for one man who killed one of Hades' sixty-something children? This is hero time, you grunts have a chance to help save what is left of this world. Now own that choice, hand me over and the world ceases to be. Don't hand me over and be the fucking heroes in this story."

That was it; the men of the brigade had decided: they were letting Marcus go.

The men of the Kappa Brigade had killed their sergeant and released Marcus from his shackles. "You men need to make this message spread. The people deserve to know that you are being led to destruction for who knows what. But it is not about one Kappa captain, it is much bigger. Make sure you are all on the right side of this story."

The men in the brigade acknowledged the information Marcus had given them. Marcus set off back towards the edge of the city and the brigade returned to the Kappa operating base. They told the story of the sergeant allowing Marcus to escape, so they executed him and returned to obtain further orders.

Outside of the city Marcus was searching for his team. He was living a charmed life – that was now twice he had gone toe to toe with Kappa brigades and made it out unscathed. He was grateful to just be alive at this point, but knew there was still a long way to go; first he needed his team. Marcus continued to wander along the path he believed the team had taken, but for mile after mile there was no sign of the team. He had passed the old stone building where he believed the team were hiding, but nothing, nobody was there. He continued and found very few spaces where the team could be hiding. With each step Marcus was becoming more concerned – he trusted Freyja and Erik to lead the team, but where were they? Had they been captured? If so by whom?

The path Marcus was travelling had been well trodden; he was no expert tracker, but he knew a group had been along the path recently, so he pressed on hoping that group to be his team. Marcus was jogging along the path and as he climbed over a small ridge he noticed a group travelling slowly to his front. It looked like a team of the Sigma armed force, who were fleeing from the fighting in Akbar. If that was the group he had been tracking then where was his team? Marcus was dressed as Sigma still, so approached the team with his hands away from his weapon.

"I am Sigma," Marcus shouted. "I am looking for some friends, I was separated from them in Akbar as I fought the Kappa forces."

"We noticed a Central force retreating towards the border; it looked like they had some Sigmas with them," a man yelled back at Marcus.

"And you didn't help them?" Marcus asked. "Are you not supposed to defend the people of Sigma?"

"We barely escaped Akbar, we aren't in a position to fight. Undermanned and under armed."

Marcus was frustrated, but he was one man and was not prepared to create tension with the Sigma team, so he thanked the group for the information and moved off. Marcus would be going alone for the rest of the journey to Central; he just hoped his team were alright and that he could find them.

58
The people of Central

The Omega team were on the back of a cart being pulled by an animal towards the central border. They had been forced to surrender to a large central brigade that had been retreating towards their border with Sigma. The large number of forces would have been impossible to engage, so the team took the path of least resistance and submitted. They had been cared for reasonably well and it was nice not having to walk. Most of the chatter was about the fate that Marcus had undoubtably met, but Erik was doing what he could to gather intelligence from the Central soldiers, learn all he could about Central and especially the Central city.

"Can I please ask where you are taking us?" Erik politely asked the cart driver.

"To the border, we have bigger things to worry about than you and your people."

"What's at the border? Why there?"

"We have all been ordered back there; every citizen will be required to defend against the invading forces."

"Every citizen? Surely, you mean every soldier?"

"Every citizen of Central is required to defend the capital. Every child has been trained for this day. Everyone benefits, so everyone fights."

"Thousands against a few hundred Kappas sounds like good odds?"

"Thousands? Sorry but I've said enough, if you know what is good for you, keep quiet and stop all the questions."

As they continued to travel through the eastern parts of Sigma, Erik was intrigued by the comment from the Central soldier. Why did the man scoff at the notion of thousands of citizens fighting? Acting a little more cautious, Erik continued to ask questions, and although the guard suggested he wouldn't answer, the truth was in there and Erik wanted to know. The convoy had stopped to rest the animals for a few moments, and the guard approached Erik.

"Do you know of the history of Central?" the guard asked.

"I do not, sir," Erik replied.

"Central city was once a gigantic palace for our gods, the people of Central were here to serve them and care for the city. There were never very many of us, just enough to serve. When the gods left us, the population of Central state numbered under one hundred."

"But that was a thousand years ago," Erik stated. "Surely over the centuries your population grew?"

"Many of the servants were old, and many were women. Yes, the population grew, but it never exceeded a few thousand. Then when Kappa began raiding and taking our citizens, we built the navy. Ten ships took most of our adult aged males away from home and the armed force took the rest, and you cannot breed without men," the guard continued. "Now we have barely a thousand people in Central city."

"Then why invade Sigma? Why fight your allies when it takes all your men?"

"Our leaders heard of a weapon being made that would kill every impure on the planet. Our entire population is based on interbreeding, it is the only option when you have under one hundred souls. Our leaders asked Sigma to join them in invading Kappa, to make an attempt to destroy this weapon, and they just walked away; they believe in the Sigma purity so didn't care about the weapon. They turned on us and we fought back; they are weak and scared."

"Why are you treating us so well? If you hate Sigma?"

"You're not Sigma. You stand out like a sore thumb, I would bet you are Omega and your friends look like Deltas and he looks like a Kappa; but if he is with you I guess he's alright?"

Erik was amazed by the assessment of the Central guard and the information he had shared. Now he had struck up a conversation, he wanted to ask about the home of the gods. Even though currently in custody and without a Leader, the team were still planning on completing their quest and they needed to find where the gods went and where they hid all the knowledge.

"Where did the gods sit in the city? It must be truly magnificent?" Erik asked.

"It might have been once, but not in my lifetime. Most of the city is in ruins, the great tower fell after the gods left. The debris has shut off great swathes of the city for centuries, and that includes the gods' throne room and the library of the world."

"What happened to the tower? I heard it stood as tall as the sky, that it touched the heavens?"

"The stories tell us that the day it fell the gods left, that their magnificence held it up somehow."

"All that knowledge, all that history is hidden under loads of rubble?"

The guard continued to tell Erik of the history, he told of the attempts that had been made over the centuries to re-discover the library and find the knowledge. There was an unsubstantiated story from before the guard was born that one man made it through the sewers to the library, but the man disappeared and nobody ever found the same route again. All of the details were filling in some of the blanks in Erik's mind. It explained why the knowledge was gone. It now makes sense that without the books and history, states would make things up to fit with what they thought they knew. He was cheered by the thought that someone may have found the library; and if they found that, surely they could find the actual seat of the gods; the citadel where the Omega leader had foretold would provide the answers and stop the wars.

The animals had rested and the Central force were back on the move; Erik was in deep conversation with Aurora and Frode; he was relaying the information from the guard, trying to help fill in the gaps in Frode's knowledge and what he had managed to decipher from the book. The group were approaching the Sigma-Central border; within minutes the team would be in their final state, now they had to escape their central captors and find the seats where the gods once sat.

59
The Book part II

Frode had been deciphering more of the book. He had managed a few hours of work over the previous days and had made some good realisations. With the information from Erik, those details were now adding to what was in the book and creating a bigger, more detailed picture. These items were clear; Testament was not a weapon, it was an offering, a reward from the gods, but the book told that it was only for those pure of heart. Frode assumed this actually meant pure of lineage. The book also told that the gods left because they were unhappy with the world, they left the people and society crumbled. Could this have been enough to start a thousand years of war? It also told of the states, and the purpose given to each, but that the people rebelled against their places in the world. Omegas wanted to be more than only farmers, Sigmas weren't happy only being workers, miners and builders. It was the same for all the states. Nothing in the sections of the book that Frode had deciphered was telling a story that would really explain what started the wars, and although the gods were said to be unhappy with the people, would that really make them desert everyone, and just up and leave? The book did clearly tell of a citadel that was the seat of the gods, that was in the very centre of the great city; under the tower that reached the sky. "I have found a reference to Keystone with the pages of the book," Frode told Aurora. "It was said to be a final solution to the ills of their world; created by the gods to fix the people. The book references an argument about whether it was right to create something that would cause such devastation."

"Anything else?" Aurora replied.

"Just that shortly after that argument, the gods left this world."

"Does it say which god was responsible for such a thing?"

"The book often mentions Chaos, the Kappa god and Galil, the Delta god. But it does not tell of who was responsible for Keystone or Testament. Might that be what we are looking for?"

Aurora had moved away from Frode; she had moved over to help Freyja who had been feeling unwell and vomiting that morning. Freyja wasn't concerned, but the group were worried for their friend. The team were unaware of her relationship with Marcus and she believed it was his loss that made her sick. She was truly feeling sick to her stomach regarding the loss of her lover. Another of Frode's discoveries was that the book was one volume of many, and that it had referenced being from the library of the world. The historian had realised that maybe the story the guard told Erik could indeed be true. Possibly the man who found the library had used the sewer system to escape the city and found his way to Omega with a book, this book, but if that was true then surely there would be a map or a reference within the pages that could guide the team to the library, and on to the citadel? Frode was scouring the book, taking any moment of any day to decipher the first words on each page, hoping to find a clue for the entrance that the explorer must have found.

The Central troops had arrived at the border between the states; they unloaded the Omega team from the cart and moved them to a small guard house positioned at the end of a large old brick wall that marked the end of Sigma and the beginning of Central. Freyja and Inga were put together in a room, whilst the other team members were all separated in locked rooms. The Central border commander wanted to know the truth before deciding the fate of the group. He wanted to speak first with the group leader, and Freyja took responsibility in the absence of Marcus.

"I do not wish to harm any of your team, but I must know what your purpose here is?" the commander asked.

Freyja was unsure if the whole truth was the best approach – she knew that the Central forces weren't buying their cover story; but the truth was a little far fetched to be totally believable. "We are refugees from all over the world. We have amongst us Omega, Delta and Kappa. Before our Omega leaders were slaughtered by the Kappa armies of General Hades, we were tasked to find help for our cause; help stop Hades and his merciless killers."

"You think we are in a position to help?"

"Sir, if you would please excuse my ignorance. I am just a farm hand from Omega thrust into a war I wanted no part of. We have travelled from the Omega capital Khristade, through Omega and Kappa; across the eastern sea and through Sigma. We have lost many friends along the way, and rid the world of many evil Kappas in the process. The mission we started, ended some hundreds of miles ago when we realised Kappa were too strong and determined to destroy this world. If we could ask for shelter from your good selves, in return my team and I would fight next to you, stand with you when Kappa arrive and the end comes."

The commander uncomfortably shuffled in his chair. "I will take this to my leaders," he stated as he stood and left the room.

The commander next spoke with Erik to try and ascertain the true reason for their mission, but Erik only asked for shelter in return for fighting with Central when the inevitable Kappa invasions came. It was the same story throughout the team, until the Commander sat down with Frode. "You carry that book like it is the most precious object in the world?" the commander asked. "May I take a look?"

Frode was hesitant but what choice did he have? Unlike his team, Frode wasn't quick to fabricate a story and what excuse could he have for not showing the commander his book? "Please be careful, it is very old," Frode stammered. "I am, well was an Omega historian,

I rescued this book when Khristade, when our capital fell to the Kappa soldiers. It is all that is left from our historical artefacts. It is very important to me."

"You have done well to keep it safe throughout your journey," the commander replied. "What language is this?" he asked as he wrenched the book open to a random page.

"I have always assumed it is the language of our gods."

"You can read this garbage?"

"I have been able to translate a few small sections. There is nothing of great interest so far, but I remain hopeful that one day it might tell us of our history."

The commander kept flicking through without much care. "And this language, what is this?"

Frode was taken a little by surprise, their commander unknowingly had found a small section of writing hidden in plain sight; Frode must have looked at that page ten times, but never seen the variation in the text. "It is ancient Omega language," Frode told the commander.

"What does it say?"

"Sorry but I would need to study it, translate it. I am not fluent in our ancient written text."

Frode was lying – with only a small glance he was already starting to decipher the text in his head. It was exactly what he had been looking for. A text map to the library of the world.

Frode tried his best to not outwardly show his joy, he knew the team were so close to the end. The commander had become bored with Frode, and left the room.

A Central Guard approached him. "Sir, we have caught a Kappa spy. He handed himself in to one of our roving patrols."

"Take me to this man," the commander ordered.

The guard showed the commander to a small dark room where the Kappa spy was being held. The commander approached the spy.

"Kappa spy, state your business?"

"I am no Kappa spy. My name is Captain Marcus, I believe you are holding my team?"

"You sure look Kappa."

"My team? Are they alright?"

"They are just fine for now," the commander stated menacingly.

"Please don't threaten my team, sir. They mean you, nor Central, any harm. We would very much like to be freed to go about our mission."

"The pretty young girl said your mission was over?"

"Yes, sir, our original mission has ended; this is a new mission. To find a peaceful corner of the world and live as much as we can before the inevitable end," Marcus was now making it up, but hoping Freyja had a similar idea.

"Your men said they would fight with us?"

"That is their choice, if that is what they decide then my team are free to do so."

The Commander was reticent with Marcus, he was not sure he was being completely truthful. "I will be making a decision regarding your fate and that of you team, you will be appraised of that decision by morning."

The commander left the guard house and proceeded to Central city where he relayed the information about the Omega team to his superiors. It was them that would be deciding the fate of Marcus and the Omega team.

60
Border crossing

Captain Marcus had released himself from his rope shackles that he was placed in when he surrendered to the Central armed force, now all he had to do was figure a way out of the room that was holding him. Several options passed through his mind; but there was one overriding thought: the team needs to take any decision about their fate out of the hands of Central. They need to escape their captivity and make their way to the city, where they can hide and re-group. Marcus began making a fuss, screaming and shouting to attract the guards, he lay on the floor in a ball, he acted like he was in pain. "Someone please help me!" he cried.

The door unlocked and two guards entered the room. "What is up with you?"

"I have a bomb in me," Marcus shouted. "Those damn Kappa fools captured me and cut me open. Get me out of here quick, unless you all want to die!"

In the guards' rush to take Marcus outside and away from the guard house, they neglected to either shackle him or blindfold him. As Marcus was dragged along the corridor he was mapping out the internals of the guard station. Every detail and room and its position was being mapped into Marcus's brain. He waited until the guards had taken him to the building exit before making his move, he elbowed one guard with extreme force in the temple, knocking him out cold and likely cracking his skull. Marcus quickly reached down and took the sidearm of the stricken guard and before the other Central soldier had a chance to draw a weapon Marcus had the pistol pressed against his head.

"Lock the entrance please," Marcus ordered to the guard, who unsurprisingly did as he was asked. "Is there a back entrance?"

"There is a door into a secure yard at the back, and a gate out of the yard," the guard stuttered.

"Please get in the room," Marcus ordered as he gently shoved the guard into an open room, taking his keys and locking the door.

Marcus proceeded to the first locked door, and knocked. "It is me," he stated before he unlocked the door.

Erik was stood ready to leave. "How many lives you got, boss?" Erik asked cheekily.

Marcus just smiled, before going to the next door. "It's me and Erik," he said before again unlocking the door.

Marcus was greeted by his girls; within a moment Freyja was wrapped around his neck and Inga around his legs. Freyja kissed and kissed Marcus. "I was convinced Hades got his hands on you," she said between the kisses. "I've got some news for you," she whispered before finally releasing Marcus from her hug.

They continued to release the entire team from their cells. Reunited again, they headed to the yard at the back of the guard house, gathering their belongings and weapons on the way out the door.

In the yard there was a single gate that would take the team into Central state. The gate was guarded but only by a handful of Central soldiers. Marcus didn't want to harm them if at all possible.

"To the Central men outside the gate, we are not here to hurt you or your state. Please put down weapons and let us pass. We do not want to fight you, but will if we must," Marcus shouted through the gate.

There was no verbal response from outside the gate, so Marcus gave Erik a boost to the top of the wall. He was lucky to not have his head blown off – the guards on the outside were not laying down their arms. Marcus dropped Erik back to the floor quickly.

"I guess we are going to have to fight," Erik stated whilst making sure his head was still firmly attached to his shoulders.

"One more try," Marcus suggested. "Men of the Central armed force; I am a Kappa Captain, commander of the notorious brigade 66 Kappa secret police. If you are not sure what that means? It means you will all be dead in moments if you insist on fighting my men and me. I implore you, please put down your guns and let us pass. Don't make me kill you today."

On this occasion there was obvious murmurs from the other side of the gate. "You can pass," a voice shouted.

"Stay alert and keep your eyes peeled, I will go first. Blank, bring up the rear," Marcus commanded quickly.

The team slowly opened the gate, and it did appear as though all the central soldiers had dropped their weapons to the ground. The team slowly moved out past the guards and into Central state. Blank was the last man who passed the guards; there was lots of twitching and nerves, but he passed without incident.

The team dived off into the Central country, escaping view within just a few moments.

"We have made it to Central; we have made it to Central!" Erik stated. "Where now?"

"I know where," Frode said with a big smile. "The Central commander unwittingly showed me the way."

"Which way do we head?" Marcus asked.

"There is a sewer entry approximately 400 metres outside the city walls to the south-west of the city, and from there I have all the directions right here in the book."

"Lead the way, old man," Marcus ordered as Frode led the team on the final leg of the long journey.

61

A Nation Surrenders

T he dead and wounded were lying all about the streets of Akbar,
the Kappa war machine had relentlessly driven through the
city and murdered anyone they deemed unfit. The Kappa soldiers
had torn through the capital under the orders from Hades, in a vain
attempt to capture Marcus and the Omega team. When Kappa had
taken Delta many years before it was much the same: you didn't
need to be a threat, to be a target. All it took to be a target was
to be alive and not be Kappa. Sigma never thought they could be
invaded – Kappa had no ability to cross the sea and the great Central
navy was waiting for anyone who attempted to cross. They never
prepared for this day, but the day had come and in less than 40 hours
the state had lost all of its armed force; they had either been killed
or deserted. Their society had crumbled, with very few standing
against the onslaught, the people of Sigma state had no fight. The
state leaders were in hiding, although they were across the sea and
two states away from Omega, stories in this world spread fast. The
leaders had heard of the end afforded to their Omega counterparts
and weren't going out the same way.

The city square was busy with activity; Hades was prowling
around, barking orders to his men. He was keen to find someone who
he might take out his frustrations on. His men had not been able to
capture Marcus and the Omega team and Hades' temper was fit to
burst. With Sigma taken, Hades was looking to turn his attentions to
their neighbours in Central. With the vast spy network that Hades
maintained within the eastern states, he was confident that Central

would be a walkover. The General ordered two battalions to move out from Sigma and approach the Central border; his orders were to start peppering the Central border with arms fire and rockets, weaken the enemy before a full scale assault. In a secure Sigma bunker the four surviving state leaders were barricaded in.

"We can't stay in here forever," Councilman Azad stated.

"If we go out there we're all dead – did you not hear what they did to those poor folk in Omega?" Councilwomen Esther responded.

"Yes I heard, but better to die quickly at the hands of that madman than slowly starve to death in here; and what about our people? They are dying whilst we cower in this bunker."

Councilman Azad moved towards the door and starting moving the furniture that had been piled up against it.

"What are you doing?" the councilwomen screamed.

"I'm going outside to surrender; at least try to save some of our people," Azad responded sternly.

He continued to move the barricade, unlocked the door and walked out of the bunker, hands raised and head slightly bowed. He was immediately confronted by a horde of Kappa soldiers.

"I, I wish to surrender the state to your General," Councilman Azad stammered.

The soldiers dragged him and the three other leaders away from the bunker and took them to Hades.

"Sir, we wish to surrender our state. Please stop killing our people, they have all laid down their arms and pose no threat to you, or your men. We will do as ordered and submit to your will" Azad stated with his head bowed.

"You think your pathetic words mean anything to me?" Hades responded.

"Sir, I merely wish to save my people. Please show us some mercy."

Hades' eyes began to twinkle, a sinister idea started to play out in his mind. He would test the resolve of the Sigma council. "Your people can live; but we live in a world where everything has a cost."

"Please sir, I will pay the cost needed to secure the safety of my people."

"Kill your fellow council members. Their death is payment for your people."

Councilman Azad began to weep – he was prepared to sacrifice himself but not have to kill. A million thoughts went through his head in a flash. Hades held out a sidearm and flicked off the safety. A group of soldiers forced the three other Sigma leaders to their knees. There were screams and prayers from the three as Azad took the gun from Hades.

"Please, sir, just take my life," Azad pleaded.

Hades stood firm. "Kill them now or my men will kill you, and all of your people."

Azad turned; he silently said sorry to his friends and through the tears now streaming down his face, he pulled the trigger three times. Each shoot hit where intended, two instant kills and as the third lay dying, Hades insisted that Azad finish her. Azad closed his eyes and again pulled the trigger.

With his friends now dead, Azad turned the gun on himself, but before he had the opportunity to pull the trigger, Hades snatched the gun from his hand. "You aren't getting off that lightly. You have to live with what you've done. If anything unnatural happens to you, your people die. If you go against my word, your people die. If you so much as speak in a way I deem unfit–" Hades paused for dramatic effect. "Your people will die!"

Councilman Azad was extremely distressed – he had saved his people, but committed a heinous crime that would stay with him forever, however long or short that may be.

General Hades stood on the top step of the council chambers in Sigma and spoke. His voice boomed out and could be heard for several blocks. "I am General Hades, the most exulted leader of Kappa and your new commander," he bellowed. "Sigma no longer exists, your freedom no longer exists. Comply or you will die. Kappa now rules this land and you will all bow down, or you will suffer."

Hades stepped down from the steps and ordered his commanders to begin processing the people. All men shall be moved to the workers camps and women and children be put to work in the Sigma factories. Food and medical rationing will begin with immediate effect and quotas will be set. Hades proceeded to a car – he was heading to the central border; he was now within a single state of taking the whole world. He would be able to control everything and everyone, remake the world in the image of Chaos, and allow his god to return. If Keystone will not work, then if Hades controls everything he will be able to test for generic purity and cull anyone who fails.

62
The Temple Attack

Bjorn had gathered some friends in the farm where he had met the Delta Scientist, Batu. The group was small but all were keen to hear what Bjorn had to say – he had promised them news that may begin the destruction of Kappa. Everyone was intrigued by what he promised to tell them.

"My friends, it is so good to see you all," Bjorn began. "It is time to begin the end of this brutal Kappa regime. I would like you all to join me on a quest to destroy what means most to General Hades, drive the first stake through the heart of Kappa." He paused for a moment before continuing with more details of his idea. "I have come to understand that Hades worships four priests of Chaos, they are hidden in the Delta temple that sits on our land's border. It is heavily guarded, but if we can strike hard, I truly believe we will be able to take the temple and rid the world of the Chaos-worshipping, death-loving monsters that inhabit it; it will strike a significant blow for all the men of this world."

There was lots of chattering in the group and most not kind to Bjorn's idea.

"I will stand with you, Father" Anders stated over the noise of all the chattering.

"I too will stand with you," Lars, another of Bjorn's sons, stated passionately.

With his sons agreeing to stand with Bjorn, others in the room also stood. Florian stood, along with his boy Ari; they were both farmers before the invasion, but would serve. Brandt stood, along with his three brothers. They were all farm hands and had served as reserves in the Omega defence force. Calder stood – he was a machinist who had lost his wife and daughter at the hands of a Kappa brigade. Annika stood – she was a wife and mother before the war, but now due to Kappa she was neither. Her husband and two sons had died when the Khristade defence wall fell. Agnatha stood – she was a young woman who had just completed her defence force training prior to the Kappa invasion. As friends and kin continued to stand with Bjorn, his heart felt bigger and stronger.

"For centuries people will talk of this moment; it will be remembered as the time when man fought back against the monsters. When ordinary people stood up against their oppressors and pushed them back."

Bjorn had 24 men and women in total, to lead into battle and destroy the evil monsters that lurk in the shadows. The puppet masters who pull Hades' strings. Bjorn described his plans to the group – they were not strong enough for an all-out assault, so they would attack in the margins. Pick off guards in small numbers whilst maintaining cover and only when the guards were weakened would they launch a full offensive. The one advantage Omega had, being farmers and outdoorsmen, was their ability to hunt. Every man and woman in Bjorn's team was a crack shot, everyone could kill at several hundred metres. This was their advantage, and this is how they would succeed.

After Bjorn had finalised the planning, he named his eldest son Anders as his second. "If anything should happen to me, there is no man I have more faith in than my son Anders. He will lead you well, he will get the job done."

The journey from the farm to the Delta border was not long, maybe a day's strong hike. Staying to cover and not exposing themselves before time was important, and Batu offered to show them the route he followed from Delta. It was a quiet path and mostly stuck to forest areas where the team could remain concealed. The temple was perched atop a hillside, so the team would have to attack from the flanks; a frontal assault up a hill would put the team at a great disadvantage. Half the squad led by Anders would make their way round to the far side of the temple, whilst Bjorn's team would position themselves on the near side. With a fair wind and some good luck, the team should create an inescapable kill box from which to pick off the guards. The team set out just before dusk; with a 24-hour hike in front of them they should arrive at the temple just as darkness set in the following day. Spirts were high as they left. Bjorn was excited by the prospect of striking right at the heart of the Kappa war machine. He had seen so many of his friends and kin killed in the recent days and months, they had all lost so much, but now they finally had found a weakness in Kappa and could strike back with purpose.

Bjorn's team were in position just after dark the day after they had left the farm. The path Batu had shown the team was absent of any Kappa and the journey had been without incident. Bjorn's team were waiting for a signal from Anders that he was in position. They were benefiting from the temple being lit; they could make out several guards patrolling around the outside. Bjorn saw a small glint in the distance on the far side of the temple – this was the signal. Anders and his team were ready, it was time to strike. Both teams readied their rifles, each took a target.

"Fire on the count of three," Bjorn whispered to his team. "One, two, three."

Each of the team fired, and shortly after they saw the muzzle flashes from the other team. Kappa guards fell, they fired again. More Kappas fell.

"And again!" Bjorn shouted.

They all fired again and more Kappa guards fell. It was time; the team had the advantage and attacked.

Guns were fired in retaliation and two Omegas on Bjorn's team were killed, but they kept attacking. Three more were shot, but they did not stop. At the end of the battle nine brave Omegas had lost their lives, but all the Kappa guards were dead. Nobody was there to protect the priests. Bjorn took the remaining members of the group through the doors to the temple. They saw the opulence of the temple, the gold depictions and the crystal statues. They pressed on, until they found the room in which the priests were holed up. It was the room of knowledge, the depository for all the artefacts stolen from the states. Bjorn entered the room first. He quickly had to avoid a swinging sword blade thrust at him by one of the priests. Bjorn staggered back as Anders took aim and killed the first priest. A second came running towards the team with a spear, Bjorn steadied himself and hit his target centre mass, two quick shots to the priest's chest. His body fell in a heap, as blood ran from his corpse and pooled on the floor. The team had the final two priests cornered; they were begging for their lives.

"Please don't kill us, we have all the worlds' knowledge. We can serve you, like we have the General."

Bjorn wasn't interested in any bargains, he was seeking one thing: the death of Hades' priests. Bjorn turned his back as his team set about beating the remaining priests. They were old and weak so it did not take much of a beating to end their lives. The priests were dead, but that was not statement enough. Bjorn ordered his team to sever their heads and display them on pikes to the front of the temple.

"Let it be known that on this day we made the first strike against Kappa, against General Hades. I will ask you all, that when you leave this place, go far and go wide, spread the news of what has happened here. Tell the story of the day, when a group of Omega farmers severed the heads of General Hades' four headed beast."

Bjorn's team left the temple, but not for home. They each travelled a different path and with each person they met they told the story as Bjorn had asked. They told of the day when Omega farmers killed the beast of Kappa.

63
Central City

The Omega team led by Captain Marcus had reached the outer wall of Central city; the wall was broken and crumbled. The once great city was in ruins, rubble covered the streets and barely a building looked whole. The team had spread out looking for the sewer that was detailed in Frode's book, but the area surrounding the city had become very overgrown with long grass and thorns. The details in the book only gave a rough location, but it did allow the group to concentrate their search in a small area. It took some time but eventually the sewer entrance was found; the tunnel was very dark and had a truly repugnant smell. Frode was asked to lead into the sewer. Erik had fashioned two torches from wood and cloth and the light they created was enough to guide the way, and for the historian to read the instructions from the book. The sewer was narrow and uneven, which made progress slow. Turn after turn, Frode followed the instructions, the twists and turns coming thick and fast. It was becoming more complicated and difficult to move freely along the stinking sewers.

"It's no wonder nobody else found the correct route," Frode commented. "He must have spent years down here."

"Is it much fucking further?" Blank complained.

"It could be miles, it could be metres, there are no measurements in the instructions."

The smell and the dark were starting to affect some of the team. Freyja had to stop and vomit, and Inga was beginning to lag at the back.

"Let's all take a break," Marcus ordered as he approached Freyja, putting a hand on her shoulder.

"I'm alright," Freyja commented as she wiped the sides of her mouth with her shirt sleeve, before vomiting again.

"You sure?" Marcus asked, his concern obvious. "You were going to tell me something? When we were in the guard house."

"Not now. We should focus on the task at hand."

After resting for a short while, Marcus ordered his team to move out. The route was becoming more and more difficult. The tunnels had become partially blocked and it was quite a squeeze for the larger team members, especially Marcus being very tall and Frode who was a rather portly gentleman. As the team pressed on, step by step their goal was becoming closer, but the closer they got the tighter the tunnels became and the more complex the instructions.

"Who designed these bloody tunnels?" Erik moaned. "It's like a maze."

"I think that might be by design," Frode remarked. "Stop people using them to access the important parts of the city."

They had now been in the sewers for several hours, with no real idea of where they were, or how far they had to still travel to reach their target, and a small amount of dissent was beginning to set in. Inga was starting to complain.

"I'm tired," she grumbled.

Marcus picked up the young girl and carried her for a little while to allow her to rest, but it wasn't just Inga who was complaining. "How much further can it be?" Astrid complained.

"Sure we've gone the right fucking way?" Blank moaned.

"That's enough," Marcus barked, though even he was starting to become annoyed with the constant smell and darkness. "Frode, do you have any idea how much further?"

"There are only a few directions left, so I think we might be close. We need to go down here. Then this right and we should be there."

The team had arrived at what appeared to be a dead end.

"That surely can't be right?" the historian asked himself out-loud.

The instructions had ended but there was no visible exit, no door or obvious escape route. The team began searching the walls for a button or lever, something that might open a hatch or cover, but found nothing. Frode read the instructions again, but there was nothing that might be translated to guide them on the last step. The team were exhausted and frustration was starting to boil over.

"You fucking fool, you've led us to nowhere," Blank shouted.

"No, this is right. We followed the instructions exactly as they are written. This must be the correct place."

"We are going to die in this stinking, shit-filled tunnel."

"All of you stop!" Marcus shouted. "You must have missed something? Please check the instructions again," he continued in a much calmer tone.

Frode began reading through the text, making gestures as he thought about the route taken and how that mirrored the instructions. Everyone was watching him intently as he wagged his finger and moved left and right, remembering every twist and turn. Frode stopped moving; his facial expression changed, like he had solved the puzzle. He pushed past the rest of the team and back down the tunnel.

Moments later there was a loud clunking noise, and then a thud as the end of the tunnel began to move.

"It was right here in front of me," Frode shouted as he marched back past the team. "Right here in the written word, the clue was there all along," he continued as he pushed the through the opening that had appeared. The team followed Frode who had already begun to climb a long ladder at the end of the next compartment. "Our explorer friend worked it out and closed the door when he left," Frode yelled from the top of the ladder. "The doors form a directional valve system to prevent back-flow."

None of the team had the slightest clue what Frode was talking about, but they didn't care as they climbed the ladder that would lead them out of the sewers.

As the team emerged from the long climb up the ladder they were greeted by the most magnificent sight. The most enormous room filled with row after row of books, stacks of books from floor to ceiling.

"Welcome to the library of the world," Frode proudly proclaimed.

As the team stood in awe of their surroundings, Frode began to search the books, running up and down each stack. He was giddy like a child with a new toy.

"Look at all this knowledge. Everything you see is at least a thousand years old!" he yelled in an overly high-pitched voice. "Think of all the history that is contained in these volumes!"

Frode continued to look at all the books as the others rested. Most were too overwhelmed to speak; the library was a true wonder, a living remnant of the bygone days of a once great civilisation. There was now just one step left to conclude. Within the walls of this once great city is the seat of the gods, the citadel and with it the answers that the team had been searching for.

64
Hades' Rage

General Hades had spun into an uncontrollable rage at news of the demise of his priests. The unfortunate young messenger had taken the full brutal brunt of that rage – he was left on the floor bleeding out from the numerous bullet wounds Hades had inflicted upon him. Hades stormed down the corridors of the Sigma council chambers, looking for anyone whom he could punish, anyone fitting to receive his rage. Hades was still in a total meltdown as he reached the courtyard in the centre of Sigma. He screamed at a young soldier to find him a car and a driver. When the young man was unable to oblige, he put his mammoth hand around the young man's neck and simply squeezed the life from him. Hades yelled at another soldier, who fortunately was quickly able to locate a vehicle which whisked Hades away and back towards the Sigma shore. A Kappa ship was waiting at the shore ready to take Hades back to the shipyard from where he would journey on through Kappa and to the Delta temple.

The journey was long and throughout it Hades' temper did not improve; he was lost without the guidance of the priests. Although they had proven to be vile monsters who were responsible for countless atrocities, they did manage to partially keep a lid on Hades' unending rage. Now they were gone, who knows what Hades might be capable of? As his car approached the temple there were hundreds of Kappa soldiers around the perimeter, and then Hades saw what he had been dreading. The sight of the priests' heads, rotting in the sun, skewered to pikes. He stepped from his car and screamed for the duty commander, who duly ran forward, only to be treated to a bullet between his eyes.

"Where is the captain of the temple guards?" Hades bellowed. There was a slight pause. "No one brave enough to step forward and own the responsibility for this?"

"He is dead, sir," a voice muttered from a large group of soldiers.

"Then the commander, where is he?"

"All, all, also dead, sir," the voice stammered.

"Are they all dead?"

"Yes, sir, they were all killed in the attack."

Hades stormed towards the remains of the priests shouting out orders. "Get them down and burn the bodies. Has anyone entered the temple?"

No one had; the Kappas knew better. Hades marched up the steps and though the doors of the temple. He proceeded through the long hallways and to the knowledge room where the priests had been murdered. Hades didn't know what he was looking for, he didn't know why he had even come back to the temple; he only ever went to the temple for guidance from the now deceased servants of Chaos.

General Hades stomped around the room, hoping to get a message, a sign of what to do next, but nothing was forthcoming. There were no signs, only the voices swirling around in Hades' head. Then a moment of clarity, a moment of silence and in that moment, he knew what he had to do. There was a singular moment of calm in his head, just one second's peace and everything became clear. Hades strode from the temple with purpose, with a new confidence in himself. He marched over to a one of the remaining commanders.

"Have Captain Vesta rendezvous with me at the eastern shore shipyard, I need to speak with her as a matter of some urgency."

"Yes, sir, may I tell her what the matter at hand is?" the commander replied.

"Tell her to prepare for the final act. Now that is all, be quick."

Hades boarded his transport which immediately began the journey back towards the eastern shore.

When the General arrived at the shipyard, Captain Vesta was there to greet him.

"I came straight away, my general, I am concerned by the message that was relayed to me. The final act is not ready, sir, Keystone has not been perfected."

"You will prepare the best version you can, and we will begin the final act, and we will succeed in cleansing this world."

"Sir, I must protest. We risk killing everyone, even the purest of Kappas would be at risk."

"That is unfortunate, but we will purify this world for the return of Chaos. Don't worry yourself, Captain, you will be safe."

The general began walking towards the landing craft waiting to return him to his flagship, that would take him back to Sigma so he could lead the final assault on Central. "I am an impatient man, Captain, ensure the device is ready soon," Hades called back to Vesta.

"It will be at least six days, my general, maybe even as much as ten."

"You have five, and not a moment longer."

Hades bordered the landing craft and was ferried back to his flagship. Captain Vesta began her journey back to Omega and the science core convoy. In five days, the Kappa scientists would be responsible for the launch of Keystone and the end of the world.

65
The Battle for Central

Hades had returned to the Sigma capital Akbar; two battalions had been sent to pepper the Central border, but Hades was preparing his remaining troops to begin their assault. Hades would be throwing everything he had at Central. His plan was simple: lay waste to Central city and destroy any remnants of the Omega team that may have found their way there. Central had always stood as the pillar of society and the fight for its destruction would be the final battle before the world was cleansed. The Kappa army left a skeleton brigade in Akbar to maintain control, as the main force headed for the border. At the Sigma-Central border, the Kappa battalions had been launching rocket attacks at the Central force defending their land. The soldiers of Central were ordinary people, every remaining able-bodied citizen was stationed along the front line. Men, women and even children were armed and being asked to fight. The Central way was for all to be ready to fight; children are trained to fire weapons, women are trained to fire weapons, but none of them were soldiers. The rockets attacks had scared the life out of the Central people, many were hiding and some had already deserted. That left only a handful of fighters which would not hold back the Kappa onslaught.

The final Kappa battalion was approaching from Sigma at a pace. Rumbling towards Central with a true Kappa bloodlust, Hades had built his troops into a frenzy, ready to kill and ready to take the final state. The soldiers joined with the two battalions already at the border, and before the attack Hades addressed his troops.

"By the end of this day the mighty Kappa will rule this world. We will have completed what our history tells us we were destined for. The other races of the world will cower and grovel on their knees, subjugated as they always should have been, ruled by the hand of Kappa. The might of Kappa will once more be the predominant race, the master race. Now go forth and kill, go forth and take what is ours."

The Kappa soldiers were frothing with rage, ready to destroy the once great Central state and every person within it. The Kappa battalions attacked, swathes of soldiers pouring towards the border. Guns firing, rockets flying, all hell was breaking loose. The Central citizens fought back, and people were dropping on both sides. The smell of war filled the air, bodies littered the field of battle, but the Kappa onslaught didn't stop – for every two Kappas killed, three more attacked. Explosions were surrounding the few Central forces that were left, and the Kappa incursions continued. Unable to continue to defend the line, the Central commander ordered a retreat into the city.

"We will engage them in the streets. Everyone, pull back within the city walls."

The Central troops started to run from the front line. Some escaped back to the city, but others were not so fortunate. They were easy targets for Kappa snipers as they retreated.

The fighting continued in the streets of Central city as the Kappa rocket divisions prepared the final assault. They had hundreds of rockets that would be targeted on the very heart of the city, destroy anything that might remain of the old world, and finally destroy the Omega team. It was at that moment that the murmurs started. The grumbling within the Kappa ranks began slowly, but the rumours spread like a brush fire.

"Have you heard? He is going to kill us all."

"I heard the psycho is planning on killing everyone in this world."

"I was told that it is only days until everyone is dead."

The muttering grew, the troops slowed their attack. The rocket division began defusing the weapons. It had begun, news of Hades' plan for Keystone was sweeping through the ranks and the discontent was great. Division commanders were executing dissenters in ranks, troops were killing their officers. The fight against Central had stopped and it was now a civil war within the ranks of the Kappa armies. The commanders had been promised a place of safety when the final act was initiated, but the troops were hearing that they would all be killed. They would be killed to allow a god that none of them believed in to return to the world.

The Kappa grunts were mad and the inter-rank fighting had intensified. The Kappa commanders were surrounding the General.

"Sir, we must retreat. We must move you to safety."

"I will not let this be the end, we will finish this. We must!" Hades yelled.

But the commanders were adamant that Hades had to leave. Hades was angry, he was so close to world domination.

"Sir, you really must leave."

"I will not, I am taking this city. I will destroy it all," Hades raged.

It took ten commanders to physically remove Hades and load him on a transport.

"You must be able to initiate the final act."

Hades and the commanders were hastily retreating; they left the war zone and quickly headed back towards the eastern shore. Hades needed to return to Kappa, to the safety of his underground bunker; it was there he would launch Keystone and then all the dissenters, all the soldiers who were rising up against him, would be destroyed.

The fighting with Central had completely ceased, the Kappa battalions were hurriedly leaving the area, finding any means to rush back across Sigma and towards Kappa state; desperate to prevent Hades from killing them all. What remained of the citizens of Central were joyous, they knew nothing of what had turned the tide. They believed they had won the battle and were celebrating as if they had won the war. Little did they know that in a matter of days General Hades would be launching Keystone, firing the final shot of an endless thousand-year war. The fight with Sigma, and the battle with Kappa had left a permanent gaping wound in Central. The final count left the people of the state with little more than a few hundred citizens. The entire population could be counted in less than five minutes.

66
Keystone

News of Keystone was spreading throughout the world, Kappa soldiers stationed in every state were beginning to hear of Hades' grand plans. The final act was in play, the believers in the Kappa ranks were securing Keystone. Captain Vesta was relocating the science core to Kappa to ensure the safety of her research. The moment the murmuring started, Vesta moved the core element of the science division to Hades' bunker. It was there that the final build would be completed, and it was there that in a matter of days the end of the world would begin. A thousand years before, Chaos had become disillusioned with the world. The Kappa god wanted a world of purity, the people of each state were created for a purpose and the mixing and mingling of the gene pool began creating discontent and fighting. Chaos asked the gods to allow for the creation of Keystone; it would purify by removal. The weapon would kill any of the impure population, and for those that remained, Testament would be the reward. Those who had not tainted the world with their disgusting behaviour would receive the gift from the gods. For the last 30 years, since the discovery of Testament knowledge, Hades had been trying to create Keystone, trying to finish what Chaos had started a thousand years before.

In the 30 years of experiments and attempts to create the weapon, no perfect solution had been found. In those 30 years the closest the Kappa scientist had come to creating perfection was version 10099; it would rid the world of all the disgusting inter-bred population, but kill one in every two pure citizens. It will be 10099 that is launched, it will be this weapon that ends the world. Hades and his most trusted commanders would hide away in a secure bunker and live out the end of days in opulent luxury whilst the population suffered and died. As the news of Hades' plan spread, Kappa divisions around the world began laying down arms, abandoning their posts and heading back to Kappa state in a vain attempt to stop Hades. In the east, the defence wall camp was now deserted, the Kappa guards turned on their masters, killing the camp commanders. They all fled back towards Kappa, leaving the people and allowing them to be free. In Delta, the Kappa soldiers had left their posts in the factories and in the camps and started the journeying back to Kappa. Khristade was like a ghost town, overnight the soldiers left. The people were once again free. As the soldiers left, information on why, had started to filter through to the people. Panic had begun, some choosing to live out their last few days in peace, spend time with their families free of the grip of Kappa. Others chose to fight, bands of each state's population had begun organising.

In the safety of Hades' bunker, Captain Vesta and her fellow scientists were putting the final elements together to enable version 10099. In another area of the bunker, Kappa weapons experts were building the enormous rocket that would launch Keystone to the heavens and rain down destruction on everyone. It was only a matter of days now until these would be brought together to create the final solution. Captain Vesta needed to test 10099; although recreated precisely, she was only able to rely on her own handwritten notes – the sabotage committed by Aurora was still having a detrimental effect. Many records and test notes had been destroyed, along with the only sample of 10099.

"We must run substantial test," Captain Vesta proclaimed. "It is vital we ensure that version 10099 will not have a detrimental effect on the world, animal life, plant life. Without a sample we have to ensure that it has been created correctly."

"How long?" Hades yelled over his radio link.

"Three to four days. It is vital we do this. Unless you want Chaos to return to a barren dead world."

Although Hades was impatient, he needed the world to be prefect for the return of Chaos, so reluctantly agreed to give Vesta three days to finalise Keystone 10099.

To the eastern side of Kappa there was fighting at the border, Kappa on Kappa. The grunts returning from Omega were attempting to gain access back to their homeland. A few highly trained Hades loyalists were defending the borders with their lives. The fighting was brutal, the heavy artillery that was positioned on the Kappa border decimated the returning Kappa soldiers, but it was not as effective against the tank battalions that were starting to appear. The tanks rolled towards the border, guns firing at the defensive positions. By the end of this battle there would not be much left of these Kappa armies. To the west it was a similar story, Kappa again fighting Kappa, as the soldiers tried to return to their homes. Barbaric fighting, soldiers being cut down and torn apart by heavy machine gun fire, and brutal hand to hand combat. On the eastern shore a group of ex-Kappa prisoners had joined together; they were being led by Altan. The group was starting the trek towards the Kappa capital, they were just one of many groups eager to fight Hades, eager to prevent him from ending the world. In Delta another movement had begun, workers and slaves joining with a few Omega rebels to form what they were calling the world's army. The forces gathering had only a slim chance, three days to find and stop General Hades, but was three days enough time for the people of the world to truly come together? They needed a leader and the huge army was heading to Khristade to find such a man.

67
The Citadel

The Omega team were within the library of the world; there were 50 doors exiting the building but not one was passable or had led them anywhere. They certainly had not found the seat of the gods.

"Are we sure it still exists?" Erik asked Frode.

"I am hopeful it does, but have found nothing to suggest where it might be."

"Surely gods would have wanted to look upon their subjects, would have wanted to have gazed out across their lands from upon high?" Marcus suggested. "Surely their seat of power was at the top of the now fallen tower?"

"It just can't've been there," Frode responded. "I will find it."

He continued to search through book after book, looking for some reference to the citadel or seat of the gods. As he did that Aurora assisted him and most of the others continued to search the room, looking for anything that might lead the team to what that sought.

Freyja was the only one not searching; she was still feeling sickly and was resting in the far corner of the enormous room. She didn't want to distract anyone else from finding the clues to lead them to the citadel, so was content by herself out of the way of the others. Inga was searching near her, more playing near her.

"Will you still take care of me when we are finished with the mission?" the young girl asked as she skipped over to Freyja.

"Of course we will," Freyja responded. "I promise to you, you will be well cared for."

"Will Captain Marcus be with us too? I do hope he is."

"I hope for that too. Now run along and enjoy yourself for a little bit, but if anyone asks, you're still searching."

The young girl skipped off with a huge smile on her face, and Freyja tried to get comfortable enough to rest.

Marcus and Erik were together with Astrid and Blank, they were talking through endless possibilities of where the seat of power might be.

"It's not just going to be along a nondescript corridor, these were the gods. It would be opulent and beautiful and very secure," Marcus surmised.

"This building is grand, but certainly not opulent, and not where a god would sit," Astrid responded.

"It would have had a fancy entrance too," Erik added.

"So where could they build an opulent, beautiful, secure place with a fancy entrance fit for gods?" Astrid asked.

"Who says they built it? For somewhere to be totally secure, nobody could know about it. If it was as opulent as we are all imagining, it would have been a target for thieves. So who built it? You don't imagine the gods getting their hands dirty, do you?" Marcus commented.

"What are you suggesting?" Erik asked.

"He's suggesting it fucking magically appeared," Blank responded.

It was not quite what Marcus was suggesting but not far from it. "Where did these gods come from? The heavens, right? So, what, did they just fall from the skies?"

"You're suggesting they travelled here? You think there is some kind of vessel, and that is their seat of power?"

"What makes more sense? It would also explain why Frode and Aurora can't find anything relating to it. The records here start after the gods arrived. There would be no building record of the citadel, if nobody built it, and if it had arrived here prior to Central city being built, there is only one place it might be."

Marcus began pointing downwards. If the city was built after the gods' arrival, then the vessel that carried them to the world must be beneath the city. "We need to start looking at the floor," Marcus called out to the rest of the Omega team. "The citadel is beneath the city, and I would guess there is a grand hidden entrance somewhere in this room."

The team began searching, moving everything not bolted to the floor. They were scrambling round trying to find any clue. Almost everything had been moved, piles of books thrown out of the way, furniture pushed against walls, clearing the floor of the library. The whole group were looking but couldn't find the clue.

"That's a funny picture," Inga commented from atop the book stacks she had climbed.

"What's that, child?" Frode asked.

"There are six funny pictures on the floor, a man, a goat man, a man with wings."

"Those are the gods," Frode proclaimed, interrupting the young girl.

"Is there anything else, Inga dear?" Marcus questioned.

"They all have their arms raised, pointing over there," Inga stated whilst pointing in the same direction of the depictions.

Marcus hurried in the direction Inga was pointing; he began moving anything in his path until he was face to face to with a book stack. Marcus called for Frode and Aurora, they began scouring all the book titles, pulling each one from the shelf, hoping one would be the clue.

As Frode removed a volume titled in the laps of the gods a panel was revealed; the panel had an inscription in the identical language that was written in Frode's book.

"What does the inscription say?" Marcus asked impatiently.

"Give me a moment," Frode moaned. "It mentions a lock or latch and something relating to a path to god."

"Seems to be a good sign. Is there a button or lever?"

"There are three holes, looks like keyholes. There is more to the inscription, just give me a minute or two."

Frode continued to translate the inscription whilst the others waited impatiently. "The inscription states that three of the six races of man are required to unlock the path to the gods."

"What is that gibberish supposed to mean?" Erik complained.

"Frode, does it suggest which races of man?" Marcus asked.

"No, just three of six."

"So we need three races? We have that here: Delta, Kappa and Omega," Marcus stated, pointing to various members of the team.

"I would assume they mean genetically pure; are you or anyone here pure Delta? You sure don't look pure Delta."

"Does it suggest how many tries we get?"

"I would imagine just one," the old historian stated. "It is a lock, after all, it is supposed to be secure."

The team took some time reviewing their options. The first choice was easy: Astrid had been taken by Hades and sent to a medical station, as they believed her to be pure Omega. She would be key number one. The second was going to be Blank, he was Kappa, as far as he knew both his father, and the breeder that birthed him were both Kappa. He would be key number two. Aurora and Marcus were both half breeds, half Delta and half Kappa. Frode, Freyja, Erik and Hilda were all Omegas. That only left Inga.

"Inga, where are you from?" Freyja asked.

"From Khristade," the little girl replied with glee.

"Do you know where you parents were born?"

"They often told me a story of them growing up in a camp; they escaped so that I could have a better life," Inga said with a smile as she thought of her parents.

"There were no camps in Omega when the child was born," Marcus commented. "She must be Delta or Theta?"

The third key had been identified, the little girl would be key number three. The three keys stepped forward and each placed their fingers in the three holes on the panel.

"Ouch!" Inga shouted, as her finger felt a sharp pinch. The panel lit up, two red lights and one green appeared and a loud clunking noise.

"It's going to lock," Frode moaned.

The panel still sprung to life; it didn't lock. The floor beneath the feet of the Omega team began to move, a staircase was slowly revealed in the centre of the library. The staircase spiralled downward and was lit up with bright white lights. The team led by Marcus began the descent of the stairs, down and down they went, all the time being shown the way by the whitest of lights.

At the end of the staircase was a corridor, whitish-silver in colour and with beautifully embossed depictions. The corridor was made entirely of a metal that none of the Omega team recognised. At the far end of the corridor was a large set of doors, again made of the same solid metal. The doors appeared carved with six ornate panels. Five of the panels had pictures of the gods; the other had been defaced; scratched at, almost completely rubbed away. The doors were not secured or locked, but it took all of Marcus, Erik and Blank's effort to push one open. As they entered the next room it automatically sprung to life, lights flicked on and screens started to flicker. This was the citadel, the seat of the gods and the Omega team had found it.

68
Our so-called Gods

As the Omega team searched through the underground citadel, in room after room they discovered more and more opulence. Precious metals and stones, great statues and crystal carvings. Everything about the citadel didn't sit right with the team. How could gods live in such luxury when their people were living as slaves? Something else also made little sense – the manufacture of the citadel was strange, the metal was nothing like the group had ever seen and the technology was way in advance of their own.

"These weren't gods, these were animals," Erik commented.

"I don't understand how any of this is possible?" Marcus questioned. "All this was made a thousand years ago and it is still centuries ahead of us; and this metal? None of this makes much sense. We came here for answers and all we have found are more questions."

"The answers are here," Frode suggested. "Have a little faith; just maybe not in these gods."

The team continued their room by room sweep. They found no books, they found no artefacts, just more and more gaudy objects that had no value to the team.

To the side of the corridor were six rooms; the first a magnificent chamber, with a gigantic bed, draped in silks and positioned in the centre of the room. Marcus approached the bed.

"Don't let Inga in here," he shouted.

Marcus had found remains, the sheets still stained red, a massive skeletal figure lay in the bed with its head removed. "Who or what is that?" Marcus asked.

"It is rather hard to tell, but working from the depictions throughout this temple, the size and limb dimensions would best fit, Jengu, the goddess of Sigma."

"Where is her head?" Erik asked sheepishly.

"Another mystery, although looking at the marks on what is left of her neck. I would say her head was quite deliberately removed," Frode surmised.

Marcus left the chamber and approached Freyja and Hilda. "Please keep Inga busy for a little while. I have a feeling that this is only the first gruesome scene we are going to find. If you are going to kill one god, you'd likely kill them all."

The trio moved to the next chamber, another bedroom and another body. Another body without a head.

"Your guess on who this might be?" Marcus asked the old historian.

"I would guess Ipotane, the Omega god."

"What happened here?" Erik questioned.

"I would guess they had an argument over something," Marcus suggested. "But it must've been the argument of all arguments; you don't decapitate someone because they used the last of the milk!"

The team moved on to the next chamber, expecting to find yet another body, but the room was empty.

"Whoever slept in that bed is most likely our butcher," Marcus quipped.

Marcus and Erik had continued into the adjacent chamber where they found the most gruesome scene of all. Again, there was a body with no head, but these remains had been completely annihilated. There were body parts scattered all over the room.

"Our butcher really didn't like this guy," Erik suggested.

"Why would you do this to another person?"

"You might have noticed, boss, but these ain't people!"

Marcus called for Frode who was searching through the previous chamber. "Your thoughts on this one?"

"Too hard to tell, I'm afraid; it might be Anzu, Vlad, Galil or possibly even Chaos."

There were two chambers left; the first was again empty. The final chamber had another set of remains, again beheaded. The only difference was this one would appear to have been knelt over when the fatal blow was struck.

"This one knew it was coming. The others were probably asleep," Marcus suggested. "Any ideas who this one is?"

"I'm sure this is Vlad, the Theta god," Frode surmised.

"So the one scattered about the room was Anzu, Galil or Chaos? Central, Delta or Kappa? I'm confident it was Anzu," Marcus guessed. "But where are Chaos and Galil? There are six chambers, four bodies and two missing gods."

Exiting the final chamber, Marcus, Erik and Frode re-joined the rest of Omega team; they continued down the corridor towards what they assumed was the centre of the citadel. At the end of the corridor stood an even larger set of doors. It took the whole team to make them even budge. With the greatest amount of effort, they pushed the door open. Inside the door was the most magnificent room with six giant thrones all surrounding a console in the very centre. There sat in one of the thrones was the skeletal remains of a huge being, with horns protruding from its skull and hooves in place of feet.

"Chaos, I assume," Marcus stated.

"Almost certainly," Frode responded.

As Marcus looked around the thrones, four were not empty. Laid on each were the heads of Anzu, Jengu, Ipotane and Vlad.

"We know who was hacked into a hundred pieces; it was certainly Anzu," Frode stated.

"Where is Galil? And why the heads?" Erik asked quizzically.

"Maybe it is like the lock to enter this place. Maybe Chaos needed the other four to operate something?" Frode suggested.

"Operate what? It's a room," Marcus questioned, annoyed that they had only proven the gods never left the world. They had been hacked apart, or in Chaos's case, possibly died of old age.

Freyja, Hilda and Inga had remained outside of the room. Marcus was keen to not let the young girl have to see anything that was unnecessary, but she was eager to look at what all the fuss was about. She had sneaked away from the women when Freyja was vomiting again, and had entered the central chamber. She skipped down to the centre console where she must have inadvertently activated something. A large image began projecting in the centre of the room – the image was of the gods. It was a recording from a thousand years ago. Some buttons had lit up on the centre console; Inga pushed one of them and the image started running backwards very quickly. Marcus hurried over to where Inga was, and pushed another button – the image stopped, frozen in time.

"Is it real?" Frode asked.

"I think it is. I can make it move with these buttons. Backward and forward," Marcus replied.

"Take it to the very beginning and work forward from there."

Marcus obliged and rewound the recording to the first frame. A picture of all six gods sat on their thrones.

69
Truth

As Marcus slowly started to forward through the recordings, written information began to appear overlaid on the images. Frode did his best to translate as much as possible.

"It appears as though our so-called gods came here from another world, a world that had destroyed itself with fighting. They came to our world to start afresh," Frode began. "They created the six races of man all from the same genetic template, but altered them to best serve. Omega were made stronger to farm, Delta smarter to create industry and science."

Frode continued to translate as Marcus went through the images. "They segregated the people and each took a race to lord over."

"So who or what were the gods?" Marcus asked.

"Beings from another world. They were all different. Chaos was almost part man, part ram with a huge amount of strength. Galil was the most like us, almost normal; Anzu a mighty winged beast and Jengu was scaled like a fish. They were all very different. Their planet housed the six unique species that evolved from other creatures over millennia."

"Why did they come here? In fact, how did they come here?" Marcus questioned, stunned by what he was being told.

"This world must have suited their purpose, it could sustain them, and they arrived in a vessel; this vessel that we appear to be in right now."

The team watched on in amazed silence as Frode continued to decipher the text.

"The gods became disillusioned, they believed that their own planet was destroyed by the population ignoring their heritage. Hedonistic ways that led to inter-breeding and fighting. The people rose up against them, they wanted more than what they were designed for. The gods didn't want the same for this world, but exactly the same had happened. The population became unruly, disobedient, they wouldn't follow the rule of the gods. They began to fight in amongst themselves."

Frode paused for a moment. He was intently reading a passage of text. He asked Marcus to go back one step so he could check his translation. "Chaos asked Galil, the scientist, to create a weapon to purify everyone. He became single minded that purity was the answer to all the ills of our world."

"And that is Testament?" Erik asked.

"No, that is the keystone; but it would seem that Galil refused to create it. That then led to an argument amongst the gods."

Frode kept going, page after page, image after image. The puzzle was becoming more complete, the pieces slotting neatly into place.

"So what about Testament?" Marcus asked.

"I believe it was created soon after the gods first arrived here. It was sold to the people as a form of reward, but really it was a device that would change the population. Re-create the population in the image of their gods. It would turn the genetically pure into a mirror image of the god that designed them. For example, Kappas would have horns and hooves."

"And this is out there somewhere?" Marcus worryingly asked.

"I think Galil hid it from the other gods. No, that can't be right?" Frode questioned himself.

"What?" Erik impatiently screeched.

"Testament's purpose, why it was created; it was to allow the gods to breed. They wanted to re-create their own kind so they could breed with the population. They were ageing and wanted to continue their lineage."

"All this so they could make fucking babies?" Blank cried out.

"Does it say where the device is hidden?" Marcus questioned.

"No, I would assume the other gods never found it."

"Maybe the Galil temple in Delta? It is the only temple of the gods that still stands today," Astrid suggested.

The images kept flying past their eyes, getting closer and closer to the events that led to the decapitation of the four gods.

"Oh my!" the old man proclaimed. "Galil had a child. He took a lover, and as he was a man they conceived a child."

The historian had fumbled upon the reason why Chaos was so angry. Galil was able to continue his own lineage whilst the other gods could not. Galil hid the child away from the gods when he knew his end was coming. He foresaw his end at the hands of Chaos.

"Chaos killed Galil in the Delta temple. He wouldn't tell him where Testament was, he wouldn't admit to having a child. Chaos fell into a fit of rage and murdered him. The keepers of the Delta temple rose up at the death of their god and attacked Kappa, it's the beginning of the first war," Frode stated. "This angered the other gods. They had rules, and Chaos broke the most sacred of them all. He killed one of their own. There was a huge fight and what we've seen here was the outcome. Chaos killed them all."

"But why the heads?" Erik questioned.

"He needed them to operate the vessel. It took four of them to fly this ship. As the stories correctly told, Chaos wanted to leave this world. He tried to fly away but the force from the vessel must have toppled the tower; it fell directly onto the ship, preventing it and Chaos from leaving. He must have died shortly after."

"So that's the truth? Beings from another planet were not satisfied with destroying their own world, so they came here and did it again, to this one?" Marcus stated. "They created a powerful chemical to alter mankind to allow them to breed; sold it as a reward in an attempt to maintain order. Then got pissed off by the people wanting to grow and be more than what was designed; so tried to purify the world and start again; and when they couldn't, Chaos killed them all and then himself whilst trying to run away like a coward? How on all things holy does this help us, how does it stop the wars, stop Hades?"

"The truth is a powerful thing. Firstly, it is very important to understand that we now know all of us were created from the same genetic material. Yes, six beings played god, altered that material to create six unique groups of men; but in essence we are all the same; all equal. The point of this quest was never about finding answers. I think our great leader understood that; the questions were more important than the answers; the journey more important than the destination. The truth wasn't as important as the quest to find it; bringing the races of the world together to fight for a common cause; fight the evils of the world together. She somehow knew that to complete this journey we would need help from each race, each state. We are all the products of the same false gods, all men striving to be more than what we were created for; and the gods couldn't accept that it will be this world's diversity that will make it great. It is the willingness of man to want to be more that pushes on onwards; whilst the gods thought purity was the answer, but it was that quest, that ultimately doomed them." Frode stopped, his eyes filling with hope.

With no more images to show, the projector shut down. The whole Omega team were unsure of what to do next. They had come to Central hoping to find a miracle, and found a story of six beings trying to play god. In all of this information there had to be a key, something that would make Hades and his armies stand down and unite the people of the world. Marcus took his time, mulling things in his mind before he spoke.

"What don't we now know? We have all this information and this great hope for man; but still many unanswered questions!

Why has Hades spent over 20 years trying to create Keystone? What happened all those years ago that made him want to kill every genetically impure person of this world? He banned religious teachings in Kappa schooling, he had no faith. Why did this man suddenly want to do what his god required, and destroy the people of this world? Think, everyone," Marcus passionately pleaded.

"He invaded Delta about 30 years ago," Aurora chirped.

"And what did he find in Delta?"

"The temple of Galil!" the scientist added.

"He must have found the remains of Galil and with it, he must've found Testament?" Frode stated.

"He is trying to finish the mission of his god. He wants to release Testament; but first needs to purify the world. But to what end?" Marcus asked.

There was a total silence before Marcus answered his own questions. "Hades wants to rule, he wants to rule everything, but how does all of this matter? How does this bring him closer to being the king of everything?"

"Old Kappa history tells us our leader sat to Chaos's right hand and ruling over the world. His twisted mind thinks Chaos is coming back, and with it he will take his place to his right hand and rule over everything. He doesn't know his god is dead. Whatever knowledge he uncovered in the Delta temple would have been from before the massacre of the gods. He thinks Chaos will return," Aurora proclaimed.

With the new knowledge in hand, the team began the long journey from the citadel and back out of Central city. It gave the group time to consider their journey. They had travelled the breadth of the world for knowledge, to discover the truth and that is precisely what they had found, but did it give them the answers that they wanted? Did it give them the clues needed to save the world, and the ammunition to stop Hades?

70
Chaos head

Marcus and his weary team had re-emerged from the sewer tunnels under the Central capital. They had lost much along their journey and the truth they had discovered was short of the miracles that they had hoped for. The wars had begun due to anger and rage amongst beings who believed themselves gods, but in reality were nothing more than monsters. The team were hurrying across Central and back towards Sigma, they were searching for Hades, but had no knowledge of his retreat to Kappa. There weren't soldiers anywhere to be seen; when the team had passed through a day earlier there were soldiers by the hundreds tearing each other apart. War was raging, battalions of men were on the battlefield.

"Where has everyone gone?" Freyja asked.

"No idea! If Kappa had won this war they would be here in force, but how could they have lost?" Erik suggested.

"They couldn't. Something else happened. There are too many dead Kappas, it makes no sense," Marcus stated.

The Omega team had reached the Central border and were starting to pass a mountain of bodies strewn across the field. They were checking each as they passed, more out of hope than any real thought of actually finding someone alive to tell their tale. Body after body was checked but nothing.

"Boss, found a live one," Erik shouted.

The man was barely alive, but was able to tell his tale. "Kappa grunts rose up against him. He wants to kill us all for some god," the man grunted through his shallow breaths. "He has retreated to

Kappa, holed up in some secure bunker." That was the last word the soldier spoke before he passed. Erik held his hand and stayed for a moment after the end.

The team went to move out again, but Marcus stopped them.

"I think this is as far as we go together," he proclaimed. "Erik, Blank and Aurora are going to come with me. We need to move quickly, get to Kappa and show the world what we found. I have a feeling that there won't be a race of man not on that battlefield."

Marcus turned to Freyja. "Take care of everyone. Make your way to Cyrus and find a good spot to hide. I promise to return."

"Don't make promises you can't keep," Freyja responded.

"You know me, I've already twice proven I always come back."

Marcus leant into Freyja and kissed her cheek. As he did so she whispered to him, "Make sure you do. I don't want your child to grow up without a father."

Marcus looked quizzically at Freyja who just nodded and smiled.

Marcus led his reduced team off at quite the pace. They were heading to Akbar where they hoped to find some transport to take them back to the shore. The four moved at a much faster speed than with the others, and although they were sad to leave them behind, this wasn't about them, it was about the world and trying to save every man within it. Marcus wanted his shot at Hades; he knew deep down that the knowledge he had would destroy the general.

Approaching Akbar, Marcus and his group were accosted by a group of Sigma men.

"Lay down your weapons and surrender," one of the Sigma men blurted out.

"Sir, I'm terribly sorry but we can't do that. Please move aside, or we will be forced to kill you," Marcus stated with authority.

The man chuckled. "We out-number you two to one."

"Look, you foolish man, we don't have time for this. Do you know who we are? Do you know what we are capable of? I could kill you all by myself without any of you getting off a shot. If you stop us now, you are all dead, so are all your families, and your friends. All will be dead within days. Unless you let us pass." Marcus was beginning to lose his normal cool. So he opened his bag and pulled out the head of Chaos. "Do you know what this is?" Marcus asked.

The Sigma men were shocked at the site of the enormous decaying skull with horns.

"What is that?" a worried sounding Sigma man asked.

"It is the head of Chaos the Kappa god. All of the Gods are dead. Your god Jengu is dead, decapitated by him, a thousand years ago," Marcus exclaimed whilst pointing towards the skull. "You might've noticed there is a mad man on the loose, who is trying to kill everyone, and the key to stop him is in my hand right now. You stop us, you are responsible for ending the world. What's your choice? Fight us and die, delay us much more and die, or let us pass? Take your time, I've got all day," Marcus stated sarcastically.

The Sigmas moved out of the way and the quartet was moving again, and on the outskirts of Akbar they found exactly what they were looking for, an abandoned Kappa transport. A commander's car with its commander hanging from a nearby wall and the driver shot in the driver's seat. Erik pulled the driver from the seat and started the vehicle; the others mounted up and Erik sped off towards the shore. As the transport roared past Mina it was noticeably quiet, not a soul to be seen. The once bustling little market town was now empty, abandoned by the inhabitants who had run away from the Kappa onslaught just days previous. As the car approached Cyrus there were signs of life starting to return, a few souls wandering around the outer reaches of the town. Erik continued to speed through the state and to the shore. There were still remnants of the deadly battles, bodies rotting all around the inland edge of the beach and some being washed back and forth in the surf. Hundreds of weapons were strewn around, and some patches of the sand were still red with blood, days after the battle; the sea had not managed to wash away the smell of death in the air. There was a single landing craft on the beach – that would have to be enough to get the team back to Kappa state; there were no ships in sight so it was the only option. The journey would be rough, they did not know if the craft had enough fuel or even if the craft would survive on the high seas, but the four souls, one Kappa, one Omega and two Delta half-breeds, had the fate of the world in their hands and they had to try.

71

The Rise of Delta

In the state of Delta the workers had risen against what was left of the Kappa armies, and had formed what was being called the Army of the world; a thousand-strong force currently being led by Omega resistance fighter Bjorn and his eldest son Anders. After the destruction of the Kappa priests, Bjorn and his team had spread through the world and told of their destruction. This, combined with the uprising in the Kappa ranks due to the news of Keystone, had allowed many Deltas to become free. There was only thing on all their minds: destroy what is left of Kappa and its armies. In some parts of the world, Kappa grunts were banding together with other states' citizens, to fight back against Hades loyalists, but not in Delta. Any Kappa found was being put down, whether for or against Hades. After 30 years of atrocities, the people of Delta were not accepting apologies from any Kappa soldiers. The army of the world had already fought in several skirmishes with Kappa as they proceeded towards Khristade. They had lost some fighters, but it was for the cause, for the annihilation of Kappa. The army was heading to Khristade to free the Omega defence force's Captain Balder, who was being held prisoner in the city. He had been there since a failed attempt to rescue his wife, who had fought with the resistance.

All around the world it was Delta citizens who were leading the uprisings. Altan and his group from the eastern shore defence wall had been making excellent progress towards the Kappa capital. They were now in a battle with a loyalist Hades division around ten miles outside of the city. It was a fierce battle where neither side was able to gain the upper hand. Both sides were well armed – on the Kappa side they were well trained killers, on the Delta side they were slaves fighting for their lives. The battle was intense and losses were heavy. On the eastern sea there was another battle, three Kappa ships had remained loyal to Hades, but the other four ships had turned. On Kappa ship number two, the captain and all the senior officers had been killed by the crew. A sergeant in the Kappa army was now commanding the ship, as it fought against ships three and six. Kappa ship seven had already been sunk – when the crew tried to take the ship, the captain scuttled the vessel and all hands were lost. Ships five and one had been taken by the crew and were ferrying Kappa grunts from Sigma back to their homeland. The ships were packed with soldiers and disorder reigned. Grunts fighting grunts for a space on each boat.

The world and any understanding of rules were crumbling, it felt like the whole world's population was trying to descend on Kappa in an attempt to stop Hades. The in-fighting and disorganisation of the soldiers were causing delays in their return to Kappa; and with gangs of headhunters roaming the world, being a Kappa, even if you were fighting against Hades, being Kappa was a death sentence. The fiercely loyal Kappa commanders had been working with Hades on the final act for decades. They had planned meticulously for this moment, and even with limited troops were easily defending the Kappa capital. They had formed a double defensive ring around the city, one ring at ten miles, with ground troops and large tank battalion and then a ring on the outskirts of the city with the larger, even more destructive defensive cannons and another two tank battalions. It would take a very well organised army to break this defence, and the Kappa commanders didn't believe that was possible.

Just outside Khristade the army of the world had encountered heavier resistance, a lone Kappa battalion had been left to guard the city. Neither loyal or not, their commanders had fled and without orders they had made the decision to wait. Now being engaged by a horde of angry Deltas, they had no choice but to fight. The fighting was pushing the battalion back towards the now almost deserted city. A few Kappas tried in desperation to flee but were attacked from Omegas still living within the city walls, battered to death at the hands of women and children. There were a few Kappas who tried to surrender, but they were taken and executed by the Delta army. The Kappas had no choice but to fight on, fight until they were either dead or had depleted their stock of ammunition. The battle continued; as the munitions ran low the Kappas turned to hand combat, brawls broke out throughout the streets of Khristade. Once civilised people were now savages, rampaging throughout the streets, looking to kill.

Throughout the lands every race of man was now fighting back against the tyranny and killing their oppressors. In the west, Deltas and Thetas had joined with Omegas; in the east, Deltas and Sigmas were fighting with Kappa within touching distance of the Kappa capital. In Khristade the battle was over, more bodies lined the streets but this time it was young Kappa men and women. Khristade was now free, but at what cost? The Army of the world had arrived in the city square; they had sacked the capitol building and rescued Balder. As they brought the great Omega captain from the darkness and up into the light of the day, he struggled to open his eyes. Squinting and blinking, it was Balder but he was not the same man. Older looking, weary looking, this was not the brave and honourable man that had gone to that building to rescue his wife. Balder had been repeatedly beaten and tortured since his incarceration – not for information; it had become obvious that the Omega captain was never going to talk. They tortured him for sport, for fun. Now he was free like all the men of the world.

Balder greeted Bjorn like a long-lost brother when he caught a glimpse of him. "Bjorn, my friend, what has happened here?"

"Khristade is free, the people rose up against Hades, against his plans to launch a weapon that risks us all. The people will fight against him, they want you to lead us. Lead us into the final battle, of the final war."

"What news of my team? My brave soldiers. Bjorn, has there been any news?"

"Sorry, Balder, I have heard nothing of your team."

Balder looked out across the city square; thousands had gathered. Men and women ready for one final battle, a battle for the world. Bjorn encouraged Balder to address the people.

"My friends," Balder began. "I do not care where you are from. I do not care what your beliefs are. I do not care for your position in the world, be it farmer, miner or worker. Be it Omega, Delta or Theta, I do not care. I will call you my friends, if you stand with me now, this one last time, stand against him. Against Hades and stop the annihilation of all we hold dear. Will you stand?"

There was a crescendo of cheers and roars from the crowd. The people had voiced their answer: they would all stand.

72
A Hero's Welcome

On the outskirts of Khristade, the army of the world was amassing. Delta, Omega and Theta all together, for the fight against one common enemy, and being led by Omega Defence force Captain Balder. The army numbered around two thousand strong, and news of the army was spreading fast, so there was an expectation that the ranks would swell as they passed through the Omega villages on the route to Kappa state and their capital. Balder was well respected throughout the western worlds. Stories of his exploits often found their way to workers' camps and factories. The stories were not quite as Balder remembered them, often exaggerated, but the tales had increased workers' morale. Hearing one man had slayed ten or 20 Kappas with his bare hands provided a good boost for the mentality of anyone under Kappa rule. Bjorn and some of the other commanders had cobbled together enough transports for around 600 soldiers. Old Kappa trucks, farm machinery and other military transports would carry some of the soldiers. They would form an advanced party, scout reconnaissance would be their task. The main body of soldiers would follow on foot, and be ready to engage the enemy upon arrival at the front lines. The troops had much distance to travel, but unlike when Balder had journeyed into Kappa with the Omega team, they did not have to skulk in the shadows. Not having to worry about being seen, they would be able to march at pace straight through to the Kappa defence surrounding the capital.

The advanced group led by Balder was moving along a predefined route to pass as many towns and villages as possible.

When the people heard that Balder had built an army, all the folk came out to see, crowds were waving and cheering as the army passed through their towns, and men and women alike were joining the back of the column as the army rolled through. By the time Balder and his advanced group had reached the Kappa border, the numbers had doubled, twelve hundred souls.

At the border a large group of Kappa grunts were waiting and the world's army prepared to engage. A young man stepped forward from the group of Kappas with his hands raised.

"I am unarmed," the man shouted. "We wish to join your army."

"We should kill all Kappas. Make them pay." There were cheers of agreement from the world soldiers.

"No," Balder proclaimed. "What is your name, son?"

"It is Jingle, sir," the young Kappa replied.

"Well, Jingle, what would you like to do after the war? After the fighting is done?"

"Find a pretty girl, make her my wife. Maybe have some little ones and a farm."

"A wife! That is very un-Kappa like?"

"Yes, sir. It is, sir."

"Good lad. The rest of your men; they feel the same?"

"Not sure they all want a farm, sir, but they all want rid of Kappa and be able to do un-Kappa like things."

"So they all want to find a pretty girl, do they?"

"Yes, sir, they do, sir."

"Join the ranks, Jingle, and bring your friends."

"Yes, sir," Jingle said with a smile.

With the ranks now swelled by Kappa soldiers, the advanced group numbered over 2000. They journeyed past the border and moved deeper into Kappa territory; soon they would be face to face with Hades' loyalist troops. Balder was pondering the best options to force through the Kappa defences. He was conflicted, desperate to reach Hades and intent on stopping the end of the world, but to accomplish this, many of the world's army would die on this field.

"What's the point in saving the world if nobody is left alive to live in it?" Balder questioned himself.

Balder had sent small scout parties further into Kappa state, to bring back intel from which he would devise the plans for breaking the defence around the capital. He was expecting Bjorn and the other commanders to be joining him soon, and their attack would commence shortly thereafter. The remaining Kappa armies were strong, but not infallible. The intel from the scouts suggested the outer ring was weakest near the tanks, the Kappas believed an attacking force wouldn't dare attack the tank battalions. But to Balder this was something to exploit, the tanks were slow to move laterally. So, a fast attack between the tank positions would breach the line and allow the world army in amongst the weaker Kappa positions. The transports being used by the world's army had heavy armour, and as a result were slow moving. Balder ordered the transports to be stripped bare, the removal of all the armour and heavy arms. The lighter weight vehicles would be fast enough to breach the lines, but offer no defence, no protection to those within them.

As the army prepared for the battle, Balder was already thinking ahead to the inner defensive ring. He created several small brigades of men, their sole purpose being to take a number of the tanks intact. The world's army would need the heavy artillery of the tanks to engage the Kappa capital defences; it was imperative to capture the tanks. Bjorn and the other commanders had arrived with the remaining force, the entire army was positioned ready to start their attack.

"We are one force, one world's army. We will fight together and die together. Just ten short miles from the Kappa capital, ten miles from taking Hades' head and preventing him from ending this world. We fight for a new world, a world where Kappas can take wives, where Omegas can become doctors and Deltas work farms. A world where there are one people," Balder preached. "Be safe, fight strong and we will win this day."

The transports rolled forward, building speed and charging towards the tank battalions. The battle had begun.

73
Driven Back

Attacking the Kappa capital had begun, thousands of troops from the world's army had breached the front line and fighting was now at close quarters, with those who were supporting Hades; supporting him against the rest of the world. The army commanded by the great Balder were organised; most where not soldiers and their losses were heavy, but they had the numeric advantage and were making it pay. For every world's soldier killed, two more were engaging in the fight; Kappa simply didn't have the remaining forces to hold the line, they were falling back to the inner defence ring that surrounded the capital. World's army troops continued to flood the battlefield, the outer Kappa defence ring was gone. Balder's army had won the battle and pushed Kappa back to the outskirts of the city. Balder and his commanders took stock of the troops and munitions; there was a choice to make. Push on immediately and not give the enemy time to reset, but risk exhaustion in their own troops; or rest their troops for a moment, resupply and then attack. This would offer Kappa just a modicum of time to ready themselves, but it was the choice that Balder made.

"We will rest for ten, resupply ammunition and then move on to the capital," Balder told his commanders. "How many tanks did we capture?"

"We captured six, the others were either destroyed or damaged behind usability," Commander Dawa reported. Dawa was Delta, he had been in a workers' camp all his life, born into Kappa slavery. He was not a tall man, or a strong man, but he was well respected and organised the Deltas well and fought like a wild animal.

"Six is barely enough, we lose one or two early in the engagement and we will be in trouble. Are we sure we can't scavenge together enough parts to make a couple more workable?" Balder asked his commander. "We must have some citizens who worked the tank factories. They would know best; try and round up a few men and see what you can do."

Dawa trotted off to find a tank specialist, whilst Balder and the other commanders discussed their tactics.

"I say we attempt to infiltrate the city with a small team. Try and get to Hades whilst the battle distracts the soldiers?" Bjorn suggested.

"We don't know the city, or where Hades' bunker is. It's too much of a risk. The team would be blind," Balder commented. "I know we are short on time, but we need to fell the army. Put Hades on the back foot."

"Is there not a risk he just launches the weapon as soon as we get close?" Anders chirped in. "The battle on his doorstep will draw his attention. The second he thinks the battle is lost, he will launch."

"It must be an infiltration team, it is the only way," Bjorn pleaded.

Balder pondered the thoughts of his commanders, before calling for Jingle, the Kappa soldier. "How well do you know your capital?" Balder asked.

"I don't, sir, born in a breeder station and schooled there until I were old enough to fight. Only the officers really ever go to the city."

"There are no officers amongst your number?"

"No, sir. We are all just grunts."

"The only way I allow a team to go into the city ahead of the main force, is if we know the target, and no one here knows the target."

"As soon as Hades knows our strength, he will launch the weapon," Anders passionately argued.

"He is probably correct, sir. Hades is surprisingly calculated. He won't risk losing the weapon. Even if it is not finished, if he fears a loss, he will launch," Jingle replied.

Balder was torn, he was an honourable war leader. His thoughts were of a battle with etiquette, with rules, but Hades wouldn't know the meaning of the words. He had to think like Hades, see the battle through the eyes of a monster. Hades wouldn't care if he lost every troop in his command, as long as he won the day. This was not who Balder was, better the world die, than him lose who he is, and deliberately send young men and women to their death. Balder needed to think. He went to find Dawa, to check on the progress with the tanks. Dawa had found three men who had previously worked in the tank factories, and they were confident of repairing an additional three units.

"Well done, Dawa," Balder commented. "Nine tanks is good. Will give us a much better chance of success."

The Omega captain was deep in thought. "If only my friend Marcus were here," he chirped to himself. "If only my team were here." Balder let his mind wander, his thoughts drifting to the fate of his team.

"Are you talking about Kappa Captain Marcus?" a voice asked.

"Yes, you know him, soldier?" Balder responded.

"Yes, sir, he was my commanding officer a few years back. He was a good commander, different from the others. Nicer I suppose. Didn't really fit in the Kappa army."

"Do you have news of him?"

"Just a story I heard, sir."

"Would you tell me?"

"The story tells of the captain single-handedly taking brigade 66, Hades' secret police. I heard that he killed Commander Orcus with his bare hands in the mines of Kappa; he was leading a team to find the gods. Hades was really pissed, chased after him personally he did."

Balder chuckled. "Good on him. Did you hear anything else?"

"Only that Hades invaded Sigma to try and find him."

"He made it across the sea to Sigma?" Balder asked.

"Must have, sir."

Balder thanked the soldier for the story. It had helped clear his mind. He marched back towards his commanders. "I will lead an infiltration team into the city," he proclaimed. "Bjorn, you will command the main force. Only light attacks with minimal troops, just enough to keep them distracted."

"What changed your mind?" Bjorn asked.

"A story of hope and determination," Balder said before wandering off again.

74
All at Sea

On the eastern sea the remnants of the Omega team were sailing towards the Kappa shore. The landing craft was very uncomfortable and was not designed for the high seas, but the four remaining team members were braving the very choppy ride. They were praying the fuel and the vessel held out long enough to reach land. The sea was very rough, causing Aurora and Blank to vomit.

"Kappas weren't designed to be fucking sailors," Blank complained between bouts of being sick.

"You're doing a good job of proving that, Blank," Marcus quipped.

"How much further do you think we have to travel to reach land?" Erik asked.

"I'm sure it's not far," Marcus replied with little confidence.

At times the vessel was struggling to move forward against the mighty waves. Marcus was trying to steer around the largest of these, but none onboard had much experience of sailing on the high seas. The first time any of them had seen the sea was a few days earlier, when they took Kappa ship number seven. As the sea continued to become rougher there was every chance the team wouldn't it make to Kappa.

"We have to turn around, go back to Sigma," Aurora moaned.

Marcus began to think of his promise to Freyja and the thought of him becoming a father. For a second, he considered turning the vessel around, but as has been the way throughout the quest, the mission was bigger than the individuals. They were unaware that the world had risen to fight Hades, they did not know as they sailed across the sea, that Omega Captain Balder was launching a daring mission to end Hades. That Marcus' father was battling Kappa just outside their capital. So they had to keep going, they must make land. They must show the world what they had found and bring down the reign of Kappa.

It was now dark; the Omega team had been at sea for nearly a full day. Aurora and Blank were sleeping, exhausted from their continuous vomiting. Erik was on watch and Marcus was where he had been for every minute since they left, at the tiller steering the craft towards Kappa.

"Lights, I see lights," Erik yelled. "I see the wall, it is Kappa. We've fucking made it," he yelped.

Marcus steered towards the lights and soon they were sailing along the coastline, looking for a good spot to land. Where they would be able to breach the wall. It was not long until Erik saw a familiar sight, a gaping hole where the shipyard was exposed. Marcus sailed the vessel past the opening to the crack they had used to escape the camp days before. The craft was beached and the team where safely in the old workers' camp. The camp was deserted, not a prisoner or guard was left.

Finding transport to carry them quickly to the Kappa capital was a priority.

"We left a truck in the mine entrance near the breeder station, we could use that. It wasn't far through the mine," Erik suggested.

"We have a lack of options, so back into the mine. Let's hope the truck is still where we left it," Marcus responded with authority.

They moved quickly to re-enter the mine, passing through the tunnels till they reached the cavern where Marcus had left brigade 66 burying bodies. Quickly making their way through the cavern and along the next tunnel, the junction came up fast, and they took the right turn and along to the exit. The truck was still there, seemingly untouched since they left it. Erik removed the truck from the mine. It was then that Marcus noticed a shallow grave.

"Brigade 66 and a few other Kappas," Marcus grumbled sombrely. "Hades must've executed them for following my orders."

There was no time to give these poor souls a proper burial. The team climbed aboard the truck and Erik hammered the throttle. Marcus pointed his friend in the right direction and they were roaring along towards the Kappa capital. As they drove through the Kappa wasteland, bodies began to appear, the odd one, then more. It was a gruesome trail of breadcrumbs to follow. As the number of bodies continued to grow, the Captain began to feel anxious, worried at what the reaction would be to the news that his team were bringing. They were unaware of the events that had transpired over the recent days and did not know what they might find in the Kappa capital. The Omega team were about ten miles from the city when it became apparent that they were not the only ones after Hades. The battle between the army led by Altan and the Kappa loyalists was still raging; it was difficult to know who was fighting who.

"Drive through, don't stop," Marcus ordered. "If we have any chance we must get into the city tonight, before the sun rises."

Erik drove straight through the throngs of soldiers, weaving a path through the lines and out the other side. They would continue until they were within striking distance of the city, then take the last mile on foot. Marcus knew the city well and knew of every route in and out of it. He had mapped the routes in his mind. Being a non-believer in the Kappa army was a dangerous thing, and Marcus wanted to make sure he knew how to escape the city if the worst happened, and Hades' goons ever came for him.

The truck stopped a mile outside of the Kappa capital. Marcus led his team across the barren ground, avoiding detection by using the darkness as cover. A small waste outlet under one of the outer walls would be their entry point.

"More sewers, I'm afraid," Marcus quipped amusingly. "The smell is quite ripe."

"Quite ripe? It fucking stinks!" Blank responded as he ducked down into a small tunnel. The tunnel was small and the team were having to crawl through the excrement to gain access to the city. Not only were they having to cope with the smell and the shit, but also the rats and other delightful creatures that inhabit dark and dank places.

"Join the Kappa army, kill people and see the world, worst case some psycho Kappa soldier shoots me in the head," Blank moaned. "But no, I get to crawl on my hands and knees through shit. I would have rather taken the bullet!"

"Will you ever stop complaining?" Erik moaned.

"When the world ends," Blank replied.

"You might get your wish if you both don't shut it," Marcus whispered sternly.

Marcus was the first to exit the tunnel. When he was sure all was clear, he beckoned the others. There were no guards, no people. It was eerily quiet.

"Where is everyone?" Aurora whispered.

"In position to defend the outer limits of the city," Marcus responded. "There is a comms station in that tower," he said, pointing at a large tower 300 metres from their position. "We need to tell everyone our news."

"What if Hades launches the weapon anyway?" Erik asked.

"Why launch the weapon if Chaos is dead?"

"Because he's fucking crazy!" Blank mumbled.

Marcus was determined to tell the world, but maybe Erik was right. First, they should find the weapon and ensure it couldn't be launched.

Marcus, Erik, Aurora and Blank made their way through the deserted streets. Hades' bunker was at the very heart of the city, positioned under a park that commemorated all the previous Kappa Generals. Each general was entombed with only a number inscribed on their stone caskets. The number referred to the amount of people killed by their hand; this was the only identifying mark for each. In the eyes of the Kappa people, it was the only defining information. Nothing else mattered to the Kappas – a good general had blood-stained hands and had delivered unspeakable death on their enemies. Marcus and Erik took position, ready to force their way into the bunker. It was heavily guarded by elite commandos. It would take a miracle to gain entry.

75

Kappa City

Kappa city was under attack, the outer defence was gone, decimated by the world's army. Bjorn was leading the attack on the inner defensive ring, small attacks just as Balder had ordered. The intention was not to breach the defence, but keep the remaining Kappa soldiers occupied long enough to allow Balder to infiltrate the city and find Hades' bunker. It was a very dark night which had allowed Balder and his small team to reach the outskirts of the city undetected. Bjorn was using the captured tanks' large artillery to attack the city defences, disguising their intentions, hiding their true infiltration plans. Balder and his team were moving around the city's outer limits, looking for any weak point they could use to make their way within the walls. Bjorn was launching wave after wave of attacks, never getting too close to the city and not causing any real damage. The attacks were using only a fraction of the total force of the world's army. Keeping the Kappas occupied but not under any real threat, luring them into a false sense of security, whilst Balder strikes at their very heart. Balder had taken six men with him. He had handpicked Jingle and Dawa to accompany him on the mission. Dawa had recommended Batzorig and Bayalag, two Deltas who had grown-up with Dawa in the workers' camps. Like their friend, they had been born to slavery and only ever knew life within the camps. Jingle had brought one of his fellow Kappas along, a woman named Livia, who was extraordinarily strong and was the reigning battalion fighting champion. The final member of the team was Anders.

They had worked their way around much of the city and the sun was beginning to rise; they had to find an entry point soon.

"Sir," Jingle called out. "This might work, a sewer tunnel."

Balder entered the tunnel first, crawling on his hands and knees through the waste-filled hole. The others followed, no comment or complaints. As Balder emerged from the tunnel he noted the lack of guards. "These Kappas are so overconfident. Where are all the guards?" Balder asked.

"They will be out defending the city," Jingle responded. "The distraction must be working?"

"Either that or they believe the city to be impenetrable."

Anders interrupted the others. "Which way do we go?"

"If we head towards the city centre and look for guards. There is no possibility Hades leaves the bunker unguarded."

As Balder and his team made their way through the city it was empty, devoid of anything.

"There are soldiers near that park," Dawa whispered.

"A park?" Balder questioned.

"It is a monument to all the fallen Kappa generals. It is mentioned in our schooling," Jingle responded.

"That must be the place; where better to hide a bunker than under the vile monsters of Kappa history?"

Balder ordered his team to gather alongside the park with a clear view of the guards.

"Stay in cover," the captain ordered.

As the team approached the park, Dawa spotted something. "There are more people. Though they don't look like Kappas."

It was still quite dark and very difficult to see the two men crouched just beyond the edge of the monuments. The team moved around the men to approach from their rear, only to be confronted by two more strangers.

"Stop there, don't fucking move a muscle," one of the strangers ordered in a whisper.

Balder had a sensation of déjà vu. He recognised the voice and the choice of curt words. "Blank, is that you?"

"Balder? No fucking way!" the stranger responded.

Balder stepped past his team and into a small ray of light emanating from a building.

"It bloody is you!" Blank stated, as he and Aurora also stepped forward.

"I have so many questions," the captain stated in the most joyful way. "Who else is with you?"

"Marcus and Erik are over there. It is just the four of us; we left the others in Sigma."

"Everybody is alright? You all made it?"

"Sorry, Balder, but Torsten was taken from us in Sigma," Aurora stated solemnly.

Blank called to Marcus, who moved from his position back to the group. He was greeted with a most huge hug from Balder.

"You damn well made it! I am so very pleased to see you are well. I have heard stories of your exploits, but did you find it?"

Marcus explained what they had found. That the so-called gods were dead, and had been for a thousand years.

"I know how to unite the people, but you seem to be doing a good job of that yourself. What looks like Kappa, Delta and Omega in the same team! We need to deal with Hades first, we believe he means to launch a weapon."

"He is," Balder replied. "And we mean to stop him."

Balder and Marcus put their heads together to devise a plan of attack. Marcus, Balder and Aurora would need to gain entry to the bunker. Aurora was the key to destroying the weapon – she had seen the development of Keystone and was the only one who knew enough to render the weapon useless.

The now expanded team attacked the bunker to draw the guards from the facility. Marcus moved forward and destroyed the outer locks. He and Balder moved inside the bunker, where they encountered minimal resistance. What enemies they did find were swiftly dealt with. When it was clear, Aurora joined them inside; their priority was to find the weapon and prevent Armageddon.

76
Final Roll of the Dice

Hades had seen his empire crumble; he had lost his army and his vision of control for the world. Keystone was moments from being ready to launch; he had planned this moment over and over in his head, but it somehow felt different, somewhat less satisfying than he had thought. He had strived for perfection and this was less; the end result would still be the same. Only pure races of man would survive and the world would become a better place.

"Is it ready?" Hades screeched impatiently.

"We have performed significant testing, and it appears to have no detrimental effects on the world. Only the population," Captain Vesta replied.

"Then launch it, launch it now," Hades screamed.

"The rocket isn't ready, sir. We are in the final stages of preparation; it will be very soon."

Hades stormed off in a petulant rage shouting obscenities. He stormed into the bunker control centre. "Update now," he shouted at his nearest commander.

"There is a force to the east which is engaged with our outer defence. The battle is fierce. We should reinforce if you don't want to lose the position and the men?"

"That position is of no consequence, let them rot," Hades snapped.

"Very good, sir," the commander responded. "Our outer defence to the west has been breached. A small force has been attacking the inner defence. There have been no losses, and no damage. Quite insignificant, sir."

"Then ignore them, you fool" Hades grumbled as he stomped out of the room.

The General was acting like a spoilt child, marching around the base shouting and cursing nonsense at the commanders and other staff. He was impatient to launch the weapon, every few minutes storming into the machine room to check progress on the rocket.

"Is it ready yet?" Hades screeched.

No one responded, scared of what Hades' reaction would be.

"Well is it? Someone answer me now!" he bellowed.

"Soon, it will be soon, sir," the lead commander suggested. "The final preparations are being made."

"What is taking so long?" Hades yelled.

"We must be precise, sir. If the rocket doesn't reach the correct altitude the keystone will not spread as designed. Just a few more moments."

Hades groaned with disgust as he shuffled off.

Marcus, Balder and Aurora were working their way through the bunker. They had managed to silently dispose of any enemies that crossed their path, but the further in they moved, the heavier the Kappa presence became. It was becoming more difficult to be quiet, to kill silently. As they rounded a bend in the corridor, they were confronted by a group of Kappa soldiers, a ten-strong force. Balder's natural reaction was to raise his weapon and shoot twice at the nearest soldier, both hits, centre mass, the soldier grabbed his chest. Blood was soaking through his tunic as he collapsed to the floor. The noise of the gun shots echoed down the corridor as Marcus jumped into action, killing two grunts; he ran his knife along the throat of the first and stabbed the second in the eye, his knife penetrating his enemy's skull down to the hilt of his blade. The soldier died instantly as the other choked on his own blood. The remaining Kappas took position to return fire, Balder had no option but to fire again. A fire fight ensued. Hades would now know his bunker had been infiltrated.

"Aurora, find another route. Get to that weapon," Marcus ordered as he glanced across at Balder. "Cover me."

Marcus leapt forward toward the Kappa soldiers, shooting two at close range with his sidearm before kicking another so hard he was knocked clear off his feet.

As Hades left the machine room, he thought he heard gun fire. "Was that inside the building?" he said to himself. He took a couple of steps towards where the noise had emanated from. More gunfire followed. "Launch the weapon!" Hades screamed. "Launch now, launch now, launch now!"

The general ran back into the machine room and slammed the door, scrambling to lock it. "Why have you not launched?" he shouted.

"The rocket isn't ready, sir. If we launch now it will not reach the required altitude."

"Launch it now, we will destroy as many of them as possible."

One of the scientists ran into the lab for the keystone. He ran directly to the container but found it empty. "Where is the keystone?" he shouted. "The keystone is gone!"

As the scientist looked around, he saw a woman running from the room. He screamed to Hades, who came marching into the room. In the blink of an eye, Hades removed his sidearm from its holster and fired a single shot.

77
Revenge is a bitch

Aurora was crawling along the floor, grasping at the vial containing Keystone. She had been shot in the back and could not walk. She heard loud steps approaching but was unable to turn or defend herself.

"Stupid girl. Where do you think are you going?" Hades yelled.

Aurora was unable to speak, the pain from her wound was excruciating. She continued to try and crawl away from the menacing figure of Hades. He stepped on her ankle with such a force there was an audible snap. Aurora screamed in agony, and she began to weep. Hades was strutting around the young science officer.

"What made you think that you, could stop me?" Hades screeched. "This is my world, this is my destiny. Chaos will return when I purify this place of the disgusting half-bred filth."

"I doubt that very much," Marcus stated as he and Balder arrived in the lab.

"You!" Hades screeched. "Traitorous scum!"

Marcus reached into his bag and lifted Chaos's head by one of the horns. He dropped the bag and stood glaring at Hades. "Your god," Marcus stated as he tossed the head towards Hades' feet. "The psycho decapitated the other beings because of jealousy. In a fit of rage he murdered everyone, then tried to run away."

"It can't be," Hades groaned. "Lies, this is all lies."

"Look at it!" Marcus yelled. "Chaos is dead, and he has been dead for a thousand years."

Hades refused to look down, refusing to believe the truth even though it was staring straight at him.

Balder had moved around Hades, gun trained on him. He checked on Aurora. She was in a bad way, and Balder did his best to stabilise the young woman. Marcus and Hades continued their stand-off; Hades' hand was twitching on his sidearm, whilst Marcus stood stoically. Staring through Hades like he was nothing.

"All the deaths, all the destruction, it was for a being who'd been dead for a millennium."

Hades still refused to look at the head, shaking his own as his temper began boiling up.

"How stupid do you feel? Believing in a false god for all these years," Marcus commented as Hades completely flipped; he threw his sidearm to the ground and charged at Marcus. Balder aimed his gun towards Hades, but Marcus shook his head, waving off the Omega Captain. He wanted to end Hades himself.

Marcus ducked away from Hades' advance and threw a punch to his left knee. He didn't flinch and the knee didn't move. Marcus skipped back, before landing a back kick; it bounced off Hades like he was a brick wall. The captain jumped and threw a punch which connected with Hades, flush on his jaw – Hades' only reaction was to blink. The General swung at Marcus and caught him with a glancing blow, the force was still such that it sent Marcus tumbling across the room. After standing and brushing himself down, Captain Marcus charged the General, he connected with a series of punches to Hades' abdomen and then a fierce punch to his throat. Hades stumbled. Marcus continued with his attack, blow after blow he connected with the General – a normal man would have been on the floor in pieces, but Hades was still somehow on his feet.

The ex-Kappa captain was exhausted; he had been pummelling Hades and not left a mark. Hades saw his opportunity and once again lunged at Marcus. This time Marcus was slower and was unable to jig out the way. Hades landed a forceful blow to Marcus's body, sending him sprawling across the floor. The General strode forward, grabbing at Marcus before he had a chance to rise. He picked him up from the floor and knocked him straight back down; he straddled the prone captain and began landing punches to his head. Striking hard at one side then the other. Captain Marcus blacked out, he was in serious trouble. Hades stopped, he lurched forward, then looked back over his shoulder to see Balder stood there with the handle of a knife in his hand, the blade was buried in the General's back. Hades rose to his feet and turned to face Balder; he towered over the Omega. He swung his arm but missed, he stumbled towards him throwing punch after punch, but not one landed. Balder took out his sidearm, but Hades quickly knocked it away. Hades lurched forward again and grabbed Balder by the throat; he began choking the life from him. Balder kicked out as he struggled, caching the General in the groin. The General released Balder and winced, stumbling once more. The Omega attacked, repeatedly kicking the General's knees.

"You killed my wife, you monster," Balder screamed as he kicked and he kicked until the General was finally down.

Balder casually walked back to where Aurora was prone on the floor and picked up his gun. He calmly turned to face Hades, cocking the weapon.

"This is for all the Omegas, but especially my wife," Balder yelled as he spun around. He felt a sharp pain run through his body as Hades had got to his feet, and plunged a knife deep into his gut. Balder could feel the blood running from his body as he stood eye to eye with the monster. Balder pull the trigger of his gun, point blank range and both men dropped to their knees. Balder dropped the smoking gun from his hand as he fell back. He was barely able to lift his head to see Hades prone on the floor with a pool of blood growing around him.

"For my wife," Balder spluttered before closing his eyes for the final time.

When Marcus came-to, he had awoken to see the bodies of Balder and Hades. He moved quickly to check on his friend, but he was gone. He checked Aurora, who was still alive, if barely. He stood over Hades' body and looked down at the monstrous man – he looked smaller now, less imposing. Marcus secured Keystone and staggered to the front of the bunker where he found Anders, Blank and Erik; they were the only survivors from the fight with the Kappa guards. Marcus hurried them to help Aurora. Marcus staggered through the streets of the city and to the comms tower. He reached the equipment and switched it to local broadcast.

"Hear me, hear me. General Hades is dead. Chaos, your god, is dead. Keystone is gone," he stated over the loud speakers. He slumped into a chair and just sat there, not knowing whether to be happy, or sad or whatever else.

The battle outside of the Kappa capital ceased, as Marcus's message was heard; the Kappa loyalists stopped fighting and laid down their arms. The wars were over, for the first time in a thousand years there was no fighting. As Marcus sat in his chair, his mind went to Freyja and Inga – although the quest was finished, his journey was not complete. He had to return to Sigma and reunite with the rest of his team.

78
Hades is dead

There was rejoicing as the news spread of Hades' death. All over the world the people came together to celebrate the slaying of the monster. In Khristade the mood was more sombre, the streets were lined but not for a party. The people of Khristade were on the streets to mourn the death of their hero. Balder was being laid to rest with his wife in a tomb that had been erected in the city square. It would stand as a monument to all the brave soldiers who had lost their lives fighting the war with Kappa.

Bjorn was leading the service. "We stand here today to honour all those who died, who gave us all a chance to live. We especially honour those brave souls who travelled the breadth of the world to end this war. We remember Balder, Torsten, Ivar, Sten and Ulf. We remember those brave enough to fight close to home: Stellen, Ava, Bo and Arne. We remember their sacrifice and their bravery. They will forever be remembered." Bjorn paused to compose himself before continuing. "We must also give great thanks to those that stood for us, stood for freedom. We thank Captain Marcus, Blank and Aurora. We thank Freyja, Erik, Hilda, Frode, Astrid and Inga. There are no words that could ever be enough to show our thanks to you all."

The Omega team had reunited; Marcus and Erik had taken a ship to Sigma and found Freyja and the team helping the Sigmas rebuild people's homes. They had travelled back to Omega in time for the funerals. All of them were keen to say goodbye to their leader, their captain, the hero of Omega. In other areas of the world, rebuilding had already begun – for the first time in 30 years Deltas were returning to their towns and villages. Reuniting with long lost kin who presumed them dead. Some people even returned to the camps – those born there who were without family had no place to go, so they returned to what they knew. It was a similar story on the eastern shore where hundreds of souls had returned to the sea defence camp, including Altan who had survived the battle with Kappa and wanted to help those who had nowhere else to go. In the eastern lands, Sigma had already repaired the motor rail and it was ferrying citizens back to their homes. The few remaining people of Central had all travelled to Akbar where they were invited to settle; for the first time in a thousand years, Central city was abandoned. The people of Central would no longer be tied to the city, be in servitude to the city, they would forge a new path with the people of Sigma.

Elsewhere, families were being reunited, and all those lost were being mourned. Only a handful of bodies of those that had perished had been found, so mourning empty graves was all that most had to say goodbye. Kappa state was deserted, the few surviving Kappas who had laid down their arms after the final battle were given their freedom and all chose to move on to other parts of the world. The Kappas that fought in the world's army had already integrated into Delta or Omega society; a few had even found pretty girls.

In the Omega villages, the people were uncovering the shallow graves where their old folk had been buried, and were giving all a proper burial. Likewise, all over the world, the battlefields were being cleared of bodies, with burials being given to all. Whether Omega, Delta, Theta, Sigma, Central or even Kappa, all the dead were being afforded peace. The munitions factories were torn down and weapons scattered across the world were being gathered and buried, buried in the Kappa mines, deep down out of everyone's reach. Never again will the world be torn apart by these weapons.

Marcus and Freyja were planning to take Inga and live somewhere quiet, away from the cities, away from all the reminders of what had gone before. Freyja thought they should move to Delta, or help Marcus's father at the eastern shore, but no decision had been made yet. Marcus was just happy to be with those he loved. Frode had taken himself to the temple of Delta; Bjorn requested he be in charge of cataloguing and studying of all the artefacts that had been found there. Aurora had survived being shot, but had been left without the use of her legs. Blank had taken it upon himself to care for her. They were offered a home in a village just outside Khristade, a thank you from the people, but they kindly declined the offer and were thinking of heading to Delta. Erik and Hilda were settling back into life in Khristade; they were keen to pick up some of the unfinished things their grandmother had started.

As Freyja and Marcus were preparing to leave the city, they were unable to find Inga – the young girl had disappeared. She had run off playing but had not returned. Inga had run to her old family home – it was now no more than a shell, ravaged by the war. She opened an internal door and skipped down some steps into a basement. The walls of the basement were covered in religious depictions and writings. In the middle of the room was a metal box; it was a shiny white colour, similar to that of the citadel. Inga placed her hand on the top of the box and it lit up, bright white light spewed from the box as the lid opened. Inside was a smaller box, which the young girl removed and placed into a small bag. She closed the lid and skipped back up the steps and into the streets of Khristade. She skipped back through the streets and found the worried Marcus and Freyja; she apologised to her new guardians. They finished loading a truck and left the city, heading towards the eastern shore. They would stop at the camp and spend some time with Marcus's father before making a decision on where they would go next.

79
A New World

Members of each race were gathering; a new government was to be formed. Elected officers responsible for the people of each state. Bjorn had been asked by the people of Omega to stand for them and he was humbled by their request. With the encouragement of his wife and children, he had accepted the role as governor of Omega. The new government would be based in the old Delta temple; it would stand for freedom, for fairness and to ensure that disagreements are settled with words, not guns. In the east the people of Sigma and Central had decided to elect one individual to represent both states. The two peoples were now living as one and should be represented by a single person. Through genetic tests they identified a number of individuals with mixed heritage, those who were both Central and Sigma. Of these, a woman was selected by the people to be their new governor. The women had been a shopkeeper before the wars, but when called upon during the fighting she had set-up and run an emergency medical station. A very well-respected woman who easily received the people's vote.

Bjorn had travelled to the east shore; he went looking for Marcus. The man who had led the Omega team was the choice of the Delta people to stand for them, to be their new governor. Bjorn had arrived in the old workers' camp that had now become a half-way station for those with no other place to go. The majority of the camp was filled with ex-Kappa grunts who had never had a home.

"Marcus, I have come to ask more of you. The people of Delta have requested that you stand for them once again, and become their governor?" Bjorn asked.

"I am flattered that the people think so highly of me, but my serving days are done. I am to become a father and I want to give my child, my family, what I never had. I do not believe it is possible to do both, to live quietly and to serve."

"I will not pretend to not be disappointed, but I understand your choice," Bjorn responded.

"There are better choices than me – my father would make an excellent governor. He has served the people of Delta his entire life, always striving to help others. There is many a Delta man who is indebted to him for their lives."

"Would he stand?"

"If he could still continue his work here, then I'm sure he would be delighted to serve the people."

Bjorn went to speak with Altan, who very quickly agreed to stand as governor, for the people of Delta.

The Theta people had elected a young woman to be their governor. She had no history that marked her for the leadership role, had not fought in any battles and not joined the world's army. The women had been a munitions worker for many years, she was known to be kind and honest. During the Kappa occupation she was known to have completed work quotas for others, and given food to those who were unable to work. A very genuine woman whom the people thought would make the perfect leader in the new world.

The people of Kappa were offered a place within the new world's government. At first they were quite reluctant to join, they were seen as the enemy, as mindless killers without so much as an ounce of compassion. They felt if the new government was to fail, they would be seen as the reason for that failure. In the new world they would have a place like everyone else. The other leaders insisted that Kappa must take their place, for the world to function all the people should be represented. The moment Kappa agreed to take their place there was a realisation of a lack of suitable candidates. Those who were loyal to Hades would not be considered, those who were recent school leavers were deemed too young. That only left the grunts and most were deemed unsuitable – there was nobody revered or well thought of. In the old world, Kappa would have fought for the privilege, but in this world that was deemed an unacceptable solution. After a tense meeting of the Kappa people, a majority voted for Aurora to be installed as their new governor. She was smart, understood Kappa history and the people. She would fit within the new leadership group and was a hero to the people of the world – it was her, after all, that had prevented Keystone and the inevitable Armageddon. Although unsure of whether she would be able to physically be part of the leadership group, Blank was more than supportive and offered to continue to help her. The grunt from the Kappa rank and file had taken to the scientist and wanted to make sure she made the most of her life.

The new leadership group was set: five elected representatives of the people, working for the people. There was a great deal of hope that the new world could be very special. Much hard work was needed to rebuild, but the citizens were eager. At the first governor meeting the tasks at hand were very lengthy and overwhelming, but they worked through the problems. There were arguments, especially over which regions to focus rebuilding efforts. There were disagreements around the schooling of children, most notably around which versions of the world's history would be taught, but these were discussed, talked though and agreements made.

Marcus and his new family left the eastern shore soon after Bjorn's visit. They caught a ship across the sea and headed to Sigma. Freyja was keen to return to help families re-build. It would not be long until her baby arrived and she wanted to help people whilst she was still able. During their stay in Sigma, they began to bond as a family; Marcus had taken to being the father figure of a ten year old well, especially considering he was a trained killer with no experience of children. His calm demeanour certainly helped. It was whilst in Sigma that Freyja began to notice a change in their young companion. Inga became noticeably edgy and impatient. Freyja and Marcus both attempted to talk with the girl, but they had little luck in deciphering her behaviour.

Epilogue

It was a very hot morning when Marcus and Freyja were awoken by their newborn daughter. It was early and the sun was just peeking over the horizon. The couple, along with their baby and adoptive daughter Inga, had settled in the Sigma town of Galia, which sat within sight of the Central border. The family had created a small garden from which they grew their own food and Marcus would offer labour to anyone who needed help. They had created a nice peaceful life for themselves. Marcus walked down the corridor of their modest home to wake Inga; she would help him with the morning chores as usual. He knocked and opened her door, but the girl was nowhere to be seen. Her bed not touched from the previous day. Marcus called to Freyja who ran into the room with her baby wrapped in her arms. Neither knew where their young dependant was; they panicked. Marcus ran outside shouting her name, he ran to their neighbours asking if any might have seen her – but she was gone.

In the old ruins of Central city, a young girl walked through the deserted streets. She was wearing a thick, long black cloak. The strange figure moved slowly towards an old well that was one of the very few things that still stood in the city. She placed her bag on the ground and knelt in front of the well. She began to pray. "My god, the almighty Galil. The father of my creation. I am the blessed who will finish your mission. I will put the world right. Do as you wanted a millennium ago and recreate this world as you saw fit."

The girl removed a small box from the bag. She placed her finger upon the box and it sprang open. Inside the box was a vial; the girl took the vial, opened it and poured the contents of it into the well.

"I am Inga, descendant of Galil. Let Testament recreate the world."

She rose and walked away, disappearing into the city.

THE STORY WILL CONTINUE IN:

GENESIS

WORLDS AT WAR 2

Printed in Great Britain
by Amazon

27343701R00189